Circling

By

Pamella Hays

This is a work of fiction. Names, characters, and places are fictitious, and any resemblance to events, locales, or persons living or dead is entirely coincidental.

Cover photo of Glacier Park by Jim Hays

Copyright © 2011 Pamella Hays
All rights reserved.

ISBN: 1466400617
ISBN-13: 9781466400610

For my family, my friends, and my students.

"Live life as if following the flight of a bird."

Laurens van der Post

PART ONE: FLIGHT

Grandmother

I often awaken in the middle of the night, troubled by my dreams. Perhaps too a nagging pain rouses me from sleep, since my old bones ache in the middle of winter. When I am awake I think about my family, especially about my son and my grandson who live far away. Over many winters one learns to be still, to be patient, to leave off worrying life like a bone. Yet I can still hear deep inside the voice of my female self, the concerns of a mother whose child is in danger. Though that is not all that I am, it is part of who I am; my duties as a shaman to my people can't erase that very human role that I chose so long ago. I struggle to disentangle my personal emotions from the wisdom life has granted me. I remind myself that my son is protected by the hawk, by his medicine. I seek to let go, to accept whatever journey his spirit guide requires; yet in the darkest part of the night I allow myself to cry the tears that no one else will see.

Molly

Molly woke up suddenly in the night, alerted to an unusual sound in the room. She sat up and groped for the flashlight that lay on the end table near her bed. The beam of light ricocheted wildly from floor to ceiling, revealing only the familiar white walls and tan carpet, and slowly she became conscious enough to realize that it had been the sound of the wind that had awakened her. Keening as if in mourning, it prowled around the windows, rattling the panes and demanding to be let in. She got out of bed and tiptoed to the window in her bare feet. As she pulled the curtain aside, she shielded her eyes with her hands, creating a tunnel of vision that allowed her to see the parking lot below. The ground was already covered in a light layer of snow. The weatherman was right; he had predicted an early winter.

She slipped back into bed and tugged the patchwork quilt up to her chin. Just before being pulled under into the riptide of sleep, she muttered aloud, "The store will be a madhouse tomorrow."

As she drove cautiously to work the next morning, Molly realized that no one was in the mood to deal with the unwelcome winter guest. Most of the drivers drove as if there were still on a dry roadbed, speeding along at their usual pace and passing her in frustration. Suddenly a small pickup truck in the oncoming lane began to swerve wildly, pulled into her lane by the snow-cone slush of the early snowstorm as if it were a child's toy. Molly froze, every cell in her body instantly aware of looming cataclysm, of the likelihood that the truck careening toward her could obliterate her like a boot randomly crushing an ant. She slammed her foot on the brake, but in that instant

Pamella Hays

the truck jerked suddenly in the opposite direction and disappeared over the edge of the embankment as if it had been a mirage conjured by the storm's magic. Her heart pounding, she glanced into the rear-view mirror just as it went down into the wide ditch on the side of the highway and saw that, miraculously, the vehicle was still upright, plowing through an open field of snow like a ship through the sea.

Once she saw that the driver was safe, she was thrilled by the notion of speeding off into the blanket of unbroken snow. If she were the young man in the truck, there would have been a temptation to keep on going, to continue careening through the white field, free and sovereign, heading for parts unknown. Her history was one of running away; she was good at it.

But right now she was heading to the gas station, general store, and gift shop where she worked. It perched in pseudo log cabin style, American and Montana flags flapping, at the crossroads of two highways, one of which led to Glacier National Park.

In the fall and winter, when the tourists had all gone, she paced the isles of the store or stood behind the counter with its brownies and doughnuts and trays of 'deli' meats and cheeses, so deeply bored that she thought she must have already died.

She turned into the circular drive and headed for the back of the store, the neglected space of overrun trash bins and miscellaneous discarded boxes where the employees were required to park. She turned off the motor and lifted her eyes for a brief moment to look at the mountain range that hung like a string of dark blue beads embellishing the sky's throat, its connection to the earth cut off by the swirling clouds of snow. Hooking the hood of her coat under her chin, she sighed, opened the car door, and felt the first wet, stinging drops of ice-snow that melted instantly on her face.

"Lovely," she thought dejectedly. The beginning of another winter. How many had she spent here now? Two or three, she couldn't remember. Each year had blended anonymously into the last, leaving no distinguishing marks, no noteworthy events that would serve as emotional mileposts. She couldn't even recall why she had come

Circling

here in the first place. Well, that was not entirely true; she had followed someone here, someone handsome and shallow and worthless and married, someone who had abandoned her within a few months time. But she repressed that memory quickly, stuffing it into her subconscious.

For a brief moment she rested her forehead on the steering wheel and allowed herself a strong dose of self-pity. A chill settled around her like a shroud. "I am an idiot," she told herself aloud. "I'm working in this job I hate, living in a stupid, ugly apartment, and not doing anything with my life. What's wrong with me? Why can't I be more ambitious? Why do I always settle for the easiest path?"

She swallowed the tears that were threatening to invade her eyes and shook herself, refusing to give in to melancholy. There was nothing to be gained by feeling sorry for oneself. She could almost hear her mother's voice sententiously intoning this advice, even though she herself, Molly thought, was constantly wallowing in self-pity. She remembered as well her father's sullen angers and her older sisters' flight from the house as soon as they were old enough to leave. Molly had followed soon after, leaving her parents to coexist in their frozen, bitter silences. She wondered fleetingly if this was all that a marriage could be, something that eventually deteriorated into an uneasy truce on the battlefield, a settled, hopeless pessimism. That had been the beginning of her running away, and she had never looked back.

Chilled thoroughly now, Molly opened the door, which was already almost frozen shut with the flakes of freezing snow-sleet. Out of stubborn pride, Molly refused to enter the store from the employee entrance at the back. Instead, she walked around to the front of the store, passing the carved wooden totem pole that stood by the front door. It was a bad replica, stained dark brown by years of rain and snow in areas where it was unprotected by the overhang of the roof. It had the forlorn, abandoned look of a puppy left standing out in the rain, its traditional tribal symbols reduced to the pathos of a carnival side show.

Inside, the store was bustling with activity. One little hint of snow, Molly observed, and people became desperate, rushing to the nearest store for reassurance of civilization and companionship, buying up junk food as if to store it up like a bear against the winter's hunger. Molly shook her head, both to rid her hair of the snow that had accumulated on it and in disbelief at people's fear-driven herd instincts.

She hung her coat on a rack behind the counter, donned an apron, and set about replenishing the trays of homemade pastries.

The isles were full of candy, crackers, chips and snacks of all kinds, batteries, fishing gear, canned goods and paper products. The shelves were flanked on each end of the store by large coolers with soda, beer and bottled water. Along with its usual smell of baked goods and a faint odor of gasoline, today the premises smelled of wet wool and damp socks, as the customers scurried about like disgruntled gnomes, snatching items from the shelves.

Suzanne, her boss, busy at the cash register, acknowledged her presence with only a brief nod. A large, sturdy, no-nonsense Montana native, Suzanne didn't waste much time in idle conversation. She was one of those phenomenal women, a blend of pioneer and pragmatist, who never questioned where she was or how she had gotten there, never casting blame on anyone else for her troubles. She appeared to accept her life with a stoic fatality, putting her shoulder to whatever task was required: she could split wood, help birth a calf, or bring down a fever with a tea made from herbs she had gathered herself. She treated the customers brusquely but not unkindly. She knew the type she was dealing with and didn't attempt to communicate much except about the current topic on everyone's mind, the weather, and everyone responded with the same head-shaking, raised-eyebrow acknowledgment of helpless resignation.

Like Suzanne, Molly was not one to muck around in self-pity. She had never allowed herself to dwell on the nagging loneliness she felt, though it sometimes bordered on despair. She knew she was attractive, even though in perhaps an unconventional way, so she assumed

Circling

that her appearance wasn't a major factor in her isolation from the male sex. It was true that she refused to wear makeup and wore her long curly hair in a haphazard French roll fastened at the top with a clip, from which long tendrils of hair escaped. She also purposefully disguised her slim, graceful figure in nondescript clothes of the sixties variety: large hand-knit sweaters over t-shirts, and long skirts with paisley or geometric patterns that swished around her ankles when she walked. Her shoes were almost invariably leather hiking boots, made even bulkier by heavy wool socks. Despite her almost pathological efforts to be invisible, however, her large, light blue eyes always attracted attention, and her mouth, wide and sensuous, formed a captivatingly enigmatic smile, simultaneously warm and sad.

Molly admired her boss enormously and envied her aplomb, her bold and steady acceptance of whatever life threw her way. Molly, on the other hand, insisted on analyzing life as if it were a math problem, trying to figure out why things were as they were. Lately she had been going to the local library and checking out books on philosophy, hoping to find in them some answer to her disgruntled questions. She persevered in wading through the books without any guide or sense of history, like a hapless explorer without a map. She couldn't have articulated why philosophy appealed to her, but she liked the mental knots the reading made, forcing her brain to come out of its stupor and struggle to untie them.

There weren't many things, or many people for that matter, who made her mind come alive that way. She had long since given up expecting life to be different, but she was thrilled that somewhere out there were others as frustrated as she was, writers whose work spoke to her of that same nagging mental itch, that unquenchable thirst to puzzle out what life meant.

A male customer, tall and self-assured in his Wranglers, cowboy boots, and sheepskin coat, was staring at her over the top of the candy isle. He observed her, she thought, in the way a male elk might watch a cow during mating season, not curious so much as objective, making an assessment of her height and weight and sexual viability.

Pamella Hays

There was a certain matter-of-factness, Molly had to admit, in the straightforward courting habits of Montana males; there was no ambiguity, no emotional foreplay, no doubt about their intentions. It was, like the popular t-shirt slogan, a matter of 'what you see is what you get.'

He wandered over to where she stood at the counter and asked her to wrap up the last brownie, observing her coolly all the while. Not one for small talk, Molly did as he asked but totally avoided making eye contact and limited her speech to counting back his change and saying, "Thank you."

Suzanne was always reminding her that it wouldn't kill her to be nicer to the customers—that was, after all, the whole idea of a service business, she would add sardonically. Molly did try. If her customer were female or elderly, she had no trouble relating to them, but with men it was another matter. She had grown infinitely tired of the calculated male-female interaction that made her feel as if she had wandered inadvertently into a bad soap opera. Until someone gave a sign that they recognized her as an individual human being instead of a piece of meat, she was content to remain aloof. Stung by her coolness, the young cowboy left without further comment.

After the morning rush of people on their way to work, the day dragged on monotonously. There were baked goods to prepare, floors to be swept, shelves to be restocked, garbage to be hauled out back. The storm continued unabated, gradually asserting itself as a serious snowstorm, the flakes becoming fluffier as the temperature plunged and the snow accumulated into a groundcover of three or four inches. Customers buying gas would come into the warm store stomping their boots and shaking their heads at this unwelcome early intrusion of winter.

Occasionally a customer Molly knew would come in, offering a conversational respite from her boredom. Whether logger or truck-driver, a mother hauling a car-full of children or a tense, rushed working-woman, each person still took the time for basic courtesies— a nod or smile, a greeting. Those she knew always inquired after her

Circling

own life, and though the expected answer was formulaic in its "Doing fine, thanks" simplicity, she appreciated their kind intent. She in fact appreciated Montanans in general: They were forthright, honest, and unassuming, very unlike, she thought, the appearance-conscious, self-obsessed urbanites portrayed in ads on television.

By the end of her shift, the store basically devoid of customers, Molly had become numb, sinking into that introspective place which was her only refuge from the mindlessness of her work. So involved was she in her thoughts that she was actually surprised when Suzanne shook her out of her reverie. " You ever gonna go home, or were you planning to spend the night?" she asked, raising an eyebrow skeptically.

Molly grabbed her coat quickly, said good-bye, and left by way of the back door. The earlier slushy snow had hardened into a layer of ice underneath the new, fluffier snow, and it took her several minutes to scrape it from the windshield. She had forgotten her gloves at home, and when the scraper bounced erratically across the uneven surface of the ice, she occasionally bloodied her knuckles. By the time she was done, she plopped down in the seat, nursing her two wounded fingers, and was thoroughly irritated at herself and at the world as a whole. And of course the heater barely functioned, so it would be a cold, uncomfortable ride home.

For the seven-hundredth time, she berated herself: "You idiot! Why do you stay here? You're not getting any younger. Are you going to work in a convenience store for the rest of your life?" No one answered. She shoved the clutch in, grinding the gear, and peeled out of the parking lot with her bald tires skidding an 's' curve into the snow.

Molly

The old man who lived in the apartment below her worked in the complex as a caretaker. He was puttering around in the driveway when she arrived home, shoveling the snow into random piles whose position had nothing whatsoever to do with the parking arrangement. Her own space was half covered with a small pile of snow, but she drove around it, causing her front wheel to veer into the neighbor's space on her left. Her neighbor would be ticked when he got home, and she would undoubtedly hear about her transgression, but she did not have the heart to scold the old fellow, who was leaning on his shovel and nodding at her as if he had just accomplished a miracle.

Molly grinned back at him. It was impossible not to respond to the bright orange, tasseled hat, the huge green army jacket and the oversized mukluks on his feet that looked like two furry, unrecognizable animals.

"Hi, Homer," she said as she unfolded herself from the small car.

Homer smiled broadly, revealing his red, toothless gums and the wad of tobacco tucked in his cheek. He nodded vigorously but did not speak, and she knew he was waiting for a compliment. "Nice job. Thanks for shoveling out my parking space." The old man gave a sweeping bow in reply, causing Molly to smile as well.

The door to her apartment, swollen by the damp cold, groaned in protest as she tried to open it. After several futile attempts to open in by tugging on the handle, she gave the bottom of the door a good strong kick, and it unglued itself reluctantly from the door-frame. When she had left for work that morning, she had not had time to

Circling

do the dishes, and they sat forlornly on the cracked vinyl counter, a testament to her neglect.

She took off her coat, throwing it onto the one armchair she possessed, and looked in a desultory way through the refrigerator, hoping to find something suitable for dinner. Eventually she settled on a carton of cottage cheese, a shriveled carrot, and two dried out pieces of pizza that lay unappetizingly in their original box.

Molly plopped down in her only comfortable chair with a paper plate of the tawdry leftovers in her lap and surveyed her tiny apartment. "I don't know what I expected Montana to be like," she thought, "but this dreary three-room apartment isn't it." With its solitary window looking out onto the back parking lot, this place was like a cookie cutter imitation of an apartment complex in any urban environment, excepting for its view of the mountain range that stood like the Great Wall of China in the distance.

She turned on the television and flipped through the channels but found nothing that interested her. Leaving a CNN broadcast muted on the screen, the talking head even more surreal than usual with her beautifully drawn mouth vocalizing silently, Molly felt tugged by the specter of depression that often haunted her, threatening to pull her under into its subterranean cave.

She would never have come here if she had not been following the footsteps of her erstwhile former lover, she reminded herself. Though large enough to provide some of the amenities of a city, this growing Montana town had another face as well, that of the judgmental small town, of the nosey intrusiveness of neighbors who knew your comings and goings, of civic-minded citizens who judged your social status by the clothes you wore and the car you drove and which church you belonged to. Everywhere you went, she reflected, you would usually see someone you knew, and this disconcerted her; she would much rather have walked through the public sphere without recognition, as she had been able to do in the city.

Strangely, she had to admit that in some ways she would have been perfectly at home in the social camouflage of the burka worn by

Muslim women. Except, of course, when she got home to her own space, a safe haven where she would never have accepted the arbitrary decrees of a male authority figure. Her father's abusive posturing as the dominant male when she was growing up, the lion of the house who demanded unquestioning obedience of herself, her mother, and her two sisters, had inoculated her forever against accepting male hegemony. Leaving that house had been her first act of rebellion, and though she knew that much of her restless wandering since then was a subterfuge for her failure to face her past, she had never regretted her decision.

So lost was she in her thoughts that, when someone knocked sharply on the door, she jumped. She seldom had visitors other than occasional visits from her female friends, and this knock sounded insistent. "I hope it's not Jehovah Witnesses," she mused, not up to the confrontation. She had to yank the door to get it open. Standing outside was a small brown-eyed Indian child, his face expressionless. On his head was an old woolen cap, and he wore a Navy pea coat that must have belonged to a much larger person. The sleeves covered his hands, and the coat itself covered his legs almost to his ankles.

Molly stood speechless, unable to absorb what she was seeing. She looked out over the child's head to the passageway, hoping to see some responsible adult who had just temporarily misplaced him, but there was no one. Instinctively, she squatted down so that her eyes could look directly into his, took the child's hand, and said, "Hello. Are you lost?"

The little boy shook his head vigorously from side to side, indicating that he was not. Puzzled, Molly then asked, "Where is your mommy then?" This last question caused the child's face to crumple, and he began to cry silently, large tears like inverted exclamation marks running down his cheeks.

Alarmed, Molly instinctively drew him to her, patting his back awkwardly, and saying that stupid thing that adults always say in such situations: "Don't cry." The child's body remained rigid in her embrace, but slowly the sobs subsided, and he became still. Then

Circling

he startled her by pulling her towards the stairs that led down into the parking lot. So insistent was his tugging that she followed him without hesitation.

Once they had reached the bottom of the stairs, he stopped and looked around, as if unsure of how to proceed. Then he made up his mind and headed towards the far end of the lot, near the laundry room, and went around the side of the building.

There, in a heap of snow that had fallen from the eves, was the body of a man or woman—Molly could not tell because the prostrate figure had its back to her, and the long black hair that fell to the waist could have belonged to either. The child looked up at her expectantly. Now it is all in your hands, his large, grave eyes seemed to say.

Overcoming her natural instinct of fear, Molly leaned over the recumbent figure. On closer examination, it appeared as if the person were breathing; she could see the rise and fall of the chest. The boy, meanwhile, stood beside her expectantly, his worried eyes revealing his obvious concern for the person before her. Reasoning that some-one inordinately dangerous would not be towing a small child with them, she got down on her knees and made a closer inspection. As soon as she got near, two things were apparent: the strong odor of alcohol, and that this was a man.

His abundant dark hair, sprinkled with powdery snow, fell like a sheet of satin down his back. He wore jeans and a plaid wool jacket and clutched a bottle of whiskey in his left hand, curled into the front of his jacket. He looked heavy, she thought, but not fat, just large and compact. Molly had no idea what to do. It was obvious that she couldn't leave him outside; he would die of hypothermia. Calling the police seemed like a logical idea, but Molly realized the probably bad consequences for this little boy if she did that. The local police force was not overly sympathetic towards Indians, and she had no doubt that the first thing they would do was to lock the man up, and the second to put the child into foster care. It didn't seem fair to take the child from his father, or brother, or uncle, or whoever this might be. She knew enough about tribal people to know that family was

Pamella Hays

sacred to them. They took their responsibility towards their children very seriously. Not that this was a sterling example of parenting, she thought. But then, on the other hand, she knew not to judge before she knew the facts.

Taking the little boy by the hand, she said, "We need help. We can't lift him by ourselves." She had no idea whether or not the child understood, but at least he did not protest, so she took him with her to the caretaker's apartment on the ground floor, to Homer.

Homer liked and trusted her and therefore did not hesitate when she explained what had happened. He shoved his hat on his head and grabbed his coat, following her out into the early darkness of the wintry night, pulling on the coat as he went. The little boy followed obediently, though he was still utterly silent.

When they got next to the man, Molly explained that she wanted to take him up to her apartment. At this Homer's mild demeanor became agitated. "What do you think you're doing?" he complained. "You can't do that! You don't know who this guy is. What if he hurt you?"

Molly countered, "But he has this little boy with him. He couldn't be that dangerous, could he?" She knew how ridiculous this probably sounded, but she was counting on Homer's basic good will towards her, their unspoken bond as fellow outcasts. Shaking his head and muttering his disapproval, Homer helped her raise the man's inert body into a sitting position. Then he instructed her to kneel down and place her arm under the man's shoulder while Homer did the same on the other side. Awkwardly they pulled the supine body through the snow, the heels of his boots dragging along behind, making a dark two-lane furrow in the snowy whiteness. It was apparent that they could never manage to get him up the stairs, so they used the handicapped elevator near Homer's apartment.

Once inside her place, they let the man fall onto the floor and both stood up, catching their breath. The child, who had trotted along behind them, now sat down beside the man and began unfastening his coat. "Homer, please would you help me get him onto the couch?"

14

Circling

Molly pleaded. Homer, now too upset to trust himself to say a word, merely dragged the man by his armpits across the floor and hoisted his torso up onto the edge of the couch. Molly ran over quickly and picked up the man's legs, lifting them awkwardly onto the cushions.

Shaking his head in vehement disapproval, Homer took his leave. He told her she knew where to find him if she needed anything and stomped out the door, leaving it ajar. In a moment, however, he returned, yelling loudly. "I just want you to know that I don't like this. I don't like it one bit. I think you're crazy!" And then, as he turned to go back down the stairs, he shouted over his shoulder. " I ain't taking no responsibility for this!" And then he was gone.

With the man safely installed on the couch, Molly considered the child. She gestured for him to come over to her, and she removed the heavy coat that hung on him like a scarecrow's garment. Underneath she was startled by the child's actual size; he was quite small, probably no more than three or four years old. That might explain his lack of speech, she thought. She pulled off his boots as well and sat him up on a stool at the kitchen counter. Then she began to heat some milk in a pan and stirred in a packet of cocoa mix. Too bad I don't have any marshmallows, she thought. He'd like that. She smiled to herself at how easily a woman could slip into a mothering role. Ashamed that she had so little else to offer, she put one of the pathetic pieces of pizza onto a plate beside the cup of cocoa.

She was going completely on autopilot. She had always trusted her instincts, despite the fact that her intuition had sometimes failed her. In one of her books on Oriental philosophy she had been reading about the idea of synchronicity, that if you get in touch with the universal energy, called the Tao, a force that was inherently centered and balanced, you would not be harmed or cause harm. She decided that this was the perfect time to practice that concept.

She chuckled ruefully at her own stubborn naiveté and watched the child busily stirring his cocoa and taking sips from the spoon while it cooled. For the moment he seemed oblivious to the slice of pizza. From the couch came the deep, raucous snoring of her

Pamella Hays

unexpected guest, his mouth open, a trickle of spit drooling down the side of his mouth. Despite his disheveled appearance, however, there was something dignified about him, and Molly felt suddenly embarrassed to be observing him in his shameful condition, his emotional nakedness.

Alone now with the little boy and feeling decidedly vulnerable, she contemplated the enormity of what she had done. In the first place, a woman living alone, as Homer had reminded her, should never take in a drunken male, especially an unknown and potentially derelict and violent person; second, she had taken in a small child as well, a child who might be an orphan, who might have been kidnapped, who might be abused. The only sensible thing to do was to go to the telephone and call the proper authorities immediately. Why was she hesitating?

Perhaps it was the complete absorption of this child, perched at her counter in his threadbare socks, earnestly and thoughtfully (she noticed that he was taking care not to spill) spooning up cocoa and placing it in his mouth with an expression of simple joy. Perhaps it was the cold, dark night outside that pressed against the window, the wind moaning like a lost spirit struggling to find its way into the room. Or perhaps it was the curiously innocent posture of the man sleeping on her couch, his arms akimbo, his face relaxed in sleep. The only article of native dress was the leather thong tied around a lock of his hair. Delicate blue beads and a small feather hung at the end of it like relics of a bygone age.

Molly found herself looking at his bronze, sculpted face, the high cheek bones and wide mouth and aquiline nose, and thinking how much he resembled the classical Indian in Westerns: a paradoxical romantic figure, alternately depicted as the devil incarnate or the noble, heroic symbol of a tradition that called to something in each of us. She wondered how much of her decision to bring him here was nothing more than the collective guilt-engendered notion that somehow native peoples, as victims of the white man's greed, were owed some special consideration.

Circling

But more than anything, Molly knew that it was her own arrogant self-assurance, her deeply felt compulsion to stick by her intuition, no matter how radical, that had impelled her to do this. Taking risks was necessary to feeling alive, she reasoned. And if she couldn't trust her own instincts, what could she trust? Molly shrugged her shoulders as if telling her conscience that the argument had ended, that her decision might be illogical, but she wasn't going to change it.

Leaving the child at the counter, where he was holding the cup now and slurping up the last drops of sweetness, she went into her bedroom and gathered extra blankets and a pillow from the high shelf in her closet. The boy had jumped down from the stool and stood quietly in the living room, watching the man as he slept.

When Molly came back, she showed him where the bathroom was, hoping he was old enough to know how to use it without her help. Then she made a simple bed on the floor beside the couch. When he returned, the child lay down on the improvised bed without question. Molly covered him with the extra blankets, and he rolled onto his side and fell almost instantly asleep.

Molly took the remaining blankets and covered the figure on the couch with one of them; the other she carried to the stuffed armchair and, wrapping herself up into it, she curled into the chair, tipping it back as far as it would go. Her last thoughts before losing consciousness were dreamlike images of high plains, snow-covered ground, and the silhouettes of wolves on the horizon, their snouts raised against the moon, and a small child running and leaping amongst them with utter abandon.

He is far from me now; I cannot reach him. I circle and circle, but he does not see me or hear my cry. The child looks up and watches me with his dark eyes. I can feel his courage flagging. He knows his father has left him alone again, and he is confused about what he should do. It is cold, and he senses that he and his father should not spend the night there, but his father does not respond to his entreaties.

I tighten my circles, descending closer and closer to the ground. I land a few feet from the child and stay very still so that he will not be afraid. He watches me guardedly, but he seems to accept my presence. After a while I approach him, being careful to keep my huge dark eyes on the ground, for I know that humans find them frightening. When I am close enough for him to reach out and touch me, I remain utterly still, my wings folded tightly against my body.

A long time passes. The snow begins to cover my head and back. At last the boy reaches out his hand, lightly brushing one of my wings. His touch is gentle and hesitant but does not show fear. Slowly I raise my head and look into his face. He seems startled by my eyes but intrigued as well, and, like a warrior, he does not look away.

I glide a short distance from him, watching him, and nodding my head.

When he does not respond, I move another few steps and once again nod my head, trying to get him to see a pattern in my behavior. Finally, to my relief, he untangles himself from his father's arm and

Circling

stands up. I repeat my awkward maneuvers, and this time he follows me, his hand stretched out as if he wants to catch me.

I continue to move slowly and systematically towards the front of the building. Gradually he follows, his eyes very attentive to my every motion. When we reach the stairway I spread my wings and glide up to the landing at the top, and he follows.

I stop in front of the apartment door, the place where the woman I have chosen is waiting. The boy is puzzled; he does not know what to do next. I rap my beak against the door, three sharp knocks, and then, flapping my wings, I ascend sharply into the air, finding a current of air that lifts me up and up, out of the sight of human eyes.

Far below me I can see the door open and the woman's dark form outlined against the light inside. She kneels down and takes the child's hand in hers, and I know I have chosen well.

Red Hawk

Just before dawn, the Indian man awoke. Though he did not move, he was instantly alert, and despite his throbbing head was aware that he lay on a couch, was covered with a blanket, and was not in a jail cell. The storm had passed, and the dark sky outside, just beginning to bleach to a muted pink on the horizon, still held the morning star captive above the mountains. He assessed further: he could hear the gentle breathing of others in the room. Fully awake now, it took all of his self-control to hold down the panic rising in his throat. Where was his son? What had he done with him? At that moment the child moved in his sleep, and the man, hearing him, put out his hand and felt the reassurance of his son sleeping peacefully on the floor beside him.

Relief, followed swiftly by a crushing agony of guilt, overwhelmed him. He silenced the groan that rose in his throat: a howl of outrage against himself and the world. He felt as if he were suffocating. Calming down, he forced himself to take stock of the other person in the room besides his son. All he could make out was the shadow of someone curled up, fetus-like, on a chair. Though he could see only a faint outline, he surmised from its small size that it was probably a woman.

Pushing aside the blanket that covered him, he swung his legs onto the floor, the muscles protesting now as if coming out of paralysis, and sat up cautiously. He shook his mane of hair, clearing his head of the whiskey cobwebs, and slowly stood up.

Circling

As his eyes grew accustomed to the gray shadows of objects in the room, he realized that he was evidently in a small apartment. A glance out of the window made it clear that they were not on the ground floor. Having little time before the sky became light, he stepped over the child and, scooping him up in his arms, blanket and all, he made his way to the door where he saw their coats hanging on hooks. He pulled these down and onto the top of his sleeping son, making sure there was a space through which he could breathe. Then he tried the handle on the door. The bottom of the door resisted his tugging, and opened finally with a shudder. The woman in the chair did not stir; he stepped outside and closed the door carefully behind him.

As soon as the cold air hit his face, he felt a wave of fear. Nate would soon awaken, and he would need food. It was not dangerously cold outside, not a problem if, like normal people, you had a warm home. But his home was almost one hundred miles away, on the Blackfeet Reservation, and he had no car. Awkwardly he removed his coat from the top of the sleeping boy and, shifting the child from one arm to the other, managed to pull the coat on. Then he stepped carefully down the stairs, cradling the bundle he carried against his chest and trying to ignore the throbbing in his head.

His head felt ten sizes bigger than usual and screamed in protest with every step he took, as if his feet were iron pistons pounding into the ground. Silently he sang his courage song, hoping that his medicine animal would hear. The sky was now lighter, a pale, clear blue, and the traffic on the road in front of the apartment was increasing, sleepy drivers on their way to work, their coffee cups in hand. Planting himself resolutely at the side of the road, the man raised the thumb of his free hand and hoped against hope that someone would stop.

After perhaps twenty minutes, an old Indian man, driving a battered pickup truck with Browning license plates, pulled over. His heart flooding with relief, Thomas Red Hawk opened the door, first placing the child on the seat and then jumping in himself. The elder nodded hospitably but made no comment. It was as if he already knew the story. In a glance he took in his passenger's condition: he still reeked of alcohol and his face was swollen and haggard. Alcohol was a familiar figure on the reservation, the hidden enemy. The old man knew first-hand that it was a destroyer of lives and homes and the untrustworthy companion of many young men. This grandfather well understood the sorrows of his people.

Meanwhile, the child slowly opened his eyes and looked around. Seeing his father, he smiled, and unwrapping the blanket around him, scooted across the seat to snuggle under his father's arm. It did not appear to matter to him to know where he was or how he had gotten there. All he needed was to have his father close.

They drove through the town and soon were out into the open meadows and fields of the valley, the mountains directly ahead growing more substantial in the increasing light. They passed by the crossroads gas station and turned north towards Glacier National Park, the old truck rattling and squeaking as it began to climb. The road followed the river that tumbled below them to the left. The highway was narrow, looping its way like a piece of ribbon candy around rocky promontories. Gradually the incline became steeper; and the truck protested as the old man ground down a gear, forcing them into a slower speed.

In a short while they were passing by the left hand turn that led to the west entrance of the park and the famous Going to the Sun Road. It had a deserted air, the road covered with still unplowed snow, the sign capped with a layer of ice.

Red Hawk broke the silence. "Are you going all the way to Browning?" he asked quietly.

The driver nodded and then added, "You?"

"I have family there," Red Hawk said. "I've been gone a long time."

"Never too late to go home," the old man offered comfortingly. As he slowed down through the town of East Glacier, he added, "I could use some breakfast. How about you?"

Circling

Not waiting for an answer, he pulled into a parking space along the main street next to a tiny diner, its one window fogged from the warmth inside.

Every seat at the counter was taken, so they settled into a tiny table jammed up against the window. The owner and chef, a young man with long hair tied into a neat pony tail, his torso covered with a grimy white apron, evidently recognized the old Indian and waved from behind the counter as he flipped pancakes. Red Hawk had not known how hungry he was until he smelled the bacon and coffee. His stomach began doing back flips in anticipation. The child's face lit up at the smell as well. Red Hawk couldn't remember when they had last eaten, probably yesterday afternoon.

He felt in his trouser pockets for money. To his relief, two or three bills remained, and he knew one of them was a ten, so he could afford breakfast. He was lucky: lucky he had not been rolled and his money stolen, lucky that the woman had taken in him and his son, an act of charity that he had been mulling over with disbelief as they rode, and finally he was lucky that an Indian had picked them up hitchhiking. The world was starting to come back into focus.

Waiting for their order to come, Red Hawk observed the characters at the counter. They were definitely locals, a motley crew of cowboys, loggers, truck drivers, and some bearded old-timers who looked like vagrants in their second-hand clothing. He realized ruefully that he looked that way as well. The critical difference, however, was that he was Indian, and that, socially speaking, took him down a notch or two, even amongst these working class white people who lived only a few miles from the reservation. He had been in Seattle long enough to have grown accustomed to curious or sometimes outright rude stares. He wondered what it would feel like to be amongst his own kind again.

When the food was set before them, they all ate in silence, rapidly and efficiently. Nate, who had always been extremely neat and precise, did not spill a drop of the precious food. His small pink tongue assiduously licked the extra syrup from each tine of his fork, and he scraped every remaining crumb of pancake carefully onto his last bite of egg.

Satisfied at last, the two men sighed, shoved their plates to the side, and stretched their legs. The coffee was wonderful, strong and hot, and between sips they finally made time for conversation. The old fellow was exceedingly polite and did not ask too many questions, but being from the same culture, Red Hawk was courteous as well, and he felt it was only proper that he let the man know something about himself. Red Hawk's months of solitude after his wife's death had made him unaccustomed to small talk; he thought his voice sounded raspy, like the throaty call of a crow.

He and his son had come from Seattle, he said, where they had been living for seven years. The boy's mother had died a short time ago, and he needed help raising the child. For that reason, he had decided to return to the reservation, perhaps leaving the boy temporarily with his mother and sister so that he could go somewhere and find work. He knew there would be no work in Browning, and he was afraid (though he did not tell the old man so) that he would be only too willing to settle into an unfocused life in Browning, sleeping the better part of the day, going out to the bars at night with his friends and playing poker and keno, drinking too much and depending on his government check to buy groceries. He had seen it happen to many of his friends—in fact, that was one of the main reasons that he had left the rez several years ago.

"What family do you have there?" the elder asked, adding, "Maybe I know them."

Red Hawk had been in an urban environment so long that he had forgotten the ingrown familiarity of a small town, especially a reservation town. Everyone knew everyone, of course. "My father died many years ago, but my mother, Stands Alone, lives there with my sister, Margaret," he offered.

The old man's face broke into a huge smile. "Stands Alone," he said. "I know her; she's a story-teller, a wisdom keeper. She has

Circling

powerful medicine. I used to court her before your father snatched her up," he said, adding ruefully, "He was a lucky man."

Red Hawk smiled as well. "What's your name?" he asked. "I'm sure my mother would have mentioned you."

"They call me Kicked by a Horse," the old fellow responded. "And you must be Red Hawk. Your mother talks about you all the time to anyone who will listen."

To this revelation, Red Hawk could only respond with embarrassment. He knew his mother had always expected great things of him, and he felt that when he left he had wounded her deeply.

He asked Kicked by a Horse if he knew anything about the job market in the area, but the old fellow was well past a working age, and he didn't know much about it. There was, however, he noted, a great amount of construction going on in the Flathead Valley; wealthy people were flocking here from all over the country, trying to grab up their own piece of paradise before it was all gone. Though the thought of so many people coming here and desecrating the land appalled Red Hawk, he was at the same time glad to hear that work was available. He did not consider himself a master carpenter, but he had worked odd jobs on construction sites much of his life; he knew how to swing a hammer, and he was a hard worker.

When they left, he insisted on paying the bill, as thanks for the ride, and even though it took all but a dollar of what he had, he was proud that he could do so.

They piled again into the truck, feeling much better than before, and as they traveled briefly through the eastern edge of the Park itself, Red Hawk felt the familiar pull of home, its unbroken solitude, low winter skies keeping watch over steep hillsides of dark green pines and occasional birches, their white bark luminous against their somber neighbors. Nate pointed with excitement to a mountain goat standing on the very edge of a large rock that perched precariously on an avalanche of scree. Absorbed in eating lichen, he didn't even bother to look up as they drove by. Red Hawk marveled at its utter

25

sense of balance, the assurance of a ballet dancer leaping through the air flawlessly, knowing exactly how it would land.

After leaving the park, they wound their way down into the valley below. Behind them were the jagged ramparts of the Glacier peaks, the giant guardians of the west, their rocky visages fierce and uncompromising as a Blackfeet warrior. Before them lay the tan grasses of the plains, rolling on forever into the distance. The town, its dwellings scattered about like randomly thrown bread crumbs, huddled at the feet of the mountains as if in fear of the vast stretches of the oceanic presence of the prairie breaking beyond. His own emotions of homecoming welling up within him, Red Hawk thought that there was no more beautiful place on earth.

Nate

It was his mother who was tucking him in, he was sure of that. But she didn't kiss him on the forehead the way she usually did. Didn't she love him anymore? Had he been bad? He knew his father was there, but then he wasn't there really. It was another man, the one who spent all day silently drinking from the brown bottle, his eyes opaque and his mouth hard and unsmiling. This father had appeared after his mother went away.

He had been told that she was dead, but he didn't believe it. Dead was like the people on the television, their bodies broken, with blood coming out of their chests. His mother hadn't looked like that. She had just looked tired, like she was sleeping. He wasn't supposed to know about dead people; his mother hadn't allowed him to watch anything but cartoons. But when she took him next door to the blonde lady's house and went away to her job and was gone for a long time, the lady sat him in front of the television, and he watched whatever she did. But he said nothing to his parents, because he did not want to upset them. His mother had told him not to be any trouble, so he did not ever question the blonde lady about the programs. He liked the parts in between the best, when they talked about peanut butter and cars. Sometimes there were puppies or children playing and riding bikes, or bright-colored, swirling patterns that came with happy music.

And now there was this warm feeling of sleep coming over him, tugging him into its embrace, and he allowed himself to be carried

Pamella Hays

there, his last vestige of consciousness wondering why he had not been kissed goodnight.

What he remembered next, after falling asleep on the floor, was waking up in the truck. His father was there, right beside him, and even though he smelled sour instead of clean like his normal self, his eyes were alright, and he smiled at him and put his arm around him. Then he knew everything was real again, at least for a while. In the restaurant, his father and the wrinkled old man with the white hair down to his shoulders ordered food, and he ate and ate and ate, thinking he was in heaven.

He watched his father and the grandfather talking. His father's voice was strong and confident, the way it was supposed to be. There were so many pancakes in his stomach that he felt like a whale that is caught on the beach and can't swim, but his father seemed to know that he felt that way and gathered him up from his chair and carried him to the truck.

Then he remembered that his father had carried him like that once before, this morning when it was cold outside and he was covered with his father's coat. Why had they gone outside so early in the morning, he wondered? Then suddenly he saw another picture of himself, sitting at a kitchen counter and drinking cocoa given to him by and a beautiful lady with curly hair that fell all around her face when she leaned over him. He couldn't understand why they had left her there.

He soon fell back asleep, lulled by the rhythmic chugging of the engine and the constant swaying back and forth like a tree blowing in the wind. When he awoke, they were in a town. There weren't a lot of people around; the streets were almost empty, and everything, he thought, the gray buildings, some of them with broken windows, the pot-holed street, and even the cars, looked old and worn-out and tired. He missed the bright signs of Seattle on top of tall buildings, the sparkling colored lights that raced up and down over the letters, the wide sidewalks filled with people always in a hurry, and the sounds of horns honking and the smell of the sea air.

28

Circling

Here it was another world: the air smelled, he thought, like the earth after a rain, clean and sharp. But it was so empty that it was like a pretend place, where no one really lived, or perhaps where they were all crouched inside the old buildings, places that seemed like a good spot for playing hide and seek.

They parked on the main street, and his father thanked the old man, shaking his hand. Then his father helped him down from the truck and took his hand and told him they had a ways to walk. That was good. He was not so sleepy now, and he liked the feeling of adventure, and his legs were strong and ready to go.

Sometimes he had to run full tilt to keep up with his father's long stride, but he didn't mind. It reminded him of when they used to go to the park together, his mother on one side and his dad on the other, and him skipping in between, and how sometimes they would suddenly lift him up, swinging, into the air with the mixture of delight and fear that corkscrewed up his spine.

Again he thought what a funny town this was. For one thing, they were hardly any cars going by, and for another, the sidewalks, when there was one, were cracked and battered. Oftentimes they simply walked along on a dirt road, skirting piles of snow and watching out for dog piles, too. There were lots of dogs, most of them skinny and mean-looking, he thought.

Hurried along so fast, he couldn't really see the houses on the street very long, but he sensed their forlornness. Many of them seemed neglected, abandoned and silent. Mostly he saw weathered boards, broken fences, and sometimes old cars or appliances lying on their sides, doors ajar, or even standing upright on the dirty snow in front of the houses. He wondered why people left their refrigerators and stoves outside. You would have to go out in the cold to get your food! But he liked the smell of wood fires in the air and the smart slap of the wind on his face and the warmth of his father's large hand in his. Sometimes his feet slipped out from under him when they hit a patch of ice, and his father always pulled him up and saved him from falling just in time.

Suddenly his father stopped in front of one of the small houses on the street that was enclosed by a fence around a tiny yard, bare except for patches of snow on either side of the walkway that had been carefully shoveled. One large pine tree stood forlornly, like a lone sentinel, its top, far above him, bending in the wind. "This is your grandmother's house," was all his father said. Then the front door opened, and a woman, small and dressed in black, her white hair wound up into a bun, stood before them. She didn't say anything he could understand, but he could sense her surprise and see the tears that welled in her dark brown eyes. Before he knew it, he was pulled up into her arms, and tears wet his cheek and he felt her skin, even softer than his mother's, so soft that it felt like a feather. Then she put him down and turned to his father, but she didn't hug him in the same way. For one thing, he was too big to hug unless she stood on tiptoe. Instead, she took his face in her small hands and looked at him for a long time as if she was trying to see inside of him. His dad stood as still as deer caught in headlights, though he took the old woman's shoulders with his hands, and his eyes were wide, sometimes sad, Nate thought, and sometimes ashamed. Nate wondered if his father had disappointed Grandmother in some way; that was how his eyes had looked when he had made his mother upset by being naughty.

At last his grandmother let go of her son and they stepped inside, where the house felt warm after the cold walk in the wind. He saw a huge wood stove, a cook stove, his father said, standing against one wall, and he smelled something being fried. Then he saw another lady, a younger lady, who came up to him and shook his hand and smiled, as if he were a grownup. His father said that this was his Auntie Margaret. He didn't quite know what an auntie was. He wondered what she had to do with those little black insects that crawled around on the floor sometimes in the spring, but he liked her eyes, which were kind, and her long black hair, like his father's. In fact, she looked quite a bit like his father, he thought, wondering why that was so.

Circling

The kitchen and living room were really just one big room. There was a table with four chairs set a little distance from the stove and counters, and a lumpy couch, covered with a bright red and blue afghan, over against the opposite wall. The couch was flanked by two leather chairs, their rusted springs pushing threateningly against the cracked, worn seats. There were only three windows, a tiny one in the kitchen, a big one behind the couch, and one over by the door. On the wood floor was a wool rug of many colors, like a picture, and across from the couch was an ancient television set, with rabbit ears perched on top. A snowy black and white picture flickered silently across the small screen.

He didn't think he was hungry again yet, but when the grandmother put a plate of fry-bread in front of him, along with a glass of milk and a pot of honey for the bread, he understood that he needed to eat in order to please her. He took a bite. What he hadn't expected was the outside crunch and the inside softness of this new kind of bread, the faint flavor of lard mixed with the sweetness of honey. Better even than pancakes, he thought.

For the rest of the day, Nate wandered about the house unheeded, allowed to poke his nose into anything that interested him. His father and grandmother and Auntie Margaret were involved in a long, boring grownup kind of conversation that seemed to leave him completely out. But he did not feel left out, because his auntie had smiled at him conspiratorially once when he sat down on the rug close to them, and he had liked the twinkle in her eye.

That evening, tired by the long day, he lay curled up in one of the old chairs, drifting in and out of sleep, warmed by the fire in the stove and the indescribable feeling of safety he felt in this house, like being rocked in someone's arms. Lots of other people came and went all night. The door would open, bringing in a gust of cold air, and there would be shouting and back-slapping and sometimes big hugs, bear-hugs, his mother had called them, and he looked over at his father and saw his face shining, the way it used to, and his mouth curled into an almost-smile, like a cat when it purred.

Pamella Hays

Images of the strange night before, of his father lying in the pile of snow, and of the pretty lady who had given him cocoa wove in and out of his mind like smoke. At last someone took note of his nodding, and carried him into a room and placed him on a big, soft bed. Before succumbing to sleep, he saw a painting on the wall, a picture of a bird, flying up into the clouds, the feathers under its wings gold from the light of the sun. He liked it immediately; it looked like the one he had followed up the stairs. The painting made him feel totally at home, and he snuggled down under the patchwork quilt and floated blissfully to sleep.

Molly

Her subconscious on high alert from the presence of her strange visitors, Molly had slept fitfully all night, dreaming of odd and unsettling images: of snow falling into the center of her house and a long-haired man shoveling it with a broken whiskey bottle, and of a hawk, who for some unfathomable reason could talk, perching itself on the arm of her chair. It quoted something that sounded like poetry in a high, shrill voice that caromed off the walls and ceiling. She could not understand the language in which he was speaking, and it irritated her. In the midst of his unsettling recital, the bird would fly up from time to time and harass the man with the bottle, who would slap at it angrily and then go back to his task, piling the snow incongruously onto her kitchen counter.

Towards dawn she fell into a deep and dreamless sleep that ended only when the bright morning sun streamed into the room. She blinked her eyes, rolling over to turn off her alarm, and then suddenly became wide-awake. She realized that she was not in her bedroom, and then the strange occurrences of the previous night flooded into her conscious mind. She sat up with a start, and taking in the scene before her, she saw immediately that her unusual guests were gone.

Unbidden, her first thought was a lament; the little boy was gone. On the heels of this emotion came anger. The man's cowardly desertion, without a word of thanks, was uncivilized, outrageous, just what she would expect of a complete asshole. She fumed and muttered as she showered, wondering despite herself where they had gone. She reflected that this served her right; she had known better, and should never have taken them in. She was fortunate that nothing worse had happened. And yet, despite all of this, something in her subconscious wouldn't accept this rational, obvious idea. She wanted to believe that the boy was safe, that the man had some sense of responsibility in him, that her bizarre but well-meant act of charity had rescued them, at least for one night. Throwing on some clothes, she left, late, for work, slamming the recalcitrant door behind her.

Suzanne seemed to accept Molly's brief excuse of "Sorry, I slept late," without comment, though Molly could not miss the frown of disapproval that furrowed her brow momentarily. Grateful for having been spared a tongue-lashing, Molly hustled more than usual and made a lame but sincere attempt to be more chatty with the customers. When she was alone, however, she stocked shelves and swept the floor robotically, her mood one of melancholy, though she could not have explained why.

It was not easy for her to admit to herself that she had felt some ties with her mysterious visitors. In the first place, neither of them had spoken, and in the second place, they were tribal people, unfathomable and unreachable as far as she was concerned. Still, the sense of loss lingered, and she was glad when her shift ended and she could go home to be alone.

But solitude was not in the cards. As she drove into the apartments' parking lot, she saw Homer there waiting for her, his face distorted with consternation and displeasure. Molly wanted to back out and drive away, but she knew she would have to face her disgruntled caretaker sooner or later. She sighed deeply, opened the door, and stepped out onto the snow. Homer was lecturing before he got within talking distance: His voice boomed as if he held a megaphone and were directing the movements of a vast crowd.

"So, you couldn't even stop by this morning to let me know you were alright? I didn't sleep a wink. Kept thinking of that savage asleep on your couch. And besides, you're breaking the rules, you know. You have to check with me if you're going to have guests.

Circling

And he wasn't exactly a guest, was he? Or that little orphan neither," Homer ranted, all in one breath.

Molly waited for him to take a breath. "Homer, I'm fine," she said, summoning calm. "I was late for work this morning. I didn't have time to stop by. And no one in this place follows that 'rule' anyway; it's probably illegal, if the truth were known. I pay my rent every month. This is my home. Don't I deserve some privacy?" By the end of her monologue, her voice had risen to a higher pitch, and her eyes flashed in anger.

Mollified, Homer lowered his head and mumbled, "I just worry about you, being alone and all. I don't mean no harm."

Molly instantly regretted her anger. This old man had indeed looked out for her wellbeing, and she knew she owed him thanks. But she also had to stand her ground and assert her independence.

"I know, Homer. I'm sorry I snapped at you. I've had a bad day." Molly lowered her eyes, embarrassed by her thoughtlessness. " I really do appreciate your help last night," she said lamely, " and my guests left early this morning, without a word. I had no problem at all with them, so you didn't need to be worried." And then, as an afterthought, she added vehemently, "And he wasn't a 'savage'."

Beaten but unbowed, Homer nodded his head in surly defeat, but he walked away still muttering his disapproval, and Molly knew she hadn't heard the last of it.

A week passed before Molly could come home without feeling the apartment's solitude like the threatening pain of a headache, but gradually everyday life took hold again. She kept busy working, shopping for groceries, cleaning house, occasionally going out to a movie or taking long walks in the nearby foothills. Winter deepened, the temperatures dropped, and the snow metamorphosed into a presence that was always around, like an annoying relative. Putting on layers of clothing, scraping windshields, driving cautiously down the highway in her car like a woman walking on ice in high-heeled shoes, became daily routines, almost comforting in their dullness.

Pamella Hays

Then one morning as Molly opened the door and stepped outside, she almost fell over a package that lay at the base of her door. It was fairly large and bulky, double wrapped in plastic grocery bags and tied with string. Her first reaction was to kick it out of the way. All she could imagine was that the next door neighbor must have dropped it when he came home late last night. Then, thinking better of her lack of neighborliness, Molly took it inside and decided she'd give it to him when she got home from work.

That day the store was particularly busy; Suzanne had taught Molly how to bake the cinnamon rolls and giant cookies that all the customers seemed to love, and now Molly baked twice a day to keep up with the demand. Her hair was pulled back and tucked into the back of her sweater, her face splotched with bits of white flour. She stopped kneading the dough momentarily and straightened up, stretching her back and surveying the crowd while breathing in gratefully the cold air that swept in as the doors swung open with each new customer.

It was at that moment she saw him. His back was to her, his long, black hair neatly braided, his large shoulders hunched over as he surveyed a lower shelf. He wore brown Carhartts, the one-piece overalls that seemed the favorite uniform for all outdoor workers. He carried a carpenter's wide leather tool belt that hung around his waist. Before she could hide her surprise, he walked over to the counter and put a supply of candy bars in front of her.

He was used to his appearance causing a variety of reactions: sometimes indifferent, as if he were invisible, and sometimes fawning, as if in apology for the white man's guilt, he surmised. But seldom did someone look as shocked as she did. It was as if she had seen a ghost.

When he came to the counter, Molly cleaned her hands on her apron and attended to his purchase, managing to run the bars through the machine and make change for the five-dollar bill he gave her. She forced herself to look him in the eye when she handed back the coins, and she was astonished at how dark his eyes were, coal-black tunnels that one could wander into and not find her way out.

Circling

He thanked her and left. It took awhile for her heartbeat to slow down and her mind refocus on her work. He had looked at her as one would a total stranger, so obviously he had not recognized her. Perhaps he had left before first light and not gotten a good look at her?

She went back to work, her hands mechanically forming the dough into cookies, but her mind leapfrogging between the past and the present. This was not the man she had pulled through the snow and onto her couch. He was nothing like what she had expected. It was apparent that he was working, and he had been polite and impeccably groomed. It was more difficult to be angry with this new person she had seen, but it was not easy to shed the hard-edged, righteous judgment that she felt towards him for his treatment of the child.

She wished that she had asked him about the boy, but then of course she would have been giving away her identity, and she was not prepared to do that, especially now that she was knew she was protected by anonymity.

At the end of her shift, she waved goodbye to Suzanne and left. When she got the apartment complex, she realized with some consternation that she had driven in a fog all the way home and had no idea what she had seen along the way. It was disconcerting to be able to drive a potentially lethal vehicle on mental autopilot, she thought.

Walking up the stairs to her apartment, she saw her neighbor coming along the walkway towards her on his way to his evening shift. She asked him to wait a minute, hurried inside, and grabbed the package from her counter. "This must be yours," she said. "I found it dropped outside my door this morning."

"Not mine," the man replied. And then, displaying some vestige of courtesy, he added offhandedly, "But thanks anyway."

Inside, Molly untied her boots, and kicking them off by the door, surveyed the mysterious package. She pulled the string around the corner of the package and opened it. Inside was a pair of beaded moose-hide moccasins, tanned to a soft pliable leather. The beadwork was sophisticated and meticulous, a red, yellow, and blue geometric

Pamella Hays

pattern typical, she knew, from pieces she had seen in the museum, of tribal artisanship. Underneath the moccasins was her blanket, the one she had wrapped the child in, washed and carefully folded.

Abruptly losing all of her usual self-control, she sank down onto the couch, holding the moccasins like icons in her palms, and cried inconsolably, for herself, for all the injustice in the world, for loneliness and abandonment and prejudice and generosity and hope and kindness, and for a mysterious man and a boy who were becoming, unbidden, more real and complex than she had ever wished or imagined.

Red Hawk

Red Hawk woke up in his rented motel room feeling unusually happy, in spite of the lumpy mattress that irritated his back, which was tired and stressed from hours of lifting boards and pounding nails. No, not happy, he thought, but peaceful. He always thought of happiness as a white man's construct. He had never believed that there was such a thing, and certainly did not believe it could be achieved somehow by one's own efforts, by going on more vacations or by buying more things. His years in the public school system had been painful and hence quickly erased, but he did remember the line from Mr. Jacobson's history class when they had studied the Constitution about 'the pursuit of happiness.' Even as a child, he had thought that was a ridiculous notion; a man could not run after happiness like a dog chased a rabbit through a field. It either came to you or it didn't. For him it came at the most unexpected times, when he had stopped yearning for it, or even when he had given up on it altogether.

He realized that, for one thing, he was no longer dreaming about his wife. She had died a year and a half ago, and though he would always miss her, he no longer felt suffocated by a heavy blanket of grief.

He knew that the sweat-lodge ceremony had helped. As soon as his mother had seen him, she had insisted that this cleansing ceremony must be performed.

As Kicked by a Horse had affirmed, his mother, Stands Alone, was a respected member of the tribe. She was renowned for her insight and knowledge as a medicine woman and was often consulted about the proper enactment of traditional ceremonies. Only a few remaining elders still told the ancient stories, myths that had never been written down but were passed along orally from generation to generation, and his mother was one of these story-tellers, a wisdom keeper. Stands Alone remembered verbatim the stories that her grandmother had told her when she was a child. Red Hawk had grown up hearing these tales, which were told only at certain seasons, in their proper context, and with great respect.

When he and Nate had arrived at her door in Browning weeks ago, she had seen her son's troubled eyes, his unkempt appearance and withdrawn demeanor, and immediately understood that he needed a purifying sweat to get rid of the heavy burdens he was carrying. She had contacted the group of men who were capable of performing such a sweat and asked for their help.

Red Hawk had not attended a sweat-lodge ceremony in many years. His last recollection, in fact, was from his adolescence, when he had gone to a recreational sweat with his father. Everything about the ceremony, from the construction of the lodge itself, with its east-facing door, to the selection of the rocks and the location of the lodge by a stream, to the ritualized behaviors of the participants, was sacred. The invited person was expected to understand this and to conduct himself with the proper respect. For Red Hawk, so alarmed by his recent neglect of his son's well-being, the sweat offered purification and redemption. He knew that the ceremony would require self-scrutiny and the sacrifice of his old ways, but that was exactly what he needed in order to put his feet back on a straight path.

As he sat cross-legged in the close darkness of the lodge, sweat running down his nose and dripping onto the tamped earth floor, he lowered his head to the cool ground and talked to the Great Spirit, asking for guidance and healing. He didn't recall ever having prayed in this way, except when he was alone in the wilderness and had received his medicine. When the heat became unbearable, he would leave the lodge temporarily, walking around it in the proper direction,

Circling

and then returning. When he emerged at the end, he felt clean, both physically and spiritually, and at the supper afterwards that he shared with the other participants, he felt a brotherhood that he had not known for many years.

Since the sweat, he had not had another drink; his conscience was still too scalded by the memory of having abandoned his son, by his utter failure as a father when he had been drinking. More significantly, he had begun for the first time in a long time to feel back in touch with his spirit, and this had given him the strength to go to Kalispell and look for work. He had found this room only a few days before.

His son, Nate, was now safe at his mother's home, warm, and well fed, thanks to the generosity of his mother and sister. He knew that the itinerant life of a carpenter had little stability for a child, especially considering that the boy would have been left in a day care of some kind while he worked, a thought that made him shiver. Now that he had gotten a job on a construction site building a series of condos, he could send them money every week and still have enough left over to live during the work-week in Kalispell. The cheap motel he had rented allowed him the solitude he needed until he could decide how to deal with the future.

While he made his breakfast on the hot plate that sat on the chipped yellow counter serving as a feeble facsimile of a kitchen, he thought about the moccasins he had made and wondered how they had been received by his mysterious guardian angel. He had thought of the charitable woman many times since the night he and Nate had spent there, but it wasn't until he had talked it over with Stands Alone that the way for him to properly thank her for what was, under the circumstances, her extraordinary generosity, was to make the moccasins for her.

He had been so panicked and hung over the morning he left that he hadn't even considered the woman in the chair, and in the dark it wasn't possible to see her anyway. Now that he was thinking more clearly, he was curious. It was unthinkable to him that a woman, especially a white woman, would take in him and Nate, especially when he was a drunk passed out in the snow. What could a white woman who would take such a risk possibly be like?

He had left the package very early in the morning before she was up and about, but he thought about stopping by on his way home from work and watching for her, or maybe even speaking to her if he got up his courage. But what if she hated him for skipping out the way he had, like a coward? What if she was a prim do-gooder who had taken them in out of pure duty but felt no charity or compassion for them? But if that were the case, why hadn't she just called the police?

Brushing these thoughts aside, he finished his breakfast, pulled on his mud-coated work boots and, grabbing his hardhat, hurried out the door. As he drove through the early morning traffic he found himself smiling at people in the next lane at stoplights. He almost laughed aloud to see their reactions, most of which were surprised but not unfriendly.

At the job site, its bare ground rutted and muddy from the scouring of huge machinery, he parked next to a dark blue pickup and walked towards the outlines of buildings, their bare plywood facades, from the distance, like a Hollywood movie set. Far in the distance the purple of the Swan Mountain Range turned pink under the sun's first rays.

The work crew stood around an outdoor fire built with the useless remains of carpentry projects, drinking coffee poured from metal thermoses. It was an accepted custom that no one had to begin working until the boss arrived, and this morning the foreman was uncharacteristically late.

Red Hawk stood on the perimeter of the circle, listening and watching. The conversation centered on the headlines in this morning's paper: The local Tribal Council was demanding that non-tribal members buy special licenses to hunt and fish on tribal land. Most of the men here were hunters or fishermen, and they resented having to pay for a second license on top of the general sportsmen's license that

Circling

the state demanded. Although the majority of his fellow workers expressed a firm belief that the reservation land the Indians had been given was more than adequate compensation, a few men spoke up about the ridiculously small amount of land the tribes now had compared to what they had once enjoyed, hinting of a certain inequity.

Though he had remained utterly silent, Red Hawk's presence had been noted, and he was dragged reluctantly into the conversation when one of his fellow workers, an Irishman named Joe who had always treated him decently, asked, "So, Thomas, as the only Indian here, what's your opinion?"

Red Hawk hated being put on the spot, but he nevertheless said, "From the point of view of my people, we are being asked to pay to hunt on the public land that once was ours but is now yours, so it does not seem unreasonable to me that we ask you to pay us to hunt on the reservation, on the land we were given by treaty."

"That's bullshit," a man with a large, beefy face and even larger frame, cut in. "The Indians didn't think of owning property until we gave them the idea. I thought 'your' land," he said, referring sarcastically to Red Hawk, "didn't belong to anybody."

Choosing his words carefully, Red Hawk answered, "That's absolutely right. We didn't think of ourselves as landowners but as tenants responsible to Mother Earth. But you're the ones telling me that the past is gone and we have to deal with the present. And the present reality is that you gave us the reservation as our property, and we're just asking that you recognize us as having the rights of any other landlord."

The beefy man's face had grown red with anger, and Red Hawk was grateful when the arrival of the boss's pickup truck on the scene broke up the conversation. Nevertheless, the atmosphere of sourness stayed around for the rest of the day like an irritating pollutant. Red Hawk was grateful when the day was over and he could escape.

The light has just begun to disappear behind the mountains when his shift ended and he headed for his old red car in the makeshift parking lot. The workers' cars were parked helter-skelter in the area

Pamella Hays

adjoining the site where the frame of the future condominium already stood two stories high, filling the air with the scent of new wood that Red Hawk loved. Construction sites were never tidy, but they exuded the clean, hopeful smell of newness, promising people the chance to start over, to live in a home untouched by the ghosts of past inhabitants, and that had always appealed to him.

Doubling his tall frame into the small compact car, he headed into the heart of town, driving past the apartment complex once before, berating himself for his cowardice, he did a U-turn and headed back. He pulled in and parked in a spot at the far end of the lot with a car on either side. His plan was to be able to spot the woman before she saw him, just in case his courage failed and he decided not to approach her.

He didn't have long to wait; Molly turned sharply into the driveway and braked abruptly as she pulled into her parking place. Red Hawk watched her as she ran up the stairs and opened the door of the apartment he remembered. "I've seen her recently somewhere," he thought in astonishment. Then, suddenly realizing where, his face broke into a rare smile. "No wonder she looked at me like that!" he said aloud, laughing.

That she had obviously recognized him at the deli made his face redden, and he felt suddenly shy. He was also trying to accustom himself to the real person he was now seeing as opposed to the image he had had of her in his mind.

For some reason he had imagined her as older, maybe even a grandmother. Nate had told him about the hot chocolate; maybe that was how he had gotten the idea. Now he saw a young, attractive white woman. This made her already unorthodox behavior the night of the storm even more mysterious. Surely a single woman raised in this era of feminism would be wary of dealing with any drunken man, and even more so an Indian? Racial prejudice aside, anyone lying passed out in the snow could be potentially dangerous. All he could think was that Nate's presence had won her over, just as his charm

Circling

had lured so many rides when they were hitchhiking on their way here from Seattle.

He watched her walk up the stairs and into her apartment, an enigma even more disconcerting than he had expected. Thrown completely off-guard, he wrestled with his first impulse, which was to drive away as fast as he could go and never come back. But something nagged at him, the thought that in his culture one gave back in return for what they had been given, and despite the gift of the moccasins, what he owed her the most was an apology. It would have been easier, he thought, if she had been older, and if he had not remembered those strangely luminous, light blue eyes he had seen at the deli, the color of the clearest, coldest river water in winter.

Drawing a deep breath, he slid across the seat of the old beater he had bought to the passenger side door, which was the only one that would open. He walked slowly up the stairs, wishing he had something to carry in his large hands, which seemed suddenly awkward and detached, as if they belonged to someone else. He hesitated at the door.

He knocked once, softly. The apartment wasn't after all very big, and he knew she was home. But when no answer came, he knocked again more loudly.

When the door opened at last, he reacted to the stunned look on her face, her obvious discomfiture, with a sudden intuition as to how startled, and possibly even frightened, she must be to see him there. He felt conspicuously large, filling the doorframe as he did, and for one fleeting moment would have given anything to have Nate beside him as a buffer.

He could not find his voice momentarily, and she, still apparently hovering between fright and surprise, said nothing. Red Hawk felt the pain of the looming silence between them and finally out of desperation asked incongruously, "Did the moccasins fit?"

He noted with relief that she shook her head. At least she was not too fearful to communicate altogether. But he misinterpreted her

45

gesture, which had been in the negative, and stumbled on, "If they're too big, I could make you another pair. I just didn't know your size. I was just guessing," he added clumsily, now totally out of balance.

"No, no…I mean they fit very well, thank you, " she said. Then, more testily, "What are you doing here?"

"My name is Thomas Red Hawk," he said, finally remembering his manners, and then added hastily, "but most of my friends call me Red Hawk. " He stumbled on, "I wanted to, I mean I owed you my thanks for taking us in, Nate and me." He spoke like a man drowning, each word a cry for help. Never before in his life had he felt so completely unmoored.

"You're welcome," Molly said, but her voice still sounded suspicious. Finally she added pragmatically, "Would you like to come in? It's getting cold in here, with the door open."

Red Hawk nodded and stepped over the threshold, a wave of something like nausea sweeping over him. He felt weak with shame remembering how he must have looked to her that night.

"Would you like to sit down?" Molly offered as he swayed slightly.

But he shook his head. "No, thank you. I have come only to apologize for my behavior the other night." He hesitated, as if searching for words. " I was not myself," he said.

Molly considered that statement, her eyes penetrating and still skeptical, and then she said, "I don't know what to say, exactly. I don't know who you are or anything about you." Despite the anger in her tone, Red Hawk saw her tense shoulders relax ever so slightly. "I'm glad you and the boy are alright," she added, her voice less harsh, as if the recollection of the child had softened her. And then she looked directly at him, her face an unreadable mask, and spoke with what seemed to Red Hawk to be deep reluctance, "I guess I can accept your apology." An awkward silence ensued before she finally asked, "Is Nate your son?"

He allowed himself the luxury of a small smile. "Yes, Nate is my son. He's with his grandmother right now." In a tone of anguish, he added, "I love him very much. I would never hurt him."

Circling

Red Hawk thought he would die with shame. The words he had just spoken had been wrenched from the deepest, most private part of his soul. He couldn't believe that he had spoken them aloud. The conversation had become so tense that for the first time he understood that saying about wanting to fall through a hole in the floor. He sensed Molly pulling away emotionally; how could she possibly understand his inappropriately intimate confession? He had a sudden vision of how he must have looked lying passed out in the snow, a derelict drunk who was an utter failure as a father. The man she had taken into her home had deserted his small, frightened son, a betrayal beyond forgiveness.

Molly' voice startled him back into the present. With a prescribed, wooden kind of politeness, she said, "He is a beautiful child. How old is he?"

But Red Hawk, having accomplished, however ineptly, what he had come to do, was already turning and heading for the door. "He's almost four," he answered as he tugged on the door handle, in full flight now. Molly walked towards him. "It sticks in the cold," she said. "Just pull hard."

Without saying goodbye, Red Hawk wrenched the door open and fled down the stairs, his braids bouncing up and down on his back as he took the steps two at a time.

Nate

When Nate's father came home that weekend, he knew right away that something was wrong. For one thing, his father didn't pick him up and hug him the way he usually did; he just patted him on the head, almost as if he wasn't even there. His father's face had that dark shadow again, as if someone had pulled a shade over a window. He ate only a little of the venison stew Grandmother had prepared and left soon afterwards, going downtown he said, to see if anything was going on.

After he left Grandma seemed out-of-herself too. She wandered around between the kitchen and the living room, turning on the T.V. and then turning it off again, and looking out the front window every other minute. His Auntie Margaret, who reminded him of his father only a girl and younger, played cards with him, just like she did every night, but his mind wouldn't stay on the game, and he couldn't remember where the Old Maid was.

Outside it began to snow hard. The wind howled around outside like a wolf, a spirit, his grandmother had told him, that couldn't find its way home. It gave him the shivers, and he felt like crawling over and getting into his auntie's lap. But that would make him a baby, and his father had said he wasn't a baby any more.

When his father was home on the weekends, he slept with him in the large old four-poster bed under the painting of the hawk. This had been his father's room when he was a boy, and the picture of the hawk (a bird whose name was just like his father's, amazingly) had been painted by his father when he was in high school. His father

Circling

had told him that someday he would explain how he had gone on a vision quest when he was eighteen and gotten his name, Red Hawk, but that the boy would have to be a little older, because you couldn't go on a quest until you were almost grown up. Still, he was intrigued that his very own father had once been a boy too, and that he himself had made this painting of a bird, and he spent long periods of time studying it until he could close his eyes and see it clearly in every detail.

Nate wondered if the high school was taller than the grade school, which was ugly and brown and only one story high. He had seen it when he went on walks downtown with his grandmother to get groceries. There were sometimes children playing in the yard, jumping and running, and yelping, and it seemed scary to think that he would be going there next year, to the littlest grade. He imagined the high school as being a skyscraper like the ones he had seen in Seattle, and that sounded even scarier. He wouldn't like being up that high.

He heard his father come into the room sometime very late that night. When he crawled into bed beside him, he smelt of cigarette smoke but not of that sour smell from the brown bottle. He was drifting back to sleep again when the bed began to shake. His father was sobbing, his big shoulders heaving up and down, his long hair rising and falling against his back, which was turned towards him. Nate thought about reaching out and patting his father's back, but something held him still; he sensed that this was one of those strange things that grownups do when they don't want anyone to notice, like when his mother had died and people talked with loud, reassuring voices, thumping him on the back and telling him everything would be alright, even though he knew they were lying.

In the morning at breakfast he searched his father's face for signs of last night's weeping. When he cried, his eyes got all red and swollen, but his father's eyes seemed just like their usual selves, although maybe a little sadder. He reached across the table and patted his father's arm, this unexpected gesture soliciting a tender smile. His father asked him if he wanted to go hunting for elk, and even though he had no idea what an elk looked like, he said "Yes," with great enthusiasm. There was nothing more wonderful than spending time with his father; he would have walked over hot coals or swum through icy rivers or climbed mountains as high as the clouds if his father wanted him to.

His grandmother, more like herself this morning, said very little but prepared them a big sack lunch that his father stuffed into his backpack. There was some fussing from the women about whether he would be warm enough, but his grandmother had bought him mittens and a wool hat with ear-flaps and a big down coat at the second hand store. Best of all, though, were the boots that had a fleecy layer inside them and laced up just like his father's.

Finally he was dressed, his auntie's scarf tied around his neck with her warning to put it over his nose and lips if the wind got too cold, and he stepped out onto the porch, his many layers of clothing making him feel stiff. He had to walk funny, his feet all splayed out like the penguins he had seen at the zoo. His father laughed at his attempt to pick up the thermos that he had offered to carry, and the unbridled joy of this laugh was worth how ridiculous he felt in his clumsy winter gear.

They drove in his father's old car to the edge of town, through the last of the houses on the street where he lived, and towards the flats beyond, climbing steadily towards the foot of the mountains.

He liked the way the road kept turning back on itself, and yet somehow it magically kept going forward as well; he could see it ahead, winding like a snake higher and higher into the mountains. His father said these were 'hair-pin" curves, but he had no idea what that meant. What did hair have to do with a road? But he thought his father liked silence more than too many questions, so he kept his questions to himself.

When they seemed to be up higher than the clouds, his father took a sharp turn off of the main road and onto a bumpy one, so narrow that the branches on the trees scraped against the window. Soon they stopped altogether, and his father scooted him out the door and

Circling

then followed him. His father gave him the thermos and a bag of cookies to carry; on his own back he had the backpack with the rest of the lunch, some extra socks and ammunition for the rifle he carried balanced in his left hand. He had grown used to how fast his father walked, but fearful that he would not seem grown up, he sprinted along, the metal thermos bumping uncomfortably against his leg.

He loved the way he felt up here. It was the way Superman would have felt, he thought, just as if you could jump into the air and fly. The sky was that clear and blue and beckoning.

Finally they came to a vast open meadow that tilted upwards, a field of shiny whiteness against the dark pines behind it. He could see animals on it, although they were far away, and he asked his father if they were elk. His father nodded, but he also put his fingers to his lips, warning him to be quiet, so he became very still and looked so hard that his eyes began to burn and tear up because of the cold air against his face.

He could see the animals moving, slowly, with their heads down, pawing at the snow to get at the grass beneath. Once in Seattle he had seen cars that looked like toys because they were so far down below him as he stood at the top of the Space Needle. But these animals, even though they were tiny because they were far away, still seemed to be immense, their racks of antlers balancing precariously, like elaborate, regal headdresses, as they bent their heads to eat. Their coats were a warm, rich red-brown, and Nate felt the urge to go up to them and stroke the dark napes of their necks.

Suddenly something rose up in him like an ancient song, something fierce and compelling and powerful that made him want to shout. He watched his father raise the rifle and heard its loud crack splitting the silence into fragments of echoing sound. The animals, torn from their pastoral still life, broke into chaotic patterns of flight and disappeared into the trees without a trace.

Red Hawk

His son was a constant source of worry, a subliminal fretting like a blister rubbing on his heel. He remembered how his wife had loved this child, her profound bond with him that had, at times, made Red Hawk jealous. And he had worried, even before she became ill, about the boy's upbringing, about how to raise him as a Blackfeet in a city that was so far away from his tribe and his land. Though his wife was Blackfeet too, and both of them made an effort to talk about their traditions to the child, it was not the same as practicing them. There was no substitute for the sense of belonging one experienced amongst one's own.

Yet he had chosen to leave his home and come to the city, and he didn't entirely regret having done so. He had encountered less prejudice here than in his own state. There were people of every color, from many different nations, and he often heard foreign languages spoken. Perhaps because of this, the presence of so many different people, everyone seemed for the most part to mind their own business. On the construction sites where he had worked, he had black friends, Latino friends, Asian friends. He loved listening to them speak, to their speech patterns and particular cultural vocabularies, all of which denoted different ways of looking at the world.

It was in the night, when he had tried to go to sleep in their tiny efficiency apartment, with the noises of the city assaulting his ears, that he missed Montana most. He began to realize that city dwellers never experienced silence, the kind of stillness that one could have

Circling

in Browning by simply walking two or three miles outside of town. Of course there were sounds in the mountains as well, but they were subtle and soothing, like a brook whispering over stones, not jarring and intrusive like the sounds in Seattle.

It was also in the night, especially after his wife had died, that he felt something he had never before known: the solitude of acute loneliness, the untethered feeling of floating unaided and unrecognized in the cosmos. When he tried to describe how completely senseless his life seemed to one of the men at the job site, his coworker had said sympathetically, "Yah, I know what you mean. Kind of like the guy who rolls the rock up the hill and then during the night it rolls back down again." And then had added reflectively, "Makes me think of that bumpers sticker, you know? The one that says 'Life's a bitch, and then you die'."

Curious about the story of the man who rolled the rock up the hill, Red Hawk had gone to the library and talked to a friendly librarian there. He asked her if she knew anything about this strange man, and she did. She steered him towards some books on Greek mythology, which, even though he did not always understand them, he liked, because sometimes they reminded him of some of his own people's stories. When he read about Sisyphus, condemned to meaningless labor rolling that huge rock up the hill forever, he was mystified. This was a concept totally alien to him. And besides, he didn't see what it had to do with his own dilemma of feeling alone, except perhaps that he was gradually realizing that his life in the city had very little purpose now that his wife was gone.

On the librarian's recommendation, he checked out some other books as well, one by a writer that the librarian said was an Existentialist, someone who, like the myth of Sisyphus, basically thought life was not very purposeful. But he only got through three or four chapters, because he could not bear the sense of black despair that was being portrayed. If this was how white people lived, and how they believed, then it was no wonder that they were so driven and angry and greedy, like ghosts wandering the world looking for something that they would never find because they did not know where they had come from or where they were going.

It was at his wife's funeral, a brief ceremony attended by only himself, his son, and two friends from work, that he began to have that same strange, detached feeling almost all of the time. He was exhausted by the ruinous stress of the last three months, when her illness had required his full-time care. He was unable to sleep. The acute sense of loss, which tumbled around in his subconscious ceaselessly, had polished his grief until its sharp edge cut into him like a knife.

Sometimes his emotional pain was so intense that the sensation of utter isolation would attack him without warning and stop him cold in his tracks. He would forget what he had been doing, would be unaware of Nate's tugging on his pant-leg, confusion and fear in his eyes.

He should never have brought her here, he thought, but now it was too late. He was the one who had insisted on coming. She had never really felt at ease here, but he knew that she had said nothing because of her great love for him. He had let her down; his sense of guilt was overwhelming. And she hadn't even been properly buried, amongst her own people. How would her spirit find rest?

He didn't remember the first time he bought a pint of whiskey. At first he just drank beer, after work with his comrades. Then he began to buy six-packs to bring home on the weekends, and he kept lonely vigils drinking while the boy slept, often until the first light of dawn crept into the sky.

But he discovered that he liked the whiskey better because it made him feel less fuzzy-headed than the beer did. Initially it sharpened his senses, making him aware of every sound and smell, every nuance of his environment. His self-perception seemed clearer, too, at least early in the evening, before had drunk most of the bottle. He could see the present from the point of view of the past, and he thought he could discern the whole picture of his life, his struggle to be both Indian and not Indian, his desire to keep with the old ways

Circling

but also to learn the white man's ways. But as the evening wore on, his sense of clarity would be taken over by a storm cloud of emotion, a mixture of self-pity and hopelessness to which he eventually would succumb. He became dependent on that bittersweet surrender to despair that obliterated all volition and responsibility, all of the nagging self-recrimination.

Then one morning he woke up sprawled across the table, his head on his arms, and saw that he had knocked over the empty bottle in his sleep. He leaned over to retrieve it but slipped sideways off of the chair, his shaky hand unable to hold on to the bottle as he fell. Appalled by his own weakness, he had one moment of lucidity. He knew that if he kept on like this, soon he would not be able to take care of his son. He knew it was time to leave, to go home. He was so relieved and grateful for this unbidden vision that he gathered himself into a ball, right there on the cracked linoleum floor, and fell into a deep sleep.

The next morning he got up, washed his face, and woke the boy. Without offering an explanation, he forced the sleepy child into his Levi jacket and shoes, which he put on over his pajamas. Nate did not protest; he had become so withdrawn into himself during his mother's illness that he was like a puppet, mind wooden and emotions numb to what was happening around him and utterly obedient, accepting whatever his father asked of him. Throwing their few possessions into a backpack, Red Hawk lifted the boy onto his shoulders, and, ducking under the door to protect the child's head, headed for the Greyhound Bus Station that was ten blocks away.

He bought them two tickets to Coeur d' Alene, Idaho, which was the farthest they could go with the money he had. Then he bought the child a breakfast of milk and doughnuts from a sleepy clerk at the station. He himself did not eat; his stomach still churned from the night's drinking, and the last thing he wanted was food. Struggling to hold on to some semblance of rationality for the boy's sake, he rejected the idea of buying a drink, even though his whole being craved it.

Pamella Hays

After the bus ride to Coeur d' Alene they hitchhiked into Montana. When they were waiting along the highway for someone to pick them up, he carried Nate on his shoulders, but sometimes the boy wanted to walk, and Red Hawk was impressed with his stamina.

Gradually the landscape metamorphosed from one of human dominance and habitation to long, unbroken stands of evergreens, somber dark hills and sometimes hard-won cattle pastures, spotted with tree stumps, or fields of hay with an isolated ranch house tucked into the folds of a hill. Beside them the river tumbled along in frothy foam, or in other stretches meandered more sedately, unwinding like a bolt of blue satin.

Most of the people who picked him up were curious but kind. He suspected that they got rides so easily because of Nate, who was, he had to admit, a charming and well-mannered child. He spoke when spoken to but never interrupted a conversation and more often that not fell asleep as soon as the car began to move.

To Red Hawk's surprise, they arrived in the city of Kalispell almost as soon as they would have by bus, in the early evening. A nasty slush storm was blanketing the area, and he put his Navy pea coat over Nate, whose own Levi jacket was totally inadequate for winter weather. The boy had to be fed, and he needed to go to the bathroom. Red Hawk chose the first pub he found, paying for a hamburger for Nate and a bottle of cheap liquor for himself with one of his two remaining twenty-dollar bills. After Nate had eaten and they had warmed up, he took the child's hand and headed east along the highway towards the reservation, hoping to catch another ride.

He couldn't believe how much things had changed in just seven short years. The "Strip," as the locals called it, was blocks longer than he remembered and now boasted several huge discount stores, their parking lots bigger than football fields. They had sprung up like corporate bullies, elbowing aside small older businesses, tire shops, dilapidated mom and pop motels, and car washes that had been there for years and now looked forlorn and wizened next to their giant neighbors. The traffic reflected the general chaos of a road too small

Circling

for the growing population and the frantic discomfort of drivers more used to a slower pace. Horns honked in irritation while cars switched lanes or took exits without signaling, their drivers apparently heedless of the driving snow.

The storm was more staid and serious now, with less wind but bigger flakes which, in the fading light, could still be seen spinning down endlessly, a plague of cold, white aliens descending upon the city. Nervous about Nate being so near the busy road, Red Hawk lifted him once again onto his shoulders.

He realized that Nate was getting tired; he could feel his head bump against his own as they walked, his fingers that clutched his father's neck loosening as he occasionally nodded off to sleep. Closer to the edge of town, aware that this time of night no one was likely to pick them up, he stopped, took the boy off of his shoulders, and carried him in his arms. When he saw the apartment complex he veered off of the road and walked towards it, his back aching from the weight of the child in his arms. For the moment his mind was too frozen to make a plan. "I'll just rest here a minute," he thought, "until I decide what to do." He sank down into the snow against a wall on the sheltered side of the building, and cuddling the boy against his chest, reached his left arm back awkwardly and pulled the whiskey bottle out of the pack.

Molly

After the second brief, uncomfortable visit with her mysterious guest, Molly felt totally irritated by the whole situation. Who did he think he was, invading her home and offering a lame apology for his unconscionable behavior several weeks ago? Yet she had to admit that, even if his apology lacked grace, it did seem sincere. And he looked very different, of course, than the first time he had been in her home. His face had more character and strength than she had expected; she reflected that anyone passed out from alcohol lost his or her identity, their face a flabby, loose mask of drunkenness, their real self masked.

And she was hugely relieved to know that the boy was all right. He had become a constant presence in her mind, though she had no idea why. She had always liked children, but she hadn't been around one in quite a long time, and she wasn't aware that she had missed them. Or perhaps it wasn't that she had missed them altogether but simply that this particular child had gotten under her skin. He was so extraordinarily beautiful. What she had said to his father about his being so striking was true. He had eyes that penetrated one's façade and seemed to see right through to one's innermost secrets. She thought that a foolish, old-fashioned notion, but the truth of it wouldn't go away. She had a thing about eyes being reflections of a person's essential being, of one's soul. It discomfited her to realize that his father had exactly the same eyes, though more wary and distrustful, and both father and son's eyes had reflected the soul of an enormously sensitive, perceptive human being. It was unsettling.

Circling

Annoyed at her unbidden train of thought, she shook her head sharply and went into the kitchen to wash the breakfast dishes. This was her precious day off, and she wasn't going to waste it by trying to figure out a man and child that she never planned to see again. She had had quite enough of the male sex to last her for, well, perhaps for a lifetime, she reflected. Nothing reassured her more than her independence, her chosen solitary life, and she banged the last dish into the rack with a force that echoed her thoughts.

She spent the day cleaning the apartment and cooking a good supper, something that she seldom took the time to do. There was something enormously satisfying about sitting in an ordered, shining home and eating a wonderful meal. To make the evening perfect, one of her favorite movies was on television, and she snuggled down contentedly into her old armchair.

She went to bed at midnight, anticipating the early morning shift that she would have to work tomorrow. Sometime during the night she felt a cold breeze across her face, and she pulled up the covers, too sleepy to wonder where the cold draft was coming from. Then she felt a presence hovering over her. It was too dark to see the form of the man, but she knew instinctively that he was there. She was complete awake now, every nerve in her body alert and humming with fear.

In an instant she felt him on top of her, one hand over her mouth and the other hand, large and rough, tearing at her nightgown. His hair brushed against her face. In her nightmare terror he seemed huge, gargantuan. She struggled, but it made no difference; his weight pinned her down to the bed, crushing her lungs. The reek of alcohol and cigarettes that seemed to emanate from every pore of his body overwhelmed her. She gagged, suppressing the urge to vomit as he violated her.

She began to feel as if she were floating somewhere above the bed. Her mind became an observer, refusing to acknowledge what was happening to her. From above she saw the large dark shadow laboring over her, his breath coming in short barks, as if he was running up a hill. But then in the midst of the nightmare of suffocating terror, an inexplicable feeling of empathy overcame her, a sudden and searing intuition that his pain was as great as hers. A great sob filled her throat and escaped through her mouth, the expression of a suffering so profound that she could not imagine surviving it.

Suddenly it was over. His heavy body lay on her for just an instant. Then he sat up, hitting her hard across the mouth with a blow that split her bottom lip open. Before she could cry out, he jumped off of the bed, running out of her bedroom and down the hall. Not a word had been exchanged between them, but she heard him slam the door as he went out, cursing at the screech it made when he pulled it shut. Her confused sense tried to recognize anything familiar in the sound. Did she know that voice?

She knew she should do something: scream for help; get up and lock the door; take a shower; call the police. But she was unable to move. Her heart pounded so hard that she thought it would explode out of her chest, leaving a gaping wound. Her limbs trembled uncontrollably, her whole body shaken by some enormous, unseen force. She had heard descriptions of rape as a violation of one's most private self, but until now she had never imagined its devastation. It was as if she no longer existed; all that was left was a pathetic body, a rag doll person with no feelings or thoughts or will, something that could be ravaged and abused and left helpless, its bright button eyes staring fixedly into a dark and violent world.

Gradually the shaking diminished, and her mind slowly crept back into her body. She moved her legs first, curling them up into the fetal position, and she lay like that for a long time. She wrapped her arms around her chest in a gesture of solidarity and comforting, as a kind friend might have done, and she felt her natural body warmth gradually suffuse her frozen torso like the small, incipient flames of an awakening campfire.

Finally she forced herself to sit up and then stand. Shambling along in haphazard fashion like a shaky patient recovering from surgery, she made her way to the bathroom. All she could think about

Circling

was to get into the shower, into hot, hot water, as soon as possible. Though her hands were still quivering, she managed to turn on the water and grab a bar of soap. Then she stood, naked and ashamed and trembling, while a stream of tears slid down her face and mingled with the cascade of water that pummeled her, burning her cut lip and leaving her skin red and raw. But her scarified heart could not be warmed. It was as numb and cold as the winter wind whistling across the plain.

Red Hawk

The cry of the hawk in his dream woke him up. He sat bolt upright in his bed, his heart racing. For a moment he did not know where he was, the dream had been that powerful. Gradually he realized he was on the single bed in the cheap motel room he rented during the week while he worked. The sky was still dark, so he figured it wasn't yet time to get up. He could hear the patter of rain on the metal roof. He shivered and pulled the covers up around his shoulders.

It had been a long time since the hawk had come to visit him. Sometimes the dreams were benevolent, full of shining white clouds and peaceful vistas, imparting a feeling of euphoria, but this one was starkly different. Red Hawk was soaring over a landscape that was black and desolate, as if everything in it had been burned by a great fire. Below he could see people scurrying to and fro in panic, carrying small children in their arms, and old people simply sitting still, their heads resting in their hands. Trees stood in scorched ruin, their charred branches lifted towards the heavens as if beseeching mercy. The air smelled of smoke and carrion.

Then he saw a man below, a white man, he surmised, because he was dressed in a long, black coat, black trousers, and a cowboy style hat. He appeared calm, almost like a statue, and his demeanor showed no sense of the chaos and grief surrounding him. In his hand he had a gun, and Red Hawk suddenly understood that he was aiming straight at him. In response, he dove towards the earth at a sharp angle, hoping to avoid the blow, but it hit him beneath his right

Circling

wing, penetrating the rib cage, and he could feel himself descending in a slow, free-falling spiral towards the earth.

Red Hawk's body trembled. Dreams like this were warnings, his mother had taught him, premonitions that were ignored at one's peril. He pushed back the tangled hair from his face and rubbed his eyes vigorously. Though it was only five o'clock, sleep was out of the question.

While he showered he tried to dissect the dream's significance: Obviously it meant that someone, perhaps himself, perhaps someone he loved, was in danger. The scorched black earth could mean many things, from holocaust to the end of the world, but he was struck by the idea that the people running in sheer terror seemed to be Native Americans. And then the symbol of the dominant power: the white man with the rifle, aiming straight at him. Was this a warning? Was something terrible going to happen?

He dressed hurriedly and drove to a nearby restaurant that he knew opened early. In the vestibule was a battered public telephone. The telephone book, torn and bereft of half of its pages, dangled from a small metal chain like a crippled appendage. He lifted the receiver and waited impatiently for the automatic message telling him to dial the number. Immediately after he did so, the same disembodied voice asked him to deposit six quarters for the call to Browning.

His mother picked up the phone and answered in a sleepy voice; he had obviously awakened her. "Mother, is Nate all right? Is everyone o.k.?" he almost shouted into the mouthpiece.

"Yes, we're fine. Everyone's asleep. What has happened? Are you sick or something?" her worried voice skipped along the line, betraying her fear.

"Yes, I'm fine. I'm sorry; I didn't think. I just had such a terrible dream!"

His mother's tone was immediately wary. "Son, you must pay attention. You must be very careful today at work. Maybe something will happen to you on the job?"

"Don't worry, I'll be careful. Sorry I woke you. Keep a close eye on Nate today, would you?"

Her calm voice reassured him. "Of course I will. He'll be fine. Call me this evening and tell me what is going on, please?"

Red Hawk agreed and hung up the phone. He walked into the café and took a booth by the window. It was still dark outside, and the neon lights were reflected in gaudy geometric patterns on the wet pavement. Inside, a few diners, mostly men, were hunched over cups of coffee. A few others, still half asleep, shoveled hash browns and eggs into their mouths hypnotically.

He felt no hunger whatsoever, but he knew he would have to eat something, or he would never endure the day's work. The waitress recognized him and asked, "The usual?" He nodded and then tried to smile at her. She had always been brusque but courteous towards him. "Bad night?" she asked.

"You might say that," he answered, smiling ruefully. He forced himself to eat slowly, and gradually the coffee and food had their effect. His thinking became more rational, steadier, and the fog of emotion that the dream had wrapped around him receded. He tried and tried to parse the dream's meaning, to interpret the symbols, but all he could come up with for certain was the tone of warning about something bad that was about to happen.

Filled with a vague but uncomfortable foreboding, he paid his bill and decided to drive to the work site. He was almost an hour early, but he didn't care; it was as if he needed to face whatever malign force was out there waiting for him. He drove in a trance through the slight early-morning traffic, surprised when he arrived at the site just on the north end of town. The three story condo they were constructing stood like the forlorn remains of a bombed building, its skeleton lit by the orange of the sunrise that had begun to push through the clouds.

Only one other man was at the construction site, the Irishman who had more or less befriended him. "What the hell's wrong with you,

Circling

buddy? You look like you've been kicked by a horse!" Joe greeted him with a laugh.

Unruffled, Red Hawk answered, "Bad dream. Couldn't sleep."

Joe shot him a suspicious look and joked, "Too much bad whiskey, huh?"

This time Red Hawk's voice was less warm. "Nah, I gave that up. It's bad for the soul. Of course you Irishmen can appreciate that," he added reproachfully.

"Touché," Joe responded, and then turned and walked away to the chemical toilet that stood at the back of the building.

Red Hawk immediately regretted his remark; it wasn't like him to be so thin-skinned, and he determined to make it up to Joe somehow.

The morning's work went relatively smoothly, and by noon Red Hawk's somber mood was beginning to lift a little. But as he sat down to eat his lunch, a police car, lights flashing in a display of official machismo, spun into the work site, kicking up mud.

He didn't know why he knew, but he knew that they were coming for him. He stood in anticipation, putting his lunch sack down on the makeshift plywood table. The officers stepped away from the car and moved towards him; evidently they were looking for an Indian, and on this site, he was it.

They approached him, bristling with hostility. He made one futile attempt at conversation. "Is there a problem, officer?" he asked in a measured tone.

"You could say that," the younger man offered sarcastically. And then he added, "You need to come with us."

Despite his resolution to remain calm, Red Hawk panicked. "What's the matter? Are you arresting me?"

The older officer, his ample belly hanging like a large double chin over the edge of his belt, took charge. "No, sir, you're not under arrest. We'd just like you to come down to the station with us for questioning; we need some information from you. We would appreciate your cooperation," he said.

65

Pamella Hays

Something inside Red Hawk turned to stone. His face became impassive, betraying no emotion. He merely nodded in assent and moved mechanically towards the waiting police car. Work on the site came to a full stop, and the resulting silence was louder than the noise of the hammers and saws that had filled the air only moments ago, as all of his co-workers stared at the scene, some curiously and others spitefully.

The younger officer led Red Hawk to the car and thoughtfully opened the back door for him. Then he got in on the passenger side in front, and the older policeman revved the engine and spun the car around adeptly.

Two distinct trains of thought kept whirling inside Red Hawk's head during the fifteen-minute ride to the station downtown. One was a kind of stoic affirmation of, and appreciation for, the warning of his medicine animal. The other was less hopeful. He understood that he was helpless, that he fit the profile of a troublemaker, guilty merely because of who he was.

Nothing good could come of this, he thought, even as he wracked his brain for some kind of logical explanation. He wondered if the girl in the apartment where he and Nate had spent the night might have reported him for harassment after his second visit. She hadn't seemed any too pleased to see him. He shook off this thought because he could see in his mind the light blue of her eyes, which had no unkindness in them. He reminded himself that she had once offered him the refuge of her home, at a time when he was the least worthy of being a guest. He shook his head in disgust and frustration, unable to unravel the knot his life had suddenly become.

The officer, typing with lightning one-finger speed on the old typewriter, began with simple questions about his name, address, etc., but gradually the questions became more troubling. He asked Thomas if he knew a woman named Molly Henderson. Red Hawk said he didn't believe he did. The officer then queried, "Do you know a woman who lives at the West Side Apartment complex?"

Circling

Red Hawk's heart jumped. "No," he answered, and then, correcting himself, he said, "Yes, in a way, I mean I don't know her name, but I was there once, uh, twice, I guess." He was aware that his answer was awkward and reeked of evasion, but he was totally unprepared for this line of questioning. Had something happened to her? Whatever it was, why would they think he had anything to do with it? Gathering his thoughts, he clarified, "My son and I stayed with her when we got here from Seattle. She let us spend the night. And then the other day I went by to thank her."

The young policeman shot Red Hawk a look full of disbelief. "Mm," he said, and then, "When was your second visit to her apartment?"

Red Hawk hesitated for a brief moment. "The last time I was there was in mid-January. I wouldn't know the exact date," he said.

"Can you tell me where you were on the night of February 6th?"

"Last night?" Red Hawk asked. "I was in my motel room here in town."

"Is there anyone who could corroborate that?" the officer added.

Red Hawk shook his head, the seriousness of his problem hitting him fully for the first time. "No," he said miserably, "I was alone."

The policeman stopped typing and looked directly at Red Hawk. "Thomas Red Hawk," he said in a tone of icy courtesy. "I'm afraid I'm going to have to ask you to come with me. I'm detaining you for twenty-four hours under the suspicion of sexual violation pending a line-up tomorrow for identification."

Red Hawk's mind somersaulted as if he had just been delivered a severe blow to the temple. As he followed the officer to the row of cells, all he could think was of the old refrain he had heard so often in Western movies: 'The only good Indian is a dead Indian.' Stories his Indian friends had told him about their encounters with the law ricocheted around in his brain, confirming his pessimism.

The cell the officer took him to was the second in a line of identical cells: tiny, claustrophobic three-sided rooms exposed like the

67

Pamella Hays

rooms in a dollhouse to the eyes of the world. He did not sleep all night long but lay on his bunk staring into space, out through the bars of the small window on the back wall. There were so many lights on in the corridor that he could not actually see the sky, but he forced himself to imagine that the stars were there, keeping the world on course, even if his own private world were in chaos.

Over and over he repeated her name, "Molly Henderson." Why hadn't he ever asked her what her name was, he wondered? He chastised himself for being so trusting of her, for imagining that she was different than other white women he had met, that she somehow was capable of compassion.

"But why would she ever have taken us in, then?" he wondered. And then, much to his dismay, because the feeling undermined his righteous, sustaining rage, he reminded himself of how much she must be suffering, that she had been raped, that she was afraid and alone and confused. His mind turned somersaults. Maybe she hadn't accused him but simply told them about him? After all, they didn't charge him right away: he was being held for twenty-four hours for questioning, and they said he was going to be in a line-up, which meant that maybe she herself didn't know who had done this to her?

By morning he was exhausted but possessed of that very clear, focused mental state that one sometimes achieves for a brief time after experiencing a trauma. He resented that he had not known where the interrogation was leading until almost the end. There was no convincing and believable way to defend oneself against the unknown.

When the public defender came to talk to him, he was much more coherent and self-defensive than he had been with the officer. The attorney, a short, round man with a bald head ringed with red hair, a pair of tortoise-shell glasses perched on his nose, explained to him that his fate rested in the hands of the victim, who would be identifying someone in the line-up. If she couldn't identify him as her attacker, Red Hawk would be released; if she did identify him, he would be formally charged and probably held without bail. All of this information was given in a matter-of-fact, impersonal way, for

68

Circling

which Red Hawk was strangely grateful. He didn't want to plead his innocence, to beg for mercy. He wanted only to keep himself together until after the line-up. Then he would face whatever came.

Later that morning, an hour or so after his attorney had left, Red Hawk was led into a small room with a long, opaque piece of glass along one side. The officer in charge handed him a number, which he was instructed to put up in front of his chest. He glanced sideways at his fellow prisoners, one other of whom was Indian, and the other two who were white, their long-hair and unshaven faces and unkempt clothing labeling them as bums or drunks.

Red Hawk had seen this situation on television, and he was perfectly aware that behind the glass Molly stood watching him and the other men. He tried to send her a mental message: "Don't do this. I am innocent. You must know that." But his thoughts merely bounced off of the glass like pebbles and fell to the floor beneath.

He was miserable and helpless and disheveled and hated the idea that she was seeing him like this. Red Hawk pulled himself up to his full height, silently intoning his medicine chant, and looked defiantly into the unseen eyes on the other side.

Now I have his attention. He still cannot hear me, but his ears are no longer stone deaf. He refuses to see the obvious. He turns away from the path he needs to follow. I am all he has to find the path again, but I can do nothing if he won't listen to me. He is in grave peril, too proud to admit that he cannot do this alone. He sings his medicine song and draws himself up, and I leave him for a moment to go to her.

I perch on the ledge next to the girl. She has the ability to see, although she does not yet know it, and her ears too are not entirely deaf. I try to fix her with my stare. I flap my wings to get her to look at me, but she is too enclosed within herself. She has wrapped grieving around herself like a shroud. I feel her wounds, but I know she must heal them herself. When she does not respond, I fly just above her head, my powerful wings creating a draft of air that lifts her hair. Finally, in desperation, I fly over and perch on her shoulder. She reacts by shrugging her shoulder and trying to shake me off, but I stay.

Then the man in the uniform asks her to identify the man who inflicted her wounds. I brush my wing against her hair and my claws curl more tightly around her shoulder. She moves her head as if to dislodge me, but I persist. At last she looks at him, and I feel a wave of blackness sweep over her. I think she is in danger of falling, but she rights herself.

I go back to him and make a vision of white light to surround him and counteract the dark; I clothe him in this light.

Circling

She blinks her eyes at this light and looks away, and then moves her head in the shape of 'no.'

I flap my wings and cry out in approval. She does not hear me, but he does. His troubled face changes into the proud, aquiline features of the hawk, and his spirit comes back into his body.

Molly

It was March, the month in Montana that could never decide whether it wanted to continue being winter or make a feeble attempt to be spring. Molly was reminded of Shakespeare's warnings about the Ides of March; this season's fitful, temperamental weather suited her own mood perfectly.

Six weeks had passed since the attack, what she had begun to cryptically refer to in her own mind as "The Defining Moment," and though she had healed physically, the psychic scars still lingered, ambushing her at the most unlikely moments. It could be something as simple as an appraising look from a man in the store where she worked or a sudden loud noise, and she would break into a sweat and begin to tremble. Suzanne had been extraordinarily kind, even suggesting that she take some time off of work, but Molly had found that, if she was alone, the memories were more frequent and painful, and so she opted to work her full schedule.

Now she locked her door with a bolt and a chain, as the police had suggested, and still she felt unsafe. Seldom did she sleep all night; most of the time she would awaken at the smallest sound, her nerves immediately on edge.

But the worst thing, aside from her permanent feeling of being unclean, a reality that made her the least desirable woman on the planet, surely unworthy of ever being loved, was the guilt she felt, the self-loathing that overcame her, when she had been asked to identify her attacker in the line-up.

Circling

She was astounded that they had so quickly rounded up Red Hawk. He had looked as bewildered and shocked as an animal caught in headlights, and her heart fell into her stomach when she saw him holding up his number, his eyes defiant and challenging.

At first, when the police answered her 911 call, it had never occurred to her to tell the officer about him, because she really had not consciously allowed herself to consider that he might be her attacker. But when the police asked her if she often invited men into her home, she was so insulted and enraged that she blurted out that no man had been there in the last year except for a Native American and his son who needed shelter.

Immediately she regretted her remark, because the office seized on it like a dog unearthing a bone. She was still shaken, exhausted, and terrified, and certainly not in any shape to parry his barrage of questions. He was scornful of her 'naiveté' (she knew he meant stupidity) in having allowed her unexpected visitors to spend the night and pointed out to her that the man had obviously come back to see her with the excuse of an apology while he was all the while planning how he would get in to her apartment.

The more he insisted and bludgeoned her with his logic, the more reasonable his argument seemed, and yet she couldn't drag her mind into acquiescence. She thought about Nate and the beautiful moccasins, and she couldn't bring herself to imagine such betrayal. On the other hand, the man who had raped her was indeed large, had long hair, and smelled of alcohol, and these facts kept her mind in a state of constant imbalance and self-doubt.

She assumed that the local police had taken her description of Red Hawk to the Browning tribal police, along with that of the child, and that they had been able to put two and two together. Still, her stomach had flipped as she looked through the glass at the men in the line, and she thought for a moment she would throw up. She tried her best to look into their souls, to imagine each one of them lying on top of her, hurting her, indifferent to her pain. She understood that this was a grave responsibility on her part, but she knew in heart that, while they all had the basic physical build and size that might have indicated her attacker, she could not honestly say that she recognized any of them without doubt. Ultimately she shook her head and repeated again that she had never seen her attacker in the dark, so she could identify no one with certainty.

The police were obviously displeased with her hesitation, but there was nothing they could do, and so they had to release Red Hawk. Molly knew that this would happen, and she prayed that she had done the right thing, the policeman's warning about serial rapists echoing in her thoughts.

But then last week the police had called and told her that they thought they had found the man who had violated her. She went down to the station again but was, as before, unable to definitively identify him. Fortunately, however, another victim was able to do so. Though her sense of relief was enormous, her sense of guilt that she had ever implicated the Native American only increased.

Despite her better judgment, she found that her subconscious was working on a plan. The idea of going over to Browning and trying to find him haunted her. He had once come and apologized to her; did she have the same courage? She wondered what had happened to him as a result of the arrest. She didn't know much about him, but the old, 'beater' car he had driven away in was evidence of the fact that he was probably working at some job comparable to her own. She made up her mind that on her next day off she would go in search of him and try to make amends for what had happened.

Nate

Grandmother was extremely quiet this morning. She set his bowl of oatmeal absentmindedly in front of him, forgetting to give him a spoon. He got up and got one for himself; he knew where they were, because one of his chores was to put away the dishes when they had dried. Somehow it didn't seem as if he should break into her thoughts, so serious was the frown on her face, so he ate quickly and quietly and, putting on his boots and jacket, went outside to play.

The snow had almost melted, but patches of ice remained on the sidewalk and under the eaves. The ground was muddy and sloppy, and the sky was low and dark. This reminded him of rainy days in Seattle, but it was much colder here. When the wind was blowing, he didn't stay outside for long, because sometimes it was so strong that he felt as if it could pick him up and blow him down the street like an empty tin can.

But today the wind was behaving itself, and the time went faster outside than when he was inside. Today was Friday. He knew that because his Auntie had told him so last night, and that meant that his father would be home in time for supper, if he were lucky. His father's homecoming always thrilled him. A pleasant sensation of warmth and security would start at his toes and wend its way up into his heart when he saw his father walk through the door. Once in a while he brought him something, a special rock he had found, or a bird's feather for good luck, or a woodcarving he had made with his carpenter tools. Still, to Nate the presents were wonderful but irrelevant. The best gift was sleeping curled up next to his father in the big bed that had seemed so lonely all week long.

He was leaning over the gate trying to get it to swing when his father's car drove up in front of the house. It was still morning, so he was amazed to see him there, but Nate immediately got down and raced over to him. Red Hawk picked up his son and swung him high in the air, as he always did, but his face was somber, and his eyes were unsmiling. He put Nate down rather than carry him into the house, and he forgot even to take his hand as they walked. Quick to read his father's moods, Nate wondered if he was going away from him again, like he used to, but he didn't smell that way, and he didn't stumble when he walked.

Auntie came to the door, opening it for them, and scrutinized her brother's face. Then Grandmother came in from the kitchen, drying her hands on her apron, and she too seemed strange. No one said so much as hello. And then his father told him to go play outside again, and he knew for sure that something was wrong—one of those grown-ups secrets that children were never supposed to hear—although he couldn't imagine why. Who would he tell, anyway? Wasn't he part of the family, too? He hesitated a little as he headed for the door and started to protest, but the impatient look in his father's eyes stopped him, and he went reluctantly into the yard.

He played outside as long as he could, peeking in the window from time to time to see that the grown-ups were still sitting around the kitchen table talking. But finally it began to get much colder; the wind picked up, and he couldn't feel his ears after a while because they were so cold. Finally he went up to the door and opened it very softly. No one seemed to notice. He sat down, took off his muddy boots as Auntie had showed him, and sat still, his back against the door, hoping he would not be scolded for coming in.

He heard words he didn't know, like 'rape' and 'arrested' and 'fired', but the way his father said them, with such bitterness and anger in his tone, Nate knew they were bad words, the kind he had been warned never to use. He felt the tension in the room. The

Circling

two women held cups of strong, black coffee in their hands, but they did not drink, and their faces were like wooden masks. His father alternated between sitting and standing up, and sometimes he would pace back and forth, gesturing like the men on television who gave speeches.

At last his Grandmother saw him there, and, nodding towards him, put out her hand for him to come to her. His father instantly stopped talking, and he saw his large shoulders sag and his head bend down, as if he had been a puppet whose strings were suddenly slackened. The ensuing silence was worse than the angry talking, and Nate wished that someone would say something.

The women got up and began preparing supper; his father went into the living room and turned on the television. It was time for what they all told him was 'the news', a time when he was supposed to be quiet. But no one needed to remind him of that tonight. He climbed up onto his father's lap, and his long arms enfolded Nate in an automatic gesture. For now that was enough, and despite his fears, Nate began to breathe easier.

The next day his father got up very early and was gone before he awakened. He was upset that his father had not told him good-bye, but his Auntie assured him that he would be back again that afternoon.

During the night his father had slept restlessly, rocking back and forth and mumbling words out loud. Once Nate heard him say "shot down, shot down." His father's apparent anguish unsettled Nate, making him feel afraid. He wanted to touch his father, to wake him up, but he thought that he might be angry if he did so. It was not until dawn that his father appeared to be sleeping deeply and peacefully.

On Sunday afternoon his father sat him down and had a talk with him. He told him that he didn't have any job, that the last one had ended, and he needed to go back to town to look for another one. He looked tired and sad, and Nate tried to reassure him by listening very seriously and not interrupting, like a grown-up. But he could not resist asking, "Did your job burn up?"

Red Hawk looked puzzled, and then, smiling a little, answered, "No, Nate, getting fired doesn't mean that anything burned up. It just means that I can't work there anymore."

This answer only made the riddle deeper, but Nate did not ask any further questions.

When his father put on his jacket and walked to the door, Nate followed him but did not hold on to his leg as he often did. Instead of the usual bear hug, his father just looked down at him and patted his head and told him to take good care of his grandmother and auntie. Nate nodded his head in assent but did not dare to look into his father's face, because he did not want him to see the tears that were filling his eyes.

Red Hawk

As soon as he walked into the store and saw her in the second aisle from the door, opening a box of canned goods, Red Hawk regretted his decision. It was not like him to be impulsive, and he didn't even know why he had come. The smoldering rage he had felt towards her after his arrest had subsided, leaving him with only a hollow feeling of betrayal. He had vowed that he would never approach her again, and he had avoided even getting gas there. He blamed his decision today on the bad night he had had, a night, to tell the truth, that was like all the other ones, full of bad dreams and weird, unsettling images. Somewhere in his dreams last night he had seen her face, or at least someone who looked very much like her, and he felt as if he had been drawn here despite himself.

Molly, absorbed in her task, did not see him at the door. A strand of loose hair kept tickling her nose as she kneeled over the box, and finally she had to step away and sneeze into her sleeve. When she looked up, she saw him watching her, and every muscle in her body tensed.

Red Hawk noticed immediately the difference in her; her skin was extremely pale, almost translucent. She had become so thin that the skin over her prominent cheekbones was pulled taut, and there were large dark circles under her eyes. He was so startled by her appearance that he realized with a start that he had been staring, and he looked immediately away.

For her part, Molly laid down the Exacto knife that she had been using to cut open the box and stood utterly still. She felt sure that he could hear her heart thumping in her chest; it filled her ears with a roar like a waterfall. She forced herself to take a deep breath. After all, she had thought about finding him more than once and apologizing, and here he was in front of her. She didn't need to stand there trembling like a schoolgirl.

He approached her slowly, his body ramrod straight, looking at her but not saying a word. The silence lengthened, becoming an unbearable weight pressing down on them. Finally Molly spoke. "I've been meaning to talk to you. I wanted….there's something I wanted to say."

Red Hawk's life was in a shambles because of this woman: he had lost his job; he was in a police file as having been a rape suspect; he had become for all practical purposes an insomniac. Yet the pathos in her face kindled a response that he did not want to feel, a response of empathy and concern, not at all the judgmental coldness that he had expected.

"Yes," he found himself saying. "I think we need to talk."

"Perhaps when I get off work you could come by the apartment?" Molly suggested.

"No!" he reacted sharply, and then, more calmly, he added, " No, not your house. Maybe we could have a cup of coffee somewhere?"

Molly couldn't believe that she had been so insensitive. Of course he couldn't come to her apartment. She blushed deeply, ashamed, but managed to add, "How about Charlie's at five thirty?"

Red Hawk merely nodded and then walked away.

Outside, he permitted himself finally to breathe. He realized that, for weeks now, he had felt as if he were drowning, being pushed down farther and farther into a bottomless river by some overwhelming and indifferent force. At least now he could perhaps start to float up to the surface, to begin some kind of healing. He intuitively knew that she must be feeling the same. It would be easy to fill up the rest of the day until she got off work. Every day he followed up on the classified ads in the paper. At first he had gone only to construction jobs, but having no luck there, he had begun to lower his sights. At

Circling

this point almost anything would do, anything, he reflected, except washing dishes, which was women's work.

He finally worked up the courage to respond to an ad that had run for two weeks, indicating that they had still not found anyone to fill the position. Maybe he would have better luck at a place like that. A home repair and upkeep business needed a handyman to do a variety of odd jobs, it said. He drove to the address given and was relieved to be greeted courteously by a large, friendly blonde woman behind the desk. The place itself was small and unassuming, but clean and upbeat, with an air of efficiency and purpose. For the first time in a while, he felt a little spark of hope rise in his chest; perhaps, he thought, his medicine had not entirely deserted him.

After a brief interview, the secretary gave him an application form and asked him to come back the next day. He left the office feeling buoyant, as if with little effort he could float above the gray March day into what he knew must be the sunny skies above the clouds.

As he got into the car to go to the restaurant where he was to meet Molly, he realized that he was looking forward to having coffee with her, even though he was apprehensive, too. He liked her name; the simplicity and matter-of-factness of it suited her well. Seated safely in the car, he allowed himself a small war-whoop of pleasure.

Molly

She couldn't believe that she had agreed to a date. Well, perhaps not a formal date; she had agreed to go snowshoeing with him in the Park. She convinced herself that her response to his invitation was nothing more than a mixture of natural curiosity about him and gratitude that he had not remained angry at her for turning him in to the police. All things considered, he had been much more sympathetic than she had imagined. Besides, she was curious to know what the Park would be like in winter; she had only ventured there in the summer, with all of the other tourists. She had warned him that she had never used snowshoes and had no gear, but he had said he would take care of everything. He would be by early on Saturday morning.

As she put in her time at work for the next two days, she found herself reflecting back on their conversation at Charlie's. He had been late, and she sat in the booth listening to the cacophony of loud talk, whispered confidences, and deliberately raucous laughter from the other tables. She had chosen this place because it was a hangout for the young crowd from the local high school—more precisely, the alternative kids, the ones who wore clothing reminiscent of the sixties Hippie movement, and who sported tattoos, earrings in noses and navels, and provocative hair styles: Afros, Mohawks, or Dreads, sometimes in iridescent green or purple or pink. Without having analyzed why, she felt comfortable with these young people, and she loved to eavesdrop on their earnest philosophical and political conversations, which, despite their overtly cynical tone, were tinged with youthful idealism.

Circling

When Red Hawk walked through the door, he caused a bit of a stir; many of the students nodded approvingly at his satin-black hair that fell almost to his waist. She had to admit that he cut an imposing figure. She had an opportunity to really study his physique for the first time, and she liked the easy, loping walk, his broad shoulders and straight back, his physical grace. There was a palpable respect, almost awe, amongst his student admirers, but he did not seem to notice. He actually looked uncomfortable at the scrutiny, and he seemed greatly relieved when he saw her sitting in the booth on the other side of the room.

At first he had been almost mute, either ashamed or angry or maybe just very shy, she thought, and her own demeanor wasn't much better. She was so nervous that she kept fiddling with her cup, stirring in so much sugar that it practically gagged her to drink the syrupy coffee. She occupied her hands by making little tents and geometric forms with her napkin.

All day long Molly had been giving herself lectures on self-control. She could not and would not talk about the violent incident itself, but she did want him to understand her state of mind at the time and how vulnerable she had been to the policeman's inferences, resulting in her exposing him to the whole terrible mess.

When she finally worked up the courage to speak, her carefully rehearsed apology came out tersely, like a spring too tightly wound. Afraid to expose her still raw emotions, she tried to be businesslike and clinical.

"The police convinced me that I should turn you in," she said, her voice low and without inflection. "They said whoever it was could strike again with out warning, and that I was foolish to have taken you in like I did. At the time it seemed logical. I mean, I was under a lot of stress, and I didn't think it through." She added the last phrase defensively, as if she assumed anyone with half a brain would understand the state she had been in. And then, lowering her eyes and taking a deep breath, she added, "I'm sorry if I have caused you any harm." Even to her ear, the words sounded tinny and shallow.

Red Hawk was taken aback. He did not know what he had been expecting, but it was certainly not this. A flash of the old anger surfaced. This was an expiation of guilt, a releasing of shame that made her feel better undoubtedly, but it did nothing for him. It was in fact as if, to her, his humiliation and incarceration were merely tangential, a sideshow to the whole tragic main event.

Before he spoke, he took a deep breath. He reminded himself that he was older than she; while he had undergone something painful, and had been a hapless victim as she was, her trauma had been even worse. While he had been driving here he had struggled to understand what she must be feeling. It helped him to imagine that this might have happened to his wife, and then he could call up genuine compassion for her.

He looked directly into her eyes and spoke bluntly, going straight to the heart of the matter. "You have had a terrifying experience," he said. "I understand now that you did not intend necessarily to implicate me. At least, that is very much what I need to believe. I am glad that you have told me this. But that is all in the past now. We have both been hurt. The question is how will you get better?"

Molly looked surprised and puzzled. Until this moment, it had never occurred to her that she could get better. She simply lived with the suffocating brew of fear and humiliation and victim-hood from day to day, imagining that this was how the rest of her life would be. She was not ignorant about the subject of rape; she knew there were therapists who specialized in that particular trauma as well as support groups for women who had gone through the same nightmare, but none of this seemed her style. She had always insisted on going it alone, on figuring out her own problems, and besides, she would have to admit that there was a kind of martyr-like satisfaction in clinging to her grief. She was not certain yet that she wanted to let it go.

Ultimately, she had answered by saying, "I haven't gotten there yet, I mean to 'better'. I still feel as if my life stopped at that moment, that time stopped, and that I'll always be stuck there somehow." She felt a rush of shame that she was talking to this man, a man she didn't

Circling

know and didn't entirely approve of, about such intimate things. She looked down and needlessly stirred her coffee.

Red Hawk's response took her aback. He told her that he understood, that until very recently he had been stuck back in the past too. He spoke, briefly but with deep feeling, about his wife's death and his many months of running away from his grief by drinking. He too was amazed at him confession, that he would speak of such private things to her, but he felt somehow responsible towards her. He had done nothing deliberately to hurt her, but he had inadvertently pulled her along into the maelstrom of that difficult period of his life, and he felt he owed her an explanation.

To his amazement, it felt good to finally put it out there, to form the words that had been shut up in his mind for so long, to speak the thoughts that had become an evil mantra that would repeat themselves over and over, chasing through his mind like a cat pursuing its tail. Despite his inherent sense of isolation, he felt lighter, as if in his talking he had broken the spell of his negative thoughts, had taken away some of their power over him.

When he finished, an awkward silence descended, but it was not as tense as before. He scrutinized her face, reflecting that, because of the light color of her eyes, he could almost watch her mind working. At last she had smiled, a sad smile that seemed to break slowly, as if it had come from a long way down.

She said only, "You have given me something to think about. Thanks." And now, thinking back over the whole conversation as she worked, she didn't regret having told him about her real feelings. What he had said about his wife had been an offering of trust, something she hadn't had much of in a very long time. Maybe it wouldn't hurt her to consider the notion of healing, of getting better. If he had been able to do it, perhaps she could, too.

85

Nate

When Nate heard about the proposed snow shoeing trip, he did something which he rarely allowed himself to do: He begged and pleaded and harassed his father at every opportunity, dogging his every move as went about preparing for the trip. He knew by heart the grown-up mantra; he was 'too little' to go, but he refused to accept it. He was stronger than they gave him credit for, and more resilient. Hadn't he kept up on the hunting trip? There was no doubt in his mind that he was up to it, especially with the woman, Molly, coming along. She wouldn't be able to keep up with his father's long legs, and so his father would have to slow down.

When he had first heard her name, he had turned it over and over again on his tongue, savoring its whimsical sound. He liked to do that with new words, trying them out so many times that they finally turned back full circle and became nonsense words again, just little agglomerations of sound. His father had carefully explained to him who she was. He had only a vague image of her, but he could remember being in her apartment, drinking the sweet cocoa and being tucked into his bed on the floor. He remembered that she had been gentle, like his mother, although she was not Indian as his mother had been.

He thought he might have a chance of wearing his father down, because he was in such a good mood. He had told them at supper the night before about his first week on his new job. He had been treated fairly, he said, just like all the other staff. He liked the variety and the challenge of confronting new tasks every day and trying to figure

Circling

out how to solve the problems they presented. The pay was not great, but it was not stingy, either, and he had real hope that the job would last. Grandmother and Auntie had been so happy that they went outside and scooped up enough clean snow for sundaes, heaping on great amounts of sugar and frozen huckleberries.

By bedtime Nate knew better than to ask again; he intuited that he needed to give his father time to think, so he went to bed quietly, without protest. When the first light of morning softened the shadows, however, he was already wide-awake. His father slept next to him, breathing softly, but he got up and tiptoed out into the kitchen, where his grandmother, her long white hair sweeping across her back like the softest goose down, was busy stoking the fire in the stove.

He loved these still, peaceful mornings with his grandmother. They seldom spoke, but, despite her silence, when he was with her he always felt welcomed and included. When she saw him, she would smile at him and nod her head, placing her hand softly on his shoulder in greeting, and her eyes, snuggled down into the folds of her wrinkled eyelids, lit up with their dark fires when she looked at him.

His father had told him that she had once been very beautiful. He thought that she was beautiful still, small and fragile and soft but also strong as the Browning wind. He could see a halo of light all around her, like an angel, though he had never mentioned that to anyone else.

But he could not, no matter how hard he tried, imagine her when she was young. He had seen the photos of her and his grandfather hung on the wall, both of them looking shy and proud at the same time, and he studied these images diligently, trying to find his now-grandmother in them. Sometimes he could see something similar in her eyes, but her erect, lithe body encased in the white buckskin dress didn't resemble the tiny, stooped figure that prepared his food every day. The person in the photograph did not have his grandmother's gentleness; this woman looked strong and defiant, almost fierce, and he couldn't imagine his grandmother that way. He wondered what he would like when he was old. Would his face change so much too?

87

Pamella Hays

After he had eaten breakfast, Nate went into the living room to watch cartoons. What he saw over by the door, leaning against the wall, was better than the presents on Christmas morning and made his heart leap with joy: three pairs of snowshoes, one of them made for someone small. This could only mean that his father had decided to take him. He raced into the bedroom and jumped full-force on his father's prone body, whooping and shouting. Red Hawk came out of his between-sleep-and-waking reverie very quickly. His son was seldom this demonstrative, and he was pleased to see him so happy.

After breakfast they began to pack the car with the snow shoes, thermos, gaiters, and extra socks to keep their feet dry. Meanwhile, Auntie prepared a lunch for them to take, fussing over what Molly might like until Red Hawk intervened. "Don't worry. She's not a typical white woman; she won't be too particular," he joked. "Just make sure there's lots of whatever you fix."

Nate was excited that he sang to himself all the way to town, wiggling around in his car seat and tapping his foot against the door. Red Hawk teased him, "You're going to be too worn out to snow-shoe," he told him, laughing, but Nate ignored him, still absorbed in his own rhythmical intonations.

Molly

Molly was so totally delighted to see Nate that Red Hawk felt confirmed in his choice to bring him. He had to admit that there had been some selfishness in his decision. Somehow the thought of being out in the wilderness alone with her had seemed a little daunting.

While Nate accepted her embrace enthusiastically, the greeting between the adults was more strained. Finally, they settled for a handshake. Red Hawk approved of the way she was dressed; she had braided her hair into one long braid down her back, and she had a wool stocking cap pulled down over her ears. She had on several layers of clothing, indicating that she must have done some backcountry hiking, since experienced backpackers understood that layers could always be removed, but too few layers could leave one dangerously exposed to unexpected bad weather. She wore her usual leather hiking boots, well broken in, and had a small pack on her back.

His cramped, noisy car felt packed to the gills by the time they and all of their supplies were inside. Red Hawk thought she might find fault with the ramshackle vehicle, but she only smiled and said, "Cozy!"

Nate's feelings were obviously hurt that she chose to sit in the front seat with his father, but she quickly reassured that she would sit with him on the way back, and this seemed to mollify him. Within a short time he had fallen asleep, and Red Hawk told her how early he had gotten up and how he had been like a whirling dervish all morning, unable to contain his excitement.

"I think its great that you brought him," Molly said. "I've missed him."

Red Hawk always found her straightforward honesty a little unnerving, not because he didn't approve of it, but because it was, in his experience, so unusual. His own people were like that, unflinchingly candid, but it was not a trait he had found as often in white people. Like all other Americans, Red Hawk had been raised watching politicians and 'talking heads' on television, and his skepticism of them, which tended to extend to others as well, ran deep.

His ancestors had been great orators, but their speech had not been deceptive or manipulative; in fact, their words were notably spare and honorable, coming from their hearts. He had always suspected this very integrity had been one of the weaknesses of the native cultures; they simply did not understand that someone in a position of power would misuse it by lying to them. Of course, they had learned differently over time, and the results were devastating.

Molly had said something, and, involved in his thoughts, he had not heard her. "I'm sorry," he said, shaking his head as if to remove the cobwebs, "What were you saying?"

"I just asked how Nate liked living with his grandmother and aunt," she replied.

Red Hawk smiled. "He loves it," he said. "He's being spoiled rotten."

"Impossible," she retorted. "There's nothing spoiled about him."

Turning more serious, Red Hawk observed, "It's been very good for him to be around family. We were very isolated in Seattle, especially after his mother died." Then, sensing that he was steering towards a conversation he was not ready to have, he asked her, "What about your family?"

Molly did not answer right away. When she spoke it was hesitantly, not in her usual frank way. "I haven't been in contact very much with them lately," she said evasively. And then, "I suppose you could say that we didn't exactly get along."

Circling

Red Hawk thought better than to pry, so they both became quiet, Molly watching the countryside, now a patchwork of melting snow and bare ground, roll past. Finally she said, "What will it be like in the mountains? How much snow will there be up there?"

"I've gone hiking there as late as April and found snow," Red Hawk replied. "Of course I'm not talking about the tops of the peaks, where the glaciers stay year round, but even the high meadows sometimes have snow until late in the spring. It shouldn't be too cold, though," he said reassuringly. "It's supposed to be sunny today, and we will probably seem almost hot once we really get going."

Molly teased, "Is this some kind of Native American clairvoyance thing? Did you study the stars last night or something?"

"No," Red Hawk said with a grin, "I watched the weather channel."

They drove up the Going to the Sun road as far as they were permitted and then parked at the end of the plowed road, which, like most of the Park this time of year, was closed and vacant. Nate woke up as soon as the car stopped and seemed totally refreshed. "I'm hungry," he said.

Molly fished an apple out of her pack. "Will this do for now?" she asked.

Red Hawk showed her how to step into the leather pouch on top of the snowshoes and lace them up tightly. Molly's and Nate's snow shoes were modern, light plastic types with an oval shape, but Red Hawk's were long 'trailers,' an old-fashioned shoe traditionally used for long treks. They were made of light wood frames with taut rawhide webbing. Their long tails stretched gracefully out behind him. Molly took a quick lesson walking around in the parking lot. With her natural good sense of balance, she learned quickly, falling only once. Nate wanted his snowshoes on too, but Red Hawk told him it would be better to wait until they were out of the trees, where the going would be tricky. He put the apple-munching Nate up onto his shoulders, and they set out.

Molly was entranced. The Park in winter was a new landscape to her, a magical kingdom. Winter's subtle beauty gradually revealed itself, the clear but softened light, tinged with a pale violet hue, brushed each snow-covered limb and rock with a muted stroke of color. She thought about the movie she had seen about the Dutch painter Vermeer, who waited for just the right kind of light and then spent hours mixing the exact color for a sleeve or a strand of hair. In this winter scene, nature's painting, the same care had been taken.

The black of the tree trunks and the white of the snow on their branches were starkly delineated, but the snow on the ground was a subtle pallet of colors, pure white, blue-gray, and violet, if one observed carefully. Here and there a rock protruded, capped with snow, and sometimes a tall wisp of yellowed grass poked through the surface. The whole effect was of an austere and secretive landscape, one that did not beckon but did not threaten either, elegant in its power, sufficient unto itself in its aura of solitude.

They trekked silently, Red Hawk taking the lead. There was almost no sound, except for the chatter of a squirrel scolding them and the occasional plop of snow that fell from a branch shaking off a too-deep layer of snow. The resulting snow ghost that sparkled as it fell through the air delighted Nate, making him laugh with a deep, spontaneous chuckle, especially when a part of the ghost fell onto his head.

At last they left the close protection of the trees and arrived at a small bridge over the creek. Before them was an unbroken field of snow, the famous Glacier peaks, like a row of otherworldly church spires, rising up behind them. Molly gasped. Turning, Red Hawk looked at her for the first time. Her cheeks were pink and her eyes alight; her pallor and the strain evident before on her face had disappeared. He smiled to himself, glad that they had come.

Molly had thought herself in pretty good shape, but she was awed by Red Hawk's stamina. She and Nate kept together, holding up the rear, and she watched her friend move rhythmically and efficiently over the crusty surface of the snow. He wore only jeans, a turtleneck, and a light wool shirt, but he had fastened bright green gaiters to his boots that protected his legs up to his knees. He had offered her

Circling

a pair, and she had demurred, but she thought at lunch she might put them on, as whenever she fell, she found getting up a very wet proposition.

Though it was not evident to the eye, Molly's tiring legs told her they were traveling gradually up hill. Sometimes she would shout at Red Hawk to wait while she caught her breath. Standing utterly still, taking in the quiet which, like an ineffable presence, seemed to be watching over them, she felt all of her cares slide off her, shedding them as the branches shed their own heavy loads of snow. The air itself, light and cold, played tag with the sunlight's shy winter warmth, energizing Molly's inner core as if she had suddenly and inadvertently stumbled into a room filled with pure oxygen.

After traveling for what Molly estimated was about three miles, they stopped to eat lunch by a small stream, its banks heavy with snow. The roots of bushes and trees, like ancient gnarled fingers, hung out over the translucent, ice blue water. Red Hawk brought out a feast of sandwiches made with fry bread and boiled beef, fruit, and chips; his sister had outdone herself. In the thermos was hot chocolate, and Molly completed the feast by offering some oatmeal cookies she had made the night before.

Stuffed and lazy, they spread a piece of plastic that Red Hawk pulled from the bottom of his pack and lay back on the ground like hibernating bears, Nate between them in utter contentment, happy to be resting for a while. Molly broke the easy silence. "I feel like I have died and gone to heaven," she said. "This place is incredible."

"Now, that's an interesting observation," Red Hawk replied. "I've read that before, but I don't think I've ever heard anyone say it. I guess I feel more like I've just come back alive, rather than died."

Molly thought for a minute. "Maybe you're right," she said. "I suppose that is a rather odd expression. I think a lot of us spend our lives in a kind of limbo, just waiting for heaven, because it's got to be better than this."

Red Hawk disagreed. "That's where you're wrong," he said. "Heaven is right here, right now." And then, pulling himself up into a sitting position, he added, "We'd probably better start back. There won't be enough daylight left if we go much farther, and I think Nate is about done in."

At this, Nate leaped up, protesting loudly. "I can go more! I can!"

Soothing his wounded ego, Molly said, "Well, Nate, maybe you can, but I think I'm getting a little tired. And we do still have to go all that way back, you know."

His honor restored, Nate helped his father clean up the lunch site. Red Hawk explained that they should leave no garbage of any kind to spoil this pristine place, although he did relent when Nate asked if he could leave a few cookie crumbs for the birds and squirrels.

Shadows were lengthening when they got back to the car, and Nate, already asleep on his father's shoulders, sank into his car chair. "I think you can ride up front with me," he said to Molly. "He's out like a light."

As they were putting the last of their gear into the hatch, they heard the distant cry of a hawk, circling high overhead. Red Hawk touched Molly's arm and pointed up to the watercolor turquoise of the late afternoon sky, where she saw the hawk above them, riding a current of air. She glanced at her companion and saw that his face was suffused with an expression she had not seen there before, a kind of self-enclosed dreaminess. She felt jealous somehow, left out, and reminded herself to ask him some day about his name.

Red Hawk

He did not know how this falling in love thing had gotten started. It was certainly not his intention, and it was far too complicated. In the first place, he still loved his wife, and how could someone love two women at once? In the second place, Molly was white, from another world, and in his experience mixed couples usually had a hard time, victims of the stereotyping that existed in both cultures. Besides, the material things that mattered so much to the dominant culture did not matter very much at all to Indians.

It was, he reflected, a problem of mythology. Tribal people had clung to their ancient rituals and stories despite the onslaught of the white culture's greedy pragmatism, their shallow myth of infinite progress. His people still sought solace in the old beliefs, and these were deeply part of their identity. Somewhere within himself, despite his years away and the relentless brainwashing of the modern culture surrounding him, he was still, proudly and irrevocably, Indian.

Tribal people were not afraid of the twenty-first century and its challenges; they simply approached them from a totally different point of view. Their own geographical bearings, their ancient origin stories, their own tightly knit family structure and sense of tribal belonging, usually pulled them back like giant magnets from wherever they had wandered, just as they had brought him back from Seattle.

It was not a matter of living in the past so much as living in a different present. Even though in the last couple of decades the Native American cultures all over the country had experienced a renaissance in native languages and tradition, they did not, nevertheless, live in some kind of nostalgic historic bubble, yearning for the buffalo to come back. What they did want was to be granted at last some dignity, some recognition for what they could contribute to white culture, for how their ancient wisdom could help. But this, Red Hawk was certain, was not going to come about in his lifetime.

And of course, above and beyond his extended family and tribal family, there was Nate to consider. He did have to admit that Nate seemed to adore Molly, following her around like a puppy whenever they were together, and the feeling was apparently mutual. But what if in the future there were other children, children of mixed race, children who would have to choose to live in one society or the other?

Red Hawk shook his head in irritation at his own wandering thoughts, at what his wife had always called his tendency to be on 'worry overload'. Here he was thinking about the worst possible outcomes, and he hadn't even slept with her yet.

Maybe, he admitted, that was the real, immediate problem. They had gone to movies, taken walks, eaten pizza in her apartment and watched television, taken Nate to the mall, but her body language was still skittish and standoffish, like a wary colt. Sex was an unspoken but enormous issue between them, and he didn't know how to talk to her about it or how to control the rising desire that he felt for her.

In desperation, he spoke with his sister about it, and she simply said, "Give her time." But that was more easily said than done.

As he drove to work, he made up his mind to talk to her today. Judging from his own experience, fears grew bigger when they were kept inside. Maybe they just needed to talk, to clear the emotional air. But at the same time that he was convincing himself of the wisdom of this course of action, his hands broke out in a sweat and his stomach churned.

Nevertheless, he called her during his lunch hour and asked if he could come over after work. She acquiesced, sounding a little puzzled, perhaps sensing a kind of urgency in his request.

Circling

When he knocked, she came to the door immediately, her hair down in the disarray of errant curls that he found so fetching. She had on her oldest jeans, faded to the palest blue, and a pink sweatshirt that said "Pink Power". He had no idea what that meant, but he surmised that it was somehow connected to her ardent feminism.

She offered him coffee, which he declined, and then without preamble he took her hand, indicating that she needed to sit. She chose one end of the couch, so he took the chair. Every instinct told him to be physically distant, unthreatening. Seeing his serious expression, Molly's eyes grew large and wary.

"Molly, I think we need to talk," he said quietly. "Or I guess maybe I think that you need to talk. Us, too, later," he stumbled, "but right now you." Then, realizing that he was making very little sense, he tried again. "Do you remember what I told you the first day we had coffee, at Charlie's, about the time after my wife died?" Molly nodded her head in assent, the expression on her face still distrustful.

"I had never spoken to anyone about that, but I felt so much better after I did, like a weight had been lifted off of my shoulders. And I think you would feel better," he was rushing, his words tumbling out helter-skelter, "if you talked about what happened to you that night." He watched her reaction, the look that flashed from disbelief to anger and then to fear.

"You need to get the poison out, Molly. I think it's the only way," he added gravely.

Sensing her immediate and total anxiety, he wished for a moment he could take back what he had said. But then he thought about the awkwardness between them, as man and woman, and that, for him, untenable situation reaffirmed his decision. He sat utterly still, waiting, forcing himself to stay where he was, to keep his mouth firmly shut.

At last, when he felt so jumpy that he thought he would simply have to get up and move around, she started to speak.

"How do I, I mean, how can I explain this to you?" she asked, her voice sounding irrevocably hurt, as if he had betrayed her trust.

Red Hawk felt turned inside out, as if all of his vital organs were now on the surface and were being scoured by her pain. He composed himself so that his voice would not sound judgmental. "Just start by talking about what happened, about the facts. Like, what time of night was it? How did he get in?"

Unable to hold her wounded gaze any longer, he bowed his head, holding it in his hands. The silence was a freight train bearing full-force down upon them. He realized suddenly that he had just gambled everything. Every chance he had of being close to her hung in the balance.

Then, so softly that he could barely make out her words, she began to talk. At first her narrative was stiff and almost formal, like a form she had filled out for the authorities, but as she went deeper into the incident, her hands talked too, and her face changed with the story, expressing first fear, then horror, then shame, her words rising and falling with the alternating shock and grief.

He summoned all of his self-control not to move towards her, not to offer words of comfort. This was the poison, vitriolic and demented, and it spewed out from her and materialized between them, an evil spirit of gigantic proportions.

Red Hawk shuddered inadvertently at the malign vision that loomed before him. But then, as suddenly as she had begun, Molly stopped. She had told him everything, even about the aftermath, when she had been stripped of all of her selfhood and dignity. And then she began to cry, great, silent tears sliding down her face, a cleansing torrent of grief. Red Hawk went to her and gathered her in his arms as gently as he would a wounded bird, and she leaned into him, weeping uncontrollably, as if he were a lighthouse in a storm.

Molly

"Leave now," Molly told herself, "before it's too late." She could not believe that she had told him everything yesterday, down to the last sordid detail. And then she had allowed him to heat up soup for her and to tuck her into bed like a child. When he told her that he intended to stay the night, at first she had felt a wave of panic, but then he had explained, "Not in your bed, on the couch. I think you shouldn't be alone tonight."

In the morning there was a prickly awkwardness between them. He sprang up from the couch as if she had poured cold water on him and, hugging her briefly, explained that they had slept so late that he was going to be late for work. He hurried out the door, promising to call some time soon.

Molly, who had waked from her first full night's sleep in months, felt as abandoned as an orphan. The warm, safe, and rested feeling she had had when she woke up dissipated quickly. She too had to hurry to get ready for work, but as the cup of coffee she drank standing by the sink hit her stomach, her pragmatic sense of reality hit her as well.

It was ridiculous to imagine, she told herself, that two such different people could every get together and live in harmony: the cultural divide between them was huge, like the Grand Canyon, and, besides, she still thought once in a while about the first time she had seen him. Even though she had never seen him drink again, it frightened her. Her father had done enough drinking to last her all eternity.

Worst of all, she didn't know if he shared her feelings, though she had to admit that his staying with her last night had said a great deal.

He was not normally very talkative; she knew that his very different background made their relationship tenuous at best. Finally, she to admit that her own emotional state was still equivocal; she alternated between dizzying moments of wanting him and sheer terror at the idea of being touched.

She calculated the amount of money she had saved and thought it would probably take her easily as far as Portland. She could get a job anywhere, she had proven that to herself, and it wouldn't take her long to pack up. She had accumulated very few things.

Slowly the old pattern of flight began to reassert its alluring power over her. As she was driving to work, prim aphorisms flitted through her mind: 'Better late than never;' 'When it doubt, don't;' 'No time like the present.' She began to imagine Portland as the Garden of Eden, a place that would offer a fresh start that might erase the past and protect her from the love she had begun to feel, from the feeling of losing her carefully constructed autonomy, her sacred self-reliance.

Besides, spring in Montana was nothing to shout about, at least not this spring. Although the rains of April had finally dispersed, and the countryside was suddenly sporting a vivid chartreuse, still there were often cold, windy days with clouds hanging low over the valley. Surely Portland would be warmer and sunnier, she thought.

At other times, especially when she was not busy at work, the other voice would emerge, the one, she taunted herself, which was her helpless twin. This voice reminded her of the last two months, when she had slowly begun to unthaw from her traumatic experience, and she had to admit that most of this progress had been made under his tutelage. And Nate's. She couldn't begin to say how much the child's presence in her life had helped, how healing his innocence and enthusiasm were, how gratifying his adoration of her.

But Molly was not a romantic; she had few illusions about how difficult it was to make any relationship work, let alone one that began with a strike against it. The tug of war between her feelings and her reason continued unabated, making her feel irritable and restless.

Circling

Meanwhile, Red Hawk had called her at lunch, as he had promised, and asked her how she was feeling. He had sounded as if he were almost afraid to hear her answer. "I'm feeling pretty good," Molly replied. "Actually," she said after a moment's hesitation, "I'm glad we talked."

Red Hawk's voice revealed his relief. "Then do you want to get together tonight, maybe go out for a burger or something?" he asked.

Despite the two voices bickering at each other in her head, Molly had accepted. Now she waited anxiously for the clock to make its creeping rotation, glacially slow today, around to five o'clock.

Since they were coming from different directions, they had agreed to meet each other at what locals called the best burger joint in town. Its red and white checked table cloths and motley collection of Montana pioneer memorabilia: gold-panning sieves, horse collars, cross-cut saws and other antiques on the walls, gave it a homely, comfortable air. They had eaten there before, and the gum-chewing young waitress recognized them, muttering a brief "How y'all doing?"

Red Hawk was in great spirits; he kept looking at her, smiling with total and unfeigned delight, and even though she found his perusal disconcerting, Molly had to admit that she was enjoying it.

Neither of them mentioned the conversation the night before; instead, they talked about easy, everyday things: their jobs, Nate's newest exploits, whether or not spring would ever come.

They both ate ravenously, the ketchup and mustard that oozed out from the bun finding its way onto their mouths and chins, making them both laugh at each other's forgotten manners.

Relaxed and satisfied by the substantial hamburger she had consumed, Molly found herself saying, even before she considered it, "Do you want to come over and watch a video?" It was too late then to regret her words, and besides, some subconscious part of her didn't want to. Maybe, she thought, she was just tired, tired of not being herself, of being alone, of wallowing in self-pity. Maybe she just wanted to feel human again.

Pamella Hays

When they got home, they sat close together for the first time on the couch, his arm around her shoulder, their hands touching. She was shaken by the heat of his body and the sculpted elegance of his hands, his fingers long and sensitive, his unblemished brown skin like a fine doeskin glove.

When he turned to look at her, something in her broke loose, an avalanche of feeling that could not be evaded. Impulsively, she took his face in her hands, exploring every ridge and hollow, tracing his very essence with her warm fingers. He sat quietly, allowing her caress as one would accept the examination of a blind person, and indeed he felt as if she were truly seeing him for the first time.

At last he pulled her to him, unable to bear any longer the desire that moved within him like a coil of lava, and he kissed her eyelids, her cheeks, her lips, with an agonized, bitter-sweet passion, bereft now of all logic, of all thought. His hands roamed her body freely, exploring her hills and valleys, opening her gift of this landscape where he could wander forever, fulfilled, affirmed, and joyful.

At his touch Molly unraveled, all her doubts and fears unspooling like loosed yarn, and she at last lost herself, consumed in the river of fire that was obliterating otherness, transforming them both into air and light.

They came together from their two different worlds, continents drifting back towards each other after millennia apart. Tectonic plates shifted; a magnetic force pulled them back into the whole, into the foreknowledge they had of one another before time, before separation, before words. Their bodies' rims and edges were the earth's, elemental and sensuous, their emotions as simple and renewing as rain falling on the land.

Sometime during the night, Molly woke with a start, the old moment of panic flooding her, but then she remembered, and she reached over and touched Red Hawk's bare brown chest, which rose

Circling

so reassuringly up and down, and felt the warmth and strength of his leg that was flung over hers, and she permitted herself a moment of rare, uncomplicated bliss. Then she rolled over to him, cupping her body against him, and fell into a redeeming sleep.

Molly

Molly felt as if she had been bewitched. Worse, she was not even sure that she wanted to return to reality. She and Red Hawk had been together now as a couple for several months. To her own astonishment, she had even asked him to move in with her, reasoning that it was silly for both of them to be paying rent. Her hunger for him, not just physically, but emotionally as well, was like a drug, an addiction that called her back to him again and again.

And then there was Nate, who, although he continued for the time being to live with his grandmother, spent almost every weekend with them, bringing out in her every motherly instinct she possessed. She in fact loved the idea of an instant family, a group that had even more strength than just two. She often thought about the wonderful old photograph she had seen in a book of three people sitting on the front seat of a hay wagon, father, mother, and child, and the inscription beneath it: "We three form a multitude."

Sometimes when the weather was bad they would go to the mall on a Sunday afternoon, the three of them holding hands, wandering around and enjoying the spectacle but with no intention of buying anything. Their finances were always tight, even now that they were sharing the rent of the apartment, and their budget allowed few luxuries other than an occasional pizza or a night at the movies. Nate, oblivious to all of these adult concerns, was entranced with the toy store and could spend hours examining the mechanical trains and the plastic action figures representing cartoon heroes. Yet Molly was amazed that he never begged for any of these toys; he merely played

Circling

with them as long as allowed, and then seemed content to leave the store without them. When she mentioned this to Red Hawk, he said simply, "I've explained that we can't afford them right now. He understands that."

For his part, Red Hawk remained for her an intriguing combination of seducer and sorcerer. She wondered often how much of her love for him was due to his kindness and sensitivity and how much to the subconscious influence of the Native American mystique in old Western movies. Despite herself, she admitted that his ethnicity, his tribal identity, had a magnetic quality that was enormously attractive.

When he asked her to marry him, on a rainy Sunday evening when they were driving back from Browning after leaving Nate at his grandmother's, he did so in a plain-spoken, straight-forward way, without preamble and certainly without candlelight and roses. He had told her before, during intimate moments, that he loved her, but this proposal seemed not a declaration of love but a statement of the obvious. There was no reason that they should continue together without making a commitment, he reasoned.

He pulled over to the side of the road and turned towards her. "I need you, Molly," he stated matter-of-factly, holding her hand. "I need a wife, a companion, and Nate needs a mother, and I know you love him." He paused for a moment and then continued. "I love you, Molly, and I don't want to spend the rest of my life without you. You're the center of my life now."

Molly, taken by surprise, sat silent for a moment. Not that she had not considered the possibility of a proposal, but simply that she wasn't prepared to make up her mind as yet. It wasn't at all as matter of fact as he seemed to imply. Where would they live, she wondered, and what were his expectations of this 'companion' he mentioned? What in fact was the role of a wife in the Indian culture? She had no illusions at least about that; Red Hawk, while an amalgam of both cultures and possessing what seemed to be a good balance of the two, was, in the final tally, Native American. Not that she would have

105

wanted him to be otherwise, it would have been like asking a plant to live without roots, but that because of this fact hers would be the conforming role. She would not have again the fierce independence and control of her life that she had so coveted and nurtured.

In the awkward silence that followed his declaration, Red Hawk studied her face, and then he got out of the car, walking to her side and offering her his hand. She followed him as he scrambled down the steep slope of the embankment to the tumbling river below. There he turned to her, both of her hands in his, his forehead touching hers, and said, "Please, please, Molly. Don't think about it. For once in your life, don't try to figure it out, to make sense of it. Just follow your heart."

When she said yes, her voice almost swallowed up by the din of the raucous river rapids, he lifted her up and swung her around, and for that brief moment their shared laughter joined with the beauty all around them.

They raced back up the hill to the car, breathless and exultant. Red Hawk turned the car around immediately, heading back to Browning, saying that a decision so momentous needed to be shared with his family.

For her part, Molly smiled at him indulgently, dizzy with a kind of unguarded elation, as if she had just climbed the tallest mountain peak in the world and was seeing a panorama of breathtaking wildness for the first time. Their unexpected return at first invoked a certain alarm, but when Red Hawk told his mother and sister his news, they were visibly pleased. Stands Alone embraced Molly warmly, welcoming her into the family, though deep in her eyes Molly thought she saw a flicker of sadness. Margaret's hug was more formal, somewhat stiff, Molly thought, but when Nate jumped into her arms, squealing with delight, it seemed as if the world were, just for that one joyful instant, in perfect balance.

Grandmother

What I felt the day they drove back to see us, to tell us that they were to be married, comes back to me now from some below-ground place, where I had put it in order to be happy for them, and especially for my son. I knew then that she had walled up her spiritual self, that she would not allow herself to acknowledge the wisdom of our people. This my inner eye saw clearly, but my outer eye concentrated only on the birth of my granddaughter and my daughter-in-law's care of both children. I watched my son's success in the world of business and saw with pride how he was gaining in esteem amongst our people, and I shut the door to any other images. Now it is clear that there has been no deep harmony, that each has been walking like a blind person, failing to see the other, to make the effort to know the inside-person, and unable to bridge the growing chasm between them.

Molly

The hypnotic rhythm of the drums seemed to come from underneath her feet, from inside of her, and from every direction, compelling as the beating of her own heart. The sun was high in the sky, hot and intense, and the air itself, filled with light and dust, smelled of fry bread and sweat and horse flesh. Molly wandered aimlessly through the powwow grounds, her sandals filling with gritty dirt stirred up from the horse races and dancing, her once blue jeans already a grimy tan. She pushed towards the front of the group watching the fancy dancers. Red Hawk had already headed for the group of men gathered inside one of the tepees for gambling, lured by the chance of earning some money in the stick game.

Molly spotted her daughter Jasmine, who was eleven, dancing beside her grandmother in the circle. Tall for her age, Jasmine already came to her grandmother's shoulders. Each of them had the inborn grace and dignity of the natural dancer. Stands Alone, of course, was quickly recognizable for her long white braids, which fell almost to her waist. Jasmine, on the other hand, thin and willowy, stood out because of the beautiful buckskin dress her grandmother had made for her, sown with thousands of beads and tiny bells. There were of course other lovely girls with brightly decorated costumes, their hair adorned with feathers and beads, but Jasmine, Molly thought, had a presence that eluded others. Her small, moccasined feet moved delicately, their cadence mirroring the drum's call, her body erect and proud, but appropriately modest as well. She seemed to be looking for her mother's face and smiled when Molly waved.

Circling

The dancing was Molly's favorite event at the powwows, not, she believed, just because her daughter participated, but because it stirred something within her, a fluttering sensation like a bird struggling to get out of its cage. She envied the women who participated, dancing gracefully, with delicate steps, heads held high. She envied their sure sense of identity that had come to them as a birthright. Though their role in the tribe was, by modern standards, circumscribed by tradition, they nonetheless possessed a genuine authority, a respect granted not only through custom, but through their roles as wife and mother and grandmother. Gradually their influence had reached out from the home, and those who wished could be teachers or nurses or clerks in the local stores or pursue other opportunities, but those roles never determined their status as much as those of the old traditions.

Their power, Molly thought, was what she most envied, because it was one granted more than earned, not that they did not deserve the respect they received, but that they began from a place of power given them by their culture and did not have to struggle constantly for recognition. Ironic, Molly thought, that she, one of the few white women on the reservation, had to earn every tiny, grudging drop of their respect. She was an anomaly, a fish out of its element, gasping for water; or, she sometimes thought, more like a ghost walking unseen through the town. Even here at the pow-wow, on a feast day when everyone was relaxed and at their ease, she walked around the area by herself, nodding to women she knew but never asked to join their group.

The shouts of the young men in the horse races woke Molly from her reverie and reminded her that she had promised Nate she would watch him ride. She quickly made her way back through the group surrounding the dancers and headed for the track.

Molly loved Nate as much as she did her biological daughter, but she supposed in a different way. Jasmine, her flesh and blood, was so much a part of her that she could sometimes hardly distinguish where she left off and Jasmine began. Having been always so fiercely independent and feminist in her thinking, Molly never attempted

Pamella Hays

to make Jasmine a clone of herself, but there was a kind of quickening, a subconscious communication between them that often took her breath away.

Nate, on the other hand, was a mystery, a puzzle she could not solve. She remembered clearly the first time she had ever seen him, when he stood at her door in the oversize coat like a little wraith conjured by the storm. Even that night, when she was so disoriented and unsure of her actions, she had recognized his extraordinary perception, his self-enclosed dignity. Now, as a boy of fifteen heading quickly towards manhood, she saw in him these same qualities, but another she had not then known. He was incredibly stubborn and willful, so competitive in any sport, but especially in basketball, that he sometimes seemed possessed. He adored his father, Molly knew, but Red Hawk, it seemed to her, was too demanding of his son. She knew the Indian expectation for young men to prove their manhood, but she also felt that somehow her husband missed their son's quiet, hidden sensitivity, the other half of his nature. He had no patience with school and did the minimum amount of work to get by, but he had a passion for drawing. He sometimes showed Molly his pen and ink drawings of reservation life, which she thought very good, but he seldom shared them with his father. And, as far as she knew, he never spoke to either of them about his most private thoughts.

Even amidst the cyclone of dust stirred up by the horses' hooves, she had no difficulty distinguishing Nate. His long, black mane of hair flew behind him like a banner, his strong bare legs gripped the side of his mount, a large chestnut mare, and he lay almost prone on her back, clutching the reins tightly. Only one rider was ahead of him as they neared the finish line, a boy at least four years his senior, and a more experienced rider, but Nate, oblivious to the roars of the crowd, had that look of concentration that Molly knew so well, and he urged his horse on. At the finish line, Nate had almost reached his rival, but his horse was a nose behind. Molly spotted Red Hawk walking towards his son and hurried to join him. He had

Circling

ridden with honor, even if he hadn't won, and she wanted him to know that they were both proud of him.

By the time she reached them, her husband and son were surrounded by a crowd of admirers, congratulating Nate on his performance. She squeezed in between them, giving Nate a discrete pat on the back. (She knew better than to be too demonstrative, and besides the small scowl on his face betrayed his annoyance with himself.) For his part, Red Hawk stood with his arm slung proudly about his son's shoulders, basking in the praise the other men were offering, while Nate stood stiffly beside him, saying not a word.

Jasmine

Though she was only eleven, Jasmine had developed a remarkable ability to see inside of people. That's what she called it, "seeing inside." Her grandmother Stands Alone had taught her that, not by speaking to her about it, but by example.

Born on the reservation, Jasmine had never known any other life. She loved the howling winter winds that brought the stinging snow, the first soft breath of spring when she could once again play outside in the sun, the protective but stern mountains nearby that she and her brother explored in the summer and autumn, Nate showing off his prowess as a guide and hunter.

Her family comprised her entire reality, and it was unthinkable that it would ever be otherwise. When they sat around the dinner table at night, the sturdy walls of the house her father had built sheltering them from the blows of the gusts of wind, Jasmine would watch each of the beloved faces, her father's enigmatic, private serenity, her mother's pragmatic exterior that hid, she knew, a volcano of emotion, her brother's contemplative solitude which he never shared with anyone, not even wholly with her. She accepted this exclusion as necessary to her brother, whom she worshipped as her hero.

But Jasmine's very favorite activity, ever since she was old enough to remember things, was to visit her grandmother's house and simply to be in her presence: sitting on her lap while she told stories, or helping her prepare supper in the kitchen, or gathering medicinal herbs on the prairie, or watching her while she put together Jasmine's new dress each year for the dancing at the powwow.

Circling

Jasmine loved her mother too, of course, but this was a different kind of feeling. What she felt for her grandmother was closer to awe, a kind of deep respect that transcended even love. There was something mysterious and unreachable about Stands Alone that intrigued her granddaughter. It was as if the elder woman was more than herself, like one of the sacred Indian maidens in the stories she told who always had some important task to perform so that the people would prosper.

Jasmine thought of her grandmother as a medicine woman, a special kind of being who was in closer touch with the spirits than ordinary people, and she believed this because her grandmother could read people's thoughts, sometimes even before they themselves knew what they were thinking. Jasmine studied her grandmother intensely, though courteously and subtly, and she noted how her grandmother was quiet and unobtrusive but extremely observant. Her sparkling black eyes did not miss anything. She did not speak a great deal, but when she did, people listened, even grown-ups like her father.

Jasmine struggled to learn these qualities, disciplining herself not to interrupt others while they were speaking, listening carefully to what people were saying and eventually realizing that what they said and what their bodies or faces were saying could be two different things. She tried to be a little invisible, like her grandmother, so that she could have a quiet space that allowed her to tune into the spirit world that she sensed was like an underground river that ran just beneath the everyday world.

As soon as her mother would allow her to do so, she took long walks alone in the hills surrounding her home, delighting in watching the activities of small animals like the prairie dogs and field mice, wooed by the delicate prairie flowers, the Paint Brush and Lupine that covered the hillsides in a quilt of red and blue in the spring. She found in all of nature a peace that it seemed to her was the same as the calm she felt when she was with her grandmother.

The time that Jasmine most cherished with her grandmother, however, was when she was allowed to brush her grandmother's silken white hair that fell in a cascade to her waist, the moment that she knew would be the time for storytelling. Jasmine would sit behind her while her grandmother sat on the bed, carefully following the instructions that Grandmother had given her. She began at the top and brushed slowly downward, careful to watch out for tangles, which her grandmother had taught her to work through with her fingers, taking apart the gossamer strands of hair one by one, gently pulling them free. Throughout this process, the old stories flowed like a river of honey, sweet and slow and deep, and Jasmine loved their comforting sameness, the words almost identical from one time to the next. When Jasmine was done brushing, Grandmother would deftly braid her hair into a long plait that fell down her back, fastening it with a beaded leather hairpiece.

It was because of her patiently learned ability to see inside of people that Jasmine knew something was wrong at home. Her father, whom she adored, was gone a lot, more even than usual. He seemed permanently preoccupied, sometimes not even remembering to tuck her into bed. She knew he had to work late sometimes at the store, and she knew he had recently become a member of the Tribal Council, but still he was gone almost every night. Her mother, who laughed less and less and scolded more and more, seemed remote, like somebody who wasn't really there.

She tried to talk to Nate about this, but he was not interested. At fifteen, he too had become a stranger who had little patience for her questions. Once in a while he still would play a card game with her or allow her on a Saturday to go bicycle riding with him, but mostly he hung out with his friends, obnoxious boys who she thought treated her rudely and were loud and boastful. When she finally cornered him one evening in his room and burst out with her theory that something was wrong with Mom and Dad, Nate dismissed her concern out of hand.

"You're always imagining things," he had said. "You have an overactive imagination." And then, with that irritating and unassailable

Circling

superiority of greater experience, he added, "All married couples fight. It doesn't mean anything. Stop worrying so much."

But Jasmine, who had learned the art of seeing inside of people, knew better. She became such a quiet observer that sometimes her parents would forget that she was in the room and argue, vehemently but without raising their voices, about a subject she had heard over and over again. In her mind she summed it up as, on her mother's part, "You don't know who I am," and on her father's part, "Quit feeling sorry for yourself and find something worthwhile to do."

She watched when, at the end of these arguments, her mother would go into the kitchen, banging pots and pans around and scrubbing the counter tops until it seemed she would remove their finish, and her father would put on his hat and coat and, slamming the door as he left, shout out, "I'm going downtown."

Jasmine thought she understood exactly what was wrong, and she wanted to tell them, but she knew it wasn't her place. Children were supposed to tend to children's things, like playing and going to school, and they weren't supposed to stick their noses in grown-ups' business. But Jasmine chafed under this artificial restriction; her inner eye saw clearly her mother's sadness and frustration, and she knew this was because she was lonely. And her father, who had a kind of elemental earthiness, a natural and profound sense of belonging, couldn't understand how her mother could be unhappy. To him, with his grounded, sensible male brain, being happy was accepting where you were and who you were. Jasmine understood that he couldn't fathom her mother's disorientation, her sense of alienation, of being an outsider. It wouldn't be until many years later, reading the works of modern writers, that she could put a name to this disease, the spiritual emptiness of that other half of her that was the legacy of modern white culture. But by then it would be too late to save her parents' marriage.

Molly

Sometimes, before she was fully awake, the nagging little voice began harping at her, questioning her judgment and stirring up the latent anger that lay coiled up in her head like a snake about to strike. She would throw aside the down comforter that covered her and, taking care not to waken Red Hawk, would pull down her soft wool robe from the door of the closet and tiptoe quietly downstairs so that she could be alone in the house.

Despite her growing and deep-seated discontent with her life, Molly had to admit that she loved the house Red Hawk had built for them. It stood on a bluff about a quarter of a mile east of town, commanding a sweeping view of the Glacier Peaks in the distance. Now that he owned Browning's only hardware store, Red Hawk had access to building materials at wholesale prices, and he had built a home that fit into the landscape as if it had been born there, its back nestled into the trees. Molly especially appreciated the design of the house with its large expanses of glass that opened it to the out of doors, while its log walls anchored it firmly to the earth, making its interior seem warm and inviting, even on the coldest winter days.

After making the coffee, she stooped to make a fire in the large stone fireplace, even though now, in mid-October, it was still not strictly necessary. She was looking forward to the first cold days of winter, which would be upon them in only a matter of weeks, and then the beginning of another basketball season. One of her greatest joys was watching Nate play. He had a grace and agility that was like his father's, but he had as well a kind of competitive ferocity that she

116

Circling

seldom saw in her husband. Nate was only in his first year of high school, but she knew he was already being groomed to be a great player, something highly valued in this Native American culture.

Jasmine, however, who had been born ten months after they had married, was very different in temperament; she had her mother's tendency to be sufficient unto herself, that kind of watchful and even wary analytical mind that seldom allowed itself exuberance. But she was Indian, too, and she possessed a grounded, natural sense of acceptance that eluded Molly.

Jasmine had been pulled into communal dancing as naturally as a fish swims in the sea. When Molly watched her in the dances, tall and elegant, she sensed in her daughter the deep and passionate core of her tribal family rising to the surface.

She had loved her daughter with utter abandon from the first moment she had held her, her abundant dark hair still wet from the delivery, a lovely mixture of the two races that had come together to bring her into the world. She had the dark black hair of her father's people, but it curled into long coils like her mother's. Her eyes were clear blue, like her mother's, her skin a silky brown.

But as Jasmine grew, Molly had to acknowledge that it was Jasmine's grandmother, not she, who had the most influence over the child. Molly had only the greatest respect for Stands Alone, so she berated herself for feeling jealous; the elder woman was sensitive in reading her daughter-in-law's mind and never interfered in Molly's raising of the child. It was Jasmine who seemed drawn to Stands Alone like a magnet, shadowing her every movement when they were together, willing to sit quietly for hours watching whatever she was doing. It was as if they were secret conspirators in a magic game that was beyond Molly's ken, two priestesses in some ancient tribal ritual in which she could never have a part. And thus, though she felt closer to her daughter than to anyone else in the world, she also recognized that she had unwittingly created a new being, a synthesis of two worlds who, however close she might be emotionally to her mother, was also forever and irrevocably different.

Pamella Hays

All of this made Molly's heart heavy on this radiantly sunny morning, with the aspen trees on the slopes of the hills resplendent in their yellow autumn finery. Refusing to be seduced by their splashy showmanship, Molly sank into the big leather sofa in front of the fire, coffee cup in hand, and bitterly contemplated her failing marriage. She didn't know if Red Hawk could see it coming, although she supposed he wasn't oblivious to their frequent clashes of will and her angry days of withdrawal afterwards. She had tried to compare her own marriage to those around her, but it was hopeless; every married couple they knew were both Indian. Molly had no girlfriend who she could talk to about her own unique problem, her different cultural background, and how being so different isolated her from everyone, even from her husband. The more she contemplated what seemed a hopeless situation, the more Molly painted herself into a corner, not allowing herself any way out except to leave.

She heard Jasmine's door open and her bare feet padding along the hallway. It was time to get up and get the kids their breakfast before school and stop feeling sorry for herself. She rose with a sigh and pushed away the voice that berated her, telling her for the thousandth time that she needed to come to a decision, to do something instead of wallowing in self-pity.

Molly

"Mom, have you seen my basketball uniform?" Nate's head appeared in the doorway of her bedroom, a note of panic in his voice.

"I just washed it yesterday; it's hanging up in your closet," Molly answered with a grin, noting her stepson's absolute helplessness at organizing his existence. Then she added, "You'd better hurry up. The Junior Varsity game starts in an hour, and you're supposed to be there early." Indian time, she added to herself silently.

In the hoop-roofed metal gymnasium the wood bleachers that ran from floor to ceiling were already packed with onlookers when Thomas, Molly, and Jasmine arrived. It was tournament time, late February, and despite the snow- storm stalking the streets outside, it looked as if virtually everyone in town had come to watch the game, which was against a team that was the Indians' biggest rival.

Thomas waved at a friend in the third row who gestured with a 'come on up', and they squeezed into the space that was made for them. Molly found herself next to Mary Crazy Fox, an influential woman whose husband was the head of the Tribal Council and a man of much power. It amazed Molly that there was so much politics on the reservation. She didn't know what she had expected, but her romanticized childhood version of Native American society conjured men in tribal dress sitting on the floor of a teepee handing around the Peace Pipe and resolving problems without argument. Instead, the town was always rife with gossip about the Council's fiery meetings and complex financial dealings. Sometimes even charges of

119

Pamella Hays

malfeasance against some powerful member would surface. Aware of the political corruption and corporate manipulation in national government, Molly felt vaguely betrayed by tribal scandal. She had expected better, somehow.

"How've you been wintering?" Mary asked, using the local expression of solidarity in assessing the effects of Browning's difficult winters. Her face looked serious, but her large brown eyes twinkled with good-natured amusement.

" Oh, o.k. I guess," Molly replied, smiling. "How are things with you?"

"Let's just say I won't mind it when spring comes," Mary replied. "Can't wait till the kids are out of school for spring break. We're heading to Spokane to visit my niece," she added helpfully.

Molly knew that this kind of trip to visit kin was a big deal, and she nodded affirmatively. "I wouldn't mind a little time away from here myself," she said, immediately regretting the comment for fear it would be misinterpreted. People here were always assuming she didn't like it here, which wasn't strictly true. Her attempt to repair the damage of her previous remark, however, was interrupted by the buzzer and the entrance of both teams from the locker rooms. A roar engulfed the gym, feet stomping on the long boards of the risers and war whoops called out from all the men. She gave up on the conversation, afraid to look at Mary's reaction to her gaffe.

Nate, his long hair braided into one thick rope, was a local celebrity when it came to basketball. He seemed to be able to be in several places at once, so nimble and swift were his movements. He drove the members of the other team wild with frustration, as whoever had the ball was almost immediately confronted with a jumping, whirling demon who possessed at least six arms. The crowd roared its approval when an opposing player was blocked from making a shot.

Molly looked at Red Hawk's face, his eyes narrowed by a frown, his mouth set in a line, the look of total concentration that was now so familiar to her. His ability to focus on concrete details, on matters substantive and real, was astonishing. On the other hand, any matter

120

Circling

with an emotional caste seemed totally beyond his ability to understand. She wondered how much of this was typical of a male and how much might be a tribal characteristic. Men here, after all, were definitely in the driver's seat. Although, she had to admit to herself, in fairness, women were not ignored nor repressed, and they were not hesitant to express their opinions. But neither were they very likely to deviate from their traditional role as wives, mothers, and grandmothers. It mystified her that women who had so much acuity seemed for the most part satisfied to be at home.

After their triumphant win, Jasmine left with her best friend, the parents promising to bring her home by eleven; Nate, his pride puffed up by having received the honor of best player of the game, pleaded to stay the night with his buddy, since it was Friday and there was no school tomorrow.

Red Hawk and Molly drove the short distance home in peaceable silence, watching the snow's slow spiral as it gently covered the landscape with its clean whiteness. Once inside the door, Thomas swooped Molly up and ran to the bedroom. Crowing, "We have the house to ourselves!" he tossed her onto the bed and immediately began removing her clothing, even as she giggled in futile mock protest, enjoying the unusual privilege of noisy lovemaking. Afterwards, sated by what Red Hawk laughingly referred to as 'having his way with her', he lay beside her, playing with her long curls, their ability to bounce back to their original shape after being pulled still fascinating to him.

Taking advantage of his mellow mood, Molly ventured, "I've been thinking about trying to find a job, some kind of work."

"Why would you want to do that?" Thomas asked in sudden irritation. "You have plenty to do around here, taking care of us, of me and the kids. And the store is doing well; we don't need the money." And then he added, wounded, "I already told you could help out at the store anytime you wanted."

"That's not the same," Molly protested. "I want to have my own money. I just feel, I don't know, bored, I guess. Keeping house isn't exactly the most mentally challenging job in the world."

"You mean, not as challenging as working as a clerk at the Crossroads?" Red Hawk scoffed, reminding her of her job at the general store when they met.

"It isn't my fault that we moved back to the Rez. I could have had a lot of jobs in Kalispell," Molly countered, her eyes beginning to tear with frustration and anger.

Red Hawk rolled over abruptly onto his side, turning his back to her. "Why do you always have to do this?" he asked, his voice low and bitter. "Why do you always have to spoil a perfectly good evening? Doesn't that ambitious white-woman's brain of yours ever turn off? Can't you ever just be content?"

Stung by the narrow prejudice of his remark, Molly did not respond but lay rigid, hoping he couldn't sense her tears.

Red Hawk

As the council meeting ended and the members walked out into the cool autumn night, calling out their good-byes, Red Hawk stayed behind in the meeting room, picking up coffee cups and sweeping the wood floor. Truth be told, he wasn't at all eager to go home. He dreaded walking into the house and seeing her pinched, inscrutable face and hearing the indifference in her voice when she asked him mechanically how the meeting had gone. He couldn't for the life of him figure out her problem; she was so hung up on not being Indian, on not belonging, and yet the longer he knew her the more convinced he was that she didn't feel she belonged anywhere. She would, he thought, even be unhappy in paradise.

For him the upshot of the problem was that he had given up on trying to talk to her about it, simply trying to keep busy and keep out of her way. He had found solace in some of his old habits, like hunting and fishing, and in his new role as a respected tribal leader. At the worst times he would feel an itch for alcohol, for hanging out at the bar and swapping war stories and enjoying the moment with men who, even if they weren't friends, were uncomplicated drinking buddies, trying to have a good time and forget their troubles, just like he was. But if for one second the urge got a hold of him, all he had to do was remember the night he had passed out in the snow and deserted Nate, and he would immediately reject the seductive escape that alcohol offered.

After the cups had been washed and left to drain and the wood stove attended to, he grabbed his jacket from the peg by the door

Pamella Hays

and stepped out into the early autumn darkness. As was often the case in Browning, the wind was keening, prowling around corners and attacking you once you stepped out into the open. He pulled the down hood from its position on his back and covered his head, although it was not cold enough to need tying. He had walked here and had rejected offers of rides because he needed the time alone to think as he walked.

He turned right at the corner onto the main street, deciding he would check out the action downtown. The council was spending a lot of time trying to deal with the problem of kids and alcohol, or 'underage drinking,' as the current buzz word called it. It had not escaped his notice that Nate, who was now fifteen, had begun to exhibit some warning signs as far as drinking was concerned. His grades at school, never great, had fallen the past semester, and Red Hawk had caught him lying a couple of times about where he had been and who he had been with. There wasn't a whole lot for young people to do in Browning, and except for basketball season, Nate seemed at loose ends, pacing around the house if forced to stay home, and hanging out with questionable kids whenever he got permission to go out.

The good thing about a small town, Red Hawk thought, was that everyone knew everyone else's business, so it was relatively easy to find out who you child spent their time with. The bad part of that, however, was a tendency to make judgments that were too harsh and too swift. He realized that his own experiences with alcohol had left him badly scalded, and the idea of his son's drinking so terrified him that he had become a tyrant, laying down rules and giving lectures that, in private moments, he admitted would have driven him crazy when he was a kid. But Nate's sassy belligerence had the response on his father's side of pushing him even further into his rigid authoritarianism. Molly was the other part of the problem; she tended to take Nate's side, not that she approved of his drinking, but that she felt her husband was being too harsh, and she tried to tell him that his attitude was just pushing Nate farther away.

Circling

Just at that moment a car full of teenagers caromed down the street, tires squealing as they made an abrupt right-hand turn onto a side street, ignoring the red light they had run. There were at least eight kids in the car, it seemed to Red Hawk, and one of them had his arm hanging out of the window, beer can in hand, defying anyone to do anything about it. Red Hawk sprinted across the street, dodging traffic, and ran full tilt down the street they had turned onto. But he was too late; the car was already a good two blocks away, flying down the middle of the street as if it were their private domain. Breathing hard, Red Hawk bent double, putting his hands on his knees, and cursed in frustration.

Until the car behind him honked, he didn't realize that he had stopped in the middle of the street. A laughing female voice called to him, "Hey, counselor, you have a suicide wish or what?"

Red Hawk looked up abruptly, prepared to offer a sharp rebuttal, but he couldn't help but grin when he saw Jen, one of the clerks at the school, a round faced, always smiling woman whose large dark eyes seemed to be perpetually twinkling.

"Guess I'm not as young as I used to be, " Red Hawk responded. "I was chasing some kids who were barreling along here in their car. Damn kids were drunk as skunks."

"Yah, I know what you mean. I live on this street and have to watch out for them if I get home late, like tonight. They think they own the place." And then, noticing Red Hawk's still somewhat breathless condition, she added, "Say, would you like a lift? I'm not in a hurry to get home, and you look pretty winded."

Red Hawk hesitated for only a moment. "Sure," he said. "That would be great. I guess I've had enough exercise for one evening."

He bent double to get his long frame into her small economy car but appreciated how warm it was. He hadn't realized how cold the wind had actually been. He smiled over at Jen, who pulled out slowly, apparently expecting the culprits to come back at any minute.

Pamella Hays

"I'm kind of glad that I got a chance to talk with you," she said. "I've been thinking about coming to a council meeting myself to talk about these kids and what they're doing to destroy themselves."

Red Hawk was sympathetic. "I know, and you're welcome anytime. That's something we have on the agenda almost every month." And then, changing the subject, he asked, "Don't I see you at all of the basketball games? Do you have a kid on the team?"

Jen shook her head. "No, just a nephew, but I really love to watch him play. Your son is pretty good, too, " she added approvingly. "It's like he's got a fire in his belly."

"Yeah, there's a fire in his belly alright, but it isn't a passion for the sport," Red Hawk growled. He hadn't spoken to anyone about his concerns about his son's drinking, and he suddenly felt embarrassed and awkward, having said it this woman who he barely knew. But he felt relaxed with her, at ease somehow. She radiated a kind of nonjudgmental quality, a kind of organic peacefulness like a slow-moving stream, the polar opposite of Molly's quick, high-strung temperament.

As they pulled up in front of his house, Jen, who had been silent for the last block or two, observed, "You know, I think we have to remember how hard it is for kids these days. You and I grew up in a different time. Sure, there was drinking and horseplay and we did some dumb things, but the world in general wasn't so crazy. Even here on the Rez, there was more of a sense of tradition and everyone knew more or less what was expected of them. Now, with a hundred channels on television and video games, and all the junk kids see, it's like we've been invaded by the white man—again. "And", she added, "this time I think there's no chance of fighting an enemy we can't even see."

Red Hawk opened the door but remained seated for a moment, leaving it ajar. "Guess I never thought of it that way," he said. "But you're absolutely right. How are we supposed to compete with the power of the media blitz, telling our kids who they should be and how to be cool?" Then, aware that the wind was coming in through

126

Circling

the open door, he ducked his head and stepped out onto the street. He turned towards her before closing the door and said, "Thanks for the ride, and for the conversation."

Jen did not reply except with a nod and a wave. As she pulled away, Red Hawk turned to look at his beautiful castle on the hill, its windows lit up from inside as if it were a citadel, a refuge from the world. Bitterly, he thought, it could have been that. It should have been. What the hell had gone wrong?

Nate

Nate waited anxiously for Molly to reply to his invitation. He would turn eighteen in two weeks, and what he wanted most in the world was for her and his sister, Jasmine, to come to his birthday party.

Since his parents had divorced almost three years ago, he had not seen much of either Molly or Jasmine; they had moved to Portland, where his stepmother had gotten a degree in medical technology and worked in the lab of a local hospital. He missed them both, of course, but especially Jasmine, his exasperating and intriguing and, he thought, stunningly beautiful little sister, three years his junior.

High School and Nate had not gotten along. The best reason for celebrating his eighteenth birthday was that it also marked his graduation from school, from the endless, boring and pointless days of sitting in a square desk, himself the proverbial round peg, enduring the nonsense not just because his father and auntie had threatened him with anathema if he didn't graduate, but because of the sheer, unequaled joy of playing basketball.

If he had been forced to describe community, he would have said it was his basketball team. As a Senior this year, he had been elected captain, and he reveled in the good-natured jokes and gibes inside the locker room at halftime, the way the other members made it clear that they respected him and looked up to him. But he also knew in his heart of hearts that his skills, while highly prized in Browning High School, were not great enough to get him a college basketball

Circling

scholarship. For one thing, he was not extraordinarily tall; he was only 5'10", and despite his considerable ability, there was no chance that he could make it in the world of giants recruited for their height as much as their skill. And anyway the thought of more school, of more studying, completely turned him off.

He tried to console himself by concentrating on the fact that he would soon be a free person, an adult able to explore the world on his own terms, able to get away from the Rez and find out what life was really like.

Tonight he was going out with his friends to celebrate the last final exam and his looming coming of age. For Nate, this meant that soon he could drink legally, and despite his father's dire warnings and morbid lectures, he intended to have one hell of a good time. When he had turned sixteen, his father had finally told him about his own tribal 'coming of age' ritual, about his three days in the mountains by himself, fasting and meditating and having his vision of his medicine bundle and medicine animal, the hawk.

Nate had listened politely but indifferently. He was not a traditionalist but a realist. In the actual world outside, he knew, young men didn't do these kinds of things. He didn't need to sit in a cross-legged position out in the middle of nowhere to have a vision: he already had one, based on the hard facts of life. Hadn't he survived the breakup of his parents' marriage? Hadn't he endured the silent agonies and emotional withdrawal of his father and the betrayal of a woman who he considered his mother, the only one he could remember ever having? And would all the rituals on earth bring back his grandmother, who had died two years ago?

He had seen a bumper sticker the other day: "Life's a bitch, and then you die." That about summed it up, as far as he was concerned. The hocus-pocus of tribal rituals were just that, meaningless attempts to forestall reality, to deal with how things really were. What good had his father's medicine dream done him? He was alone and confused and deeply unhappy, as far as Nate could see, and even though he remained a confirmed tee-totaler, Nate sensed in him a longing for something that would obliterate the pain he felt. Nate didn't have this compunction. For him alcohol dulled the edge, giving the senses a blurred and dreamy effect, as good, he imagined, as any bogus vision.

His own visions came in that translucent moment between the sober, everyday, deadening reality of his school life and the high created by the mixture of alcohol and risk when he drove his father's pickup at high speeds down the highway late at night, the windows down, the wind careening through the cab like a crazed ghost. Before he was too drunk to be aware, his senses heightened to a level almost of pain, he thought he could understand everything: his father, Molly, the divorce, the Rez, the whole goddamned world. The clairvoyance he felt then, for that fleeting moment, was equaled only when he played basketball or when he was immersed in his drawing, snippets of time carved out of the humdrum of everyday existence. Then he could feel the same harmonious sensation, the same fusion of his inner world and outer reality. But these moments were rare, and he did not know how to make them happen; they just came unexpectedly. On the other hand, he could usually depend on the alchemy of alcohol.

Once in a great while, when he woke up early in his bedroom and looked at his father's drawing of the hawk, an anomaly amongst the posters of rock stars and famous basketball players that otherwise adorned his room, he would experience a twinge of guilt, a fleeting sense of something missed, but mostly he was able to forget about it. He did have to admit, however, that he missed his grandmother.

After Molly and Jasmine had left, she had been his center, his hold on sanity. He had respected her more than anyone else in the world, even his father. She had never scolded or harangued; she had never withdrawn her affection, even when he came home drunk and woke up as ornery as a wolverine. And yet when he had done something wrong or foolish, it was her look of silent reproach that could cut him to the quick and make him feel genuine regret, could somehow pull him back into true.

Circling

Though he was still angry at Molly, whom he blamed in large part for the divorce, he also had to admit that he missed her in somewhat the way he missed his grandmother, as a source of gentleness and stability. She was someone who he knew loved him without constraint or doubt, who had attended all of his basketball games, cheering the loudest of anyone in the stands, who encouraged him in his efforts to draw, who acknowledged his own tendency to dream but focused it with her objective and pragmatic advice. The love of his father he was not so sure of, their relationship since the marital breakup having changed so drastically.

His first clear recollection of his dad was from years ago when he was still a small child and they had moved into town with Molly after his father had gotten married. He remembered sleeping on the couch in the living room watching the stars, flung randomly across the sky like sparkling confetti, white and pink and blue. He remembered picnics in the park, when he and Molly would meet his father during his lunch hour and he would play on the jungle gym and the teeter-totter while his parents talked. He could remember crawling into bed with them on Saturday mornings, snuggling into his father's arms while Molly smiled at him and played with his hair.

He remembered too, with a distant but piercing awareness, how he had worshiped his father, wanted his approval more than anything else in the world, admired and imitated his walk, his speech, his expressions. Nothing had been better then than to be permitted to go out into the mountains with his father, to hunt or fish or simply hike, immersed in the silence and majesty of the place, unafraid and confident of his father's love.

But these recreational trips had gradually become less and less frequent. His father, out of place in town, had continued to work as a handyman, but he seemed restless, in need of something more, and eventually they had moved back to the Rez. Nate remembered hearing arguments about this proposed move late at night, through the bedroom walls. Though he could never make out what they were saying, the tone of anger in his father's voice and the entreaties of his stepmother were clear, and he sensed that this was about something very big and hurtful between them.

After they moved back to Browning, his father had started his own business as a contractor. Gradually he had built up a fairly good clientele and had even been able to open a hardware and building supply store. Molly was already pregnant with his sister then, and they had moved in with his grandmother and auntie.

Later they had gotten a house of their own, the house where Nate had lived all of the years of grammar and middle school, but Nate had decided to move back to his grandmother's after the divorce. Living in the emptiness of their large family home, which had echoed with the laughter and conversation enlivening it when Molly and Jasmine were there, seemed more than he could endure.

His Auntie Margaret, who had never married, welcomed him back to his grandmother's house with open arms, spoiling him by preparing all of his favorite foods. His father had consented to this move readily: evidence, Nate thought, of his nearly total indifference to his son.

His father came over almost every night for dinner, and they made stilted conversation. His father, still handsome, Nate had to admit, even with a few streaks of gray in his long hair and the advent of a small potbelly, talked about his store, his construction projects, about phone calls from Jasmine and the current gossip about the Tribal Council, but he never mentioned Molly. It was, Nate thought bitterly, as if she had ceased to exist.

Sometimes they talked about Nate's future, about what he wanted to do with his life, and Nate came up against the now-familiar litany of staying around for a while and working for his father until he decided what to do. To this suggestion Nate was always evasive, not openly disagreeing, but being careful not to commit himself either. And then, on occasion, the stale, familiar lectures were dragged out, his father's admonitions about the evil of drink and the numbers of young Indian men who died in alcohol-related car accidents. At that point communication would totally shut down, and Nate would

Circling

politely excuse himself, inventing an errand or a study session with friends to get out of the house as soon as possible.

But now he had a plan, something that even his father would be helpless to change, and he could hardly wait to spring it on them all at his birthday party and watch their utter astonishment at his bold new strategy.

Molly

Molly turned the letter over and over in her hands. She had recognized Nate's handwriting right away, the uphill slant of the almost unintelligible scrawl, and she tried to imagine what it might hold. They hadn't seen one another for almost a year now, and she had missed him fiercely. But then Montana was a long way away, her job kept her very busy, and Jasmine had school. And besides, if she saw Nate she would see Red Hawk, and that was almost more than she could handle.

Her mind still was incapable of reconstructing the causes of the divorce. The most plausible explanation was simply attrition, like the slow, inexorable drip of water on rock. She tended to want to blame that attrition on his tribal background, on his insistence on going back to the Rez, where she had felt alone and misunderstood, out of place. It was true that his mother had welcomed her sincerely; she said very little to her, but every gesture of friendship, from invitations to dinner to offering to show her how to do beadwork, was genuine.

Red Hawk's sister, Margaret, however, was another matter. Molly thought at first that perhaps she was simply jealous; before Molly's coming, she had enjoyed the full attention of her brother, whom she obviously adored, and had not had to share him or her nephew. And perhaps, Molly reluctantly recognized, Margaret had never fully forgiven her for turning in her brother to the police years ago. But the animosity between them seemed to go deeper than that; Molly hated to admit it, but maybe they both possessed more than a little prejudice, Margaret chary of Molly's white woman's independence, and

Circling

Molly impatient with what she considered her rival's smug Indian purity.

But even this couldn't account for her having finally decided to leave her husband, and in moments of weakness she still had to acknowledge her love for him. From the moment they had first made love, she had felt an attraction so strong that to go against it would be like refusing to admit that the sky was blue. He was a paradox that never failed to intrigue her, a door that would unexpectedly open up and reveal to her another whole world.

When they were first married, this man who had always seemed serious and even solemn, to Molly's amazement, proved to be an inveterate tease, and their home often resounded with his uninhibited laughter when he finally managed to crack her perhaps exaggerated sense of dignity. He had an evenness that she valued, especially because it contrasted so much with her own volatility. While he occasionally would slip away from her, to some private spiritual place that she was never allowed to enter, he could be an extraordinary lover, his attention totally focused on her when they were together.

But all of his careful attention to her needs could not eventually make up for the Browning winters, with their heavy snow fall and shrieking, cold winds; her hurt feelings from the courteous indifference with which she was treated in the stores; her chagrin with the sudden quiet that descended on a group of women when she entered the room. She began to feel stifled, or perhaps more accurately, suffocated. She couldn't seem to keep a clear sense of her own identity; she wandered through her days when Red Hawk was at work and Nate and Jasmine were at school like a ghost haunting her own home.

She tried to explain herself to Red Hawk, but here his sensitivity closed down: why didn't she go to the local college, he offered, or join some women's group, or learn to paint? He suggested that her problem was just boredom, that she was feeling estranged because she wouldn't mingle, because she chose to be by herself so much.

She could remember with sickening clarity every word of the argument they had had the day before she left. Red Hawk had come

Pamella Hays

home at noon from the store feeling amorous, and she had rejected his advances. Hurt and angry, he had asked her what was the matter, and this time she had held nothing back.

"The matter, Red Hawk?" Molly had screeched in utter frustration. "What is the matter? The matter is that I don't belong here, that I have no identity."

She would never as long as she lived get over her astonishment at his answer. "Of course you belong here, Molly, and everyone knows who you are. You're my wife," he offered so innocently that for a heart beat she was stunned into silence.

Then the words spewed out in a furious whirlwind of self-righteous anger. She remembered feeling as if the funnel cloud of a tornado were stirring inside of her and coming out as black and ominous and uncontrollable as nature's power unveiled.

"Your wife, " she spat. "Your wife? Is that all I am to you, to them? The wife of the respected businessman and Tribal Council member, the wife of the man everyone in town greets at the basketball games. Is that who I am?"

Red Hawk responded with a nonplussed expression. Slowly the gravity of the conversation was dawning on him, but he obviously still didn't understand.

"I didn't mean it like that, Molly. Of course you're not just my wife, but it's a place to start, a place of respect in the community. What you do with that is your own business; you have to give them some time, and you have to try. You keep yourself isolated here in the house too much. You don't reach out."

Molly was beside herself with rage. She felt as if she stood somewhere outside of the house, a passer-by listening in at the window, so great was her sense of isolation and estrangement.

Finally, almost wearily, she capitulated. "I give up, Thomas. It doesn't make any difference what I say, how many times I tell you that I don't fit in, that I feel excluded, that I don't have any close women friends here. You're Indian, your skin and the way you speak, and even how you walk—everything about you fits. And you refuse

136

Circling

to see that I will never fit. I've thought and thought about this, I've read everything about the Indian culture, I've tried to figure it out, but it's too elemental. It boils down to skin and bones, and to traditions and beliefs that will never be truly mine."

"That's exactly your problem, Molly," Red Hawk said with infinite weariness. "You always trying to figure everything out, to make sense of things, instead of just being here, accepting what is. That's the difference between us: I accept life, you analyze it." And then, spitefully, he added, "So what the hell good are all of those philosophy books you're always reading?"

The next morning Molly began to pack. When he came home for lunch, she told him that she wanted a divorce. The words dropped into the room like acid, poisoning the atmosphere between them. As she told him what she intended, she watched a dark shadow fall over his face, leaving an expression of shock, as if she had told him she was terminally ill. And when they had told Nate, it was even worse. She loved Nate as her own son, and to feel his rage flare up and then almost as suddenly turn into cold, unforgiving ice, was perhaps even more painful to Molly than his father's reaction. Try as she might to explain her love for him, and that she would always be a part of his life, the wall he had instantly put up between them never again came down.

She still spoke to him on the telephone once or twice a month, and he would, with prodding, tell her about school and sports, but his voice had a cool reserve, a businesslike efficiency that was totally unlike him.

Jasmine had had a rough time too, because it fell on her young shoulders to decide which parent she wanted to stay with. Ultimately Jasmine, who was after all only fourteen, just beginning the most difficult period of adolescence, had struck a compromise: she would live with Molly during the school year, but with her brother and father in the summer. For Nate the decision was immediate and final: he would stay with his father and his school friends. His smoldering disaffection for Molly and the culture she symbolized spread like a wildfire, and he could only put it out by remaining on the Rez, by being who he was, Indian.

She and Jasmine had made a place for themselves in the city. Molly was still thrilled with her new job, with her attainment of something she had never imagined she could achieve. Her new position had increased her salary considerably, and it allowed them to move into a nicer apartment, a roomy condo, and she loved to sit on the balcony, sovereign and free, and watch the sunset as it embossed with gold the windows of the adjacent buildings.

Most of the time she refused to think about the past; her rational mind remained convinced that she had done the right thing, that she had taken the only path open to her. But sometimes her heart betrayed her, and as she watched the sun be swallowed up by the horizon, she would slip into a melancholy dreaming, a yearning sadness over what she had given up, had lost.

She was alone now more and more, since Jasmine was almost sixteen, a sophomore in high school, and very involved in drama. There was hardly a week that went by when Jasmine was home at night; mostly, play rehearsals dominated her evenings, and often Molly would go to bed even before she got home. Molly trusted Jasmine, a rare privilege in these days of youthful discontent, she knew, and she counted her blessings that Jasmine had found the theater, a source of creativity and passion that had thus far kept her out of the syndrome of angry teenage rebellion.

Finally Molly sat down at the kitchen table and opened the letter. It was not in fact a letter; it was a card, an invitation, as it turned out, to come back for Nate's eighteenth birthday celebration. There was no personal note added, but Molly could read between the lines: This was the first time since she had left that Nate had reach out to her, had offered, however hesitantly, to let her back into his life. She knew that she couldn't, that she wouldn't, say no. And she didn't even have to consult Jasmine, who spent a great deal of time waxing nostalgic about Montana, about the prairie, about how wonderful her father was and how sweet her brother. Molly always tried to take

Circling

these barely disguised hints of reconciliation with a grain of salt, but she had to admit that sometimes Jasmine's rhapsodies hit a nerve.

Without being able to acknowledge it consciously, for she always had insisted that she hated it there, Molly sometimes missed the landscape, too, the rawness and challenge of the weather, the fierceness of the soul-scouring winds, the heart-stopping beauty of driving a few miles east, outside of town, and seeing the vast expanse of the prairie for the first time. And she missed Nate. She had no trouble acknowledging that, although her feelings were always mixed. She couldn't shake her guilt, the awareness of how she had hurt him.

As for Thomas, she refused to even let him into her consciousness. The ache she felt for him was like an old scar, an unhealed wound, a discomfort so deep that it had become a constant companion, a kind of chronic emotional arthritis.

When Jasmine came home from school, Molly showed her the note. Jasmine's excitement was hard to resist. She was, Molly observed, not for the first time, a splendid combination of the best of both cultures: tall and lithe, with lovely skin the color of burnished copper, curly dark hair that fell uninhibited almost to her waist, the high cheekbones of her father's tribe but her mother's generous, wide mouth, and bringing together all of these remarkable features, her mother's clear blue eyes.

"Mom! This is fantastic! A big party. Just imagine! We need to start looking for tickets right away," Jasmine enthused. And then, seeing the hesitant look in her mother's eyes, she added, "Don't even think it, Mom. I know how you resist going back, but you don't have any choice. This is Nate's big day, and if you miss that you might as well throw in the towel as far as being his mom."

"You've never been one to mince words, Jasmine." Molly answered with some anger. Jasmine flashed her a hurt look, and she quickly added, "But of course you're also right. We can't miss this. I'll get on the Internet this afternoon and see what we can come up with for tickets."

Pamella Hays

Never one to harbor her negative feelings for long, Jasmine pulled her mother up out of her chair and danced her around the room. "You know what, Mom?" she offered. "You need to let go once in a while. You're way too serious all the time. This is going to be great!"

Infected by her daughter's enthusiasm, soon Molly found herself talking about vacation time, airline tickets, and travel plans. She permitted herself only one small dig at the short notice, evidence she said of the infamous indifference of Indian people to time, but even this critical little jibe did not ruffle Jasmine, who was bubbling over with joy at the thought of them all being together again.

Red Hawk

Nate had dropped his little bomb at suppertime, telling his father that he had invited Molly and Jasmine home for his birthday celebration. Red Hawk did not dare show his discomfort. His son's birthday was a big event this year, a symbolic coming of manhood, and it was only natural that he would want to include his stepmother and sister. But Red Hawk had simply not thought that far ahead, had not imagined what kind of party they would have, and so Nate's words left him feeling shaken and uncertain.

In the two years since she had been gone, Red Hawk had grown to love Molly even more, despite his attempts to let go of his need for her. His original hurt pride, bewilderment, and anger had slowly metamorphosed into something more like a lingering depression, a heavy encumbrance that never lifted. He went to work, he kept up his responsibilities on the Council, he tried, desperately but he knew ineffectually, to communicate with his son. But none of this was enough.

At night, when they had usually lain together, saturated and at peace after making love, he missed her the most. Not, he thought, because of the lack of physical contact, though he missed that too, but because those were the most intimate moments between them, when Molly finally seemed satisfied and content, forgoing talk, happy just to be in his arms. Her absence in his bed was a cavernous hole, a kind of hollow existential nothingness, he decided with irony, remembering his early attempts to read Sartre.

141

Pamella Hays

And now she was coming back, even though for only a short while, and he found himself feeling terrified. The worst moment would be at the airport, when he would have to go and pick them up and actually see her there, acknowledge her presence. He thought if he could just survive that, that instant of painful recognition that she still existed, then perhaps he would be all right.

Of course he was thrilled that he would get to see his daughter, he and Molly's proof of their love, of the coming together of their two worlds. Jasmine's vivacity and loving personality were like medicine for his soul. He needed to see her in the same way that he needed to breathe. She would have grown up a lot since he had seen her last summer, he reminded himself. She was almost sixteen, sixteen, he thought with helpless panic, almost a woman.

But one's heart could only bear so much at a time. Right now Jasmine, as far as he could tell, was all right: balanced and healthy and optimistic. Nate, however, was another matter. He tried over and over again to understand the metamorphosis, the enormous change from the quiet but loving and obedient child to the infuriatingly aloof, sharp-tongued, and rebellious young man he saw now, growing exponentially more angry on a daily basis. And secretive, too, Red Hawk thought, and that characteristic was the most disturbing. Where did his mind go when he put on that mask of scorn, his eyes becoming like obsidian, black and sharp and hard? Red Hawk knew he was drinking; his mother also had expressed concern about that, but nothing he said seemed to have penetrated Nate's reflective armor.

Sometimes at night Thomas would wake up with a start, thinking he had heard the phone ring, the call in the middle of the night that always meant trouble, and more often than not, tragedy. But how could he explain these fears to Nate, who was brash and young and fearless and so utterly certain that he was impregnable to harm?

Red Hawk knew too that Nate missed Molly. He hoped that at least some good might come of her visit that way. Maybe he could convince her to talk to Nate. He knew she loved him and would

Circling

immediately pick up on his outraged isolationism and dismissive superiority, traits that were so inimical to his actual self.

Red Hawk forced himself to smile. "I'm glad you want your mom and sister to come, Nate," he said. "It will be nice to see them. It's been a while."

"Your excitement is overwhelming, Dad," Nate answered sarcastically. "But at least you managed to mention that I have a mom," he offered bitterly. "Normally you just act like she doesn't even exist."

Red Hawk sighed. Pushing back his plate and thanking his sister for the wonderful meal, he put his hand briefly on his son's shoulder, feeling his immediate response as the muscles tightened, and left before his emotions could betray him.

Jasmine

Like all teenage girls, Jasmine was a hopeless romantic. She had been to see the film "Titanic" with a bevy of girlfriends three times, and each time she had wept copiously. Unlike her brother, who had lost his faith in love when his parents divorced and had become bitter and angry, her own faith in love as fate, as destiny, had been rekindled. She was convinced that her role in life was to bring her parents, the star-crossed lovers, back together.

She thought that she understood what had happened with a perceptive and brilliant clarity: Her parents had been buffeted by the crosswinds of two very different cultures, and neither of them had been willing to compromise. Her father had become even more native than before, her mother more single-mindedly feminist. Jasmine knew how proud and stubborn they both were. What she had to do was to force them to see the errors of their entrenched points of view. At the moment she had no idea how to accomplish that, but she believed Cupid himself had intervened on her behalf with the felicitous birthday invitation.

She considered talking to Nate to try to make him her ally, but after two years of witnessing his belligerent sarcasm, she had reluctantly decided that he would almost certainly reject her pleas. Nate was an annoying puzzle to her, and she didn't like feeling uncertain about people. She realized that he had an even greater attachment to his tribal roots than she did. His real mother, after all, was Indian too, and her interpretation was that Molly's leaving had forced him to become more rigid in his loyalties, more Catholic than the Pope,

Circling

so to speak. On the other hand, she also heard, in their long phone conversations, scathing criticism of their father. Even though he had chosen to stay where he was, Nate paradoxically seemed to long for something else, specifically the world beyond the reservation. It was as if, she thought, he had been cleaved in two by the divorce, and the intertwined hatred and longing that he felt for both parents seemed to be pulling his own self apart like a prisoner on the rack.

Jasmine was given to such melodramatic images because of her immersion in the theater. Here she found the solace of kindred spirits, kids who were fringe-people, some gay, some feminist, some loners, some artists, and amongst them her own exotic background was celebrated rather than looked askance at. She wasn't a flirtatious, blonde, cheerleader type, and she didn't want to be, but neither was she determined, like her brother, to feel like an outcast, to play the role of the cynical rebel. Sometimes she thought that if only Nate had come out here with them, if he had experienced the polyglot culture of the urban environment and its greater tolerance for the variety of ethnic groups in the city, then perhaps he would have become less self-absorbed, less likely to wallow in self-pity.

Though she usually managed to stuff it far inside, her concern for her brother was deeply unsettling. Sometimes she wondered how far he would be willing to go to prove his point, to demonstrate the harm that he perceived had been done to him. She knew he wasn't inherently selfish. She knew he was capable of great tenderness and sensitivity, because she had seen these traits through his drawings. And she shared his love of tribal traditions, for the spiritual reassurance of ritual and ceremony, of clear-cut celebrations of identity like the dances she had participated in during the yearly pow-wows. Nothing could compare, not even the best drama on the stage, to the mesmerizing power of the drums, of dancing in unison with all of the women of the tribe, resplendent in their elegant costumes created for the occasion. She could close her eyes and hear the bass beat of the drum reverberating under her feet and the closer, whispering jingle of bells and ornaments like the pop-can tabs which were painstakingly sewn

Pamella Hays

onto skirts and tops. She could smell the distant, voluptuous scent of fry-bread and the pungent dust of the earth raised by the delicate, intricate steps of the dance.

When she went back in the summers, she always fell easily into the old sway of the powwow, relishing the games, the gambling, the dancing, the covert but unmistakable interest of the young men who she observed were watching her while she danced. Sometimes she daydreamed about her future as a married woman. Would she marry within the tribe or instead find some urbane and sophisticated man of the world? Being her mother's daughter, possessing her mother's one-step-at-a-time common sense, she did not indulge overly long in these fantasies, and she did not above all permit herself to travel deeper into the underlying cultural conflicts, into what would inevitably be, when the time came, a wrenching choice.

Meanwhile, however, she needed a plan for the imminent celebration, and she began by nudging Molly towards something more than acquiescence, towards a genuine excitement about going home.

Nate

Molly was touched by the obvious efforts that Red Hawk had made to tidy up their house and make it seem welcoming. There were flowers on the dining room table and in their bedrooms, and the kitchen was spick and span. Though the house retained the un-lived in, indifferent air of a bachelor, she could tell that he meant well, that he had tried to recapture something of the ambience of a home.

There had been an awkward moment at the airport when she saw him waiting for them amongst the waving, smiling crowd. Unlike his counterparts, he stood in the back and did not wave, though he was obviously searching for their faces. Tall enough to be easily seen, he merely waited until they came up to him and then took his daughter into his arms and gave her a long, loving hug. Then he pushed her away to arm's length and commented, "You're a young lady now, Jasmine, a very beautiful young lady."

His daughter responded by throwing herself into his arms again, whispering into his ear, "Dad, I've missed you so much!"

Molly meanwhile stood apart, growing more nervous about the proper way she should greet her former husband. A hug? A hand-shake? No, that was too formal. She didn't want to be overly stand-offish, inappropriately cold. Red Hawk, however, solved the problem by coming up to her and giving her a kind but distant embrace, kissing her on the cheek and telling her she looked well.

Pamella Hays

Molly had some difficulty ignoring the smell of his after-shave and the simple animal warmth of his torso, but she stepped back, smiled, and greeted him with what she hoped was polite enthusiasm.

"Where's Nate? she asked. "I thought he would be here too."

"He's running around like a chicken with its head cut off getting ready for this big do," Red Hawk smiled. "I haven't seen him so excited in ages."

As they walked towards the car, Red Hawk carrying their suitcases in both hands, Molly asked, "What's he planning to do after graduation?"

"Not a clue," Red Hawk answered cryptically. "He's heavily in to the teenage rebel thing. He hardly talks to me at all." Then, with a feeble attempt at humor, he added, "You know, like his dad- the strong, silent type."

Then, hoping to lighten the moment, he smiled over at Jasmine, who was walking beside him. "How'd we manage to get one kid so withdrawn and one kid so outgoing?" he asked her, a note of playfulness laced with sadness in his voice.

After he had put the suitcases in the trunk, Jasmine took his hand. "Don't worry, Dad. Nate's just going through a phase. He'll get himself straightened out."

"I hope so, sweetheart," Red Hawk answered. "I certainly hope so."

When they arrived home, Molly had almost immediately excused herself to go get ready for the big event. Though their flight had come in early, the trip to Browning had taken over two hours, and the party was slated to begin at noon.

Jasmine, meanwhile, stood in the living room looking out the picture window at the view of the yellow prairie, its tall grasses swept by the wind's broom, calmed into stillness only when it reached the foothills covered with dark pines. In the far distance were the peaks of the park, titanic guardians of the spirits that resided there. She felt as she always did when contemplating their aloof majesty, serene and safe.

Circling

Red Hawk came up behind her, putting his hand on her shoulder. She turned to him, giving him a quick hug, and pulled him down on the couch next to her.

"Don't you have to get ready too?" he asked.

"Yah, but it only takes me a second. Natural beauty, you know?" she teased.

Red Hawk smiled. He hadn't allowed himself until that moment to fully comprehend how much he missed her. She was, he thought, like a light in the dark, like a beacon in a storm. When she entered a room, a soft glow came with her.

"I need to talk to your mom about something before the party," he excused himself. "Don't go away," he added in a playful but nostalgic tone.

Red Hawk knocked on the door of the bedroom. "Molly, you decent?" he asked. It pained him to think that he had to ask her that, this woman whose body he knew better than his own, this beloved landscape across which his hands and lips had so often wandered.

"Sure," Molly replied. "Come on in." She was dressed in a slip and high heels, holding a blue dress in front of herself, contemplating its effect in the mirror with a frown. "Is a dress too much? Should I wear slacks instead?" she queried fretfully.

"Wear whatever you feel comfortable in," Red Hawk replied, his glance taking in at once the familiar form of her, the slender grace that still moved him. Then he added, "Molly, there's something we have to talk about right away, about Nate."

"Nate?" Molly said with some alarm. "Why? What's wrong with him?"

Red Hawk smiled ruefully. "Adolescence," he said. And then, "Sometimes I think it's something more maybe, too. He's distant, angry. Nothing I say seems to touch him. It's as if he's suddenly become deaf."

Molly studied his face, seeing the palpable worry lines, sensing the hurt he wouldn't express openly. "Do you suppose he'd talk to me?" she asked. "I could try."

149

Relief flooded Thomas's voice. "I hoped you would," he said. "At this point he and I are so estranged that I might as well be invisible. But I really think he needs to talk to someone. I think something is very wrong."

A knock on the door interrupted. "Hey you two," Jasmine said. "I hate to butt in, but it's almost one o'clock."

Molly hurriedly finished dressing, grabbing the special cake that Red Hawk had remembered to order from the local bakery, and they headed out the door.

They got to the party, which was being held at Nate's request at Margaret's house (another little twist of the knife, Red Hawk thought), a bit late, but they were still some of the first to arrive. An improvised table of saw horses and sheets of plywood stood at the back of the living room, covered with a bright woven cloth and already holding plentiful quantities of food. The number of dishes would increase, Molly knew, as guests arrived with their own offerings. She placed the rectangular chocolate cake, with its red Happy Birthday message, in the middle of the table.

Nate came out from the kitchen when he heard their voices, and he gave Molly a brief hug, a gesture she thought much more suitable to a distant acquaintance than to this mother, but she did not comment. His sister he picked up and spun around, and then, placing her once again on her feet, he stood back and did a mock appraisal. "Not bad, sis," he said. "You're pretty good looking for a half-breed."

Jasmine laughed and, embarrassing him mightily, planted a long kiss on his cheek. "And you," she said lightly, "look for all the world like Dad."

At this remark, Nate winced, or at least so Red Hawk thought, but to his sister he said, "Guess it could be worse."

Their conversation was interrupted by the arrival of several guests, bearing plates of food and carrying beverages of every description. Soon the house was packed with people standing shoulder to shoulder, the conversations and laughter a loud but pleasant undercurrent of sound. Molly stood a little back from the mainstream, observing

Circling

but also enjoying; she had forgotten the hospitality and friendly spontaneity of these kinds of gatherings.

Some women came up and said hello, polite but wary, and Molly did her best to respond, steering the conversation over to questions about their families, their children's exploits, the harshness of the winter just past. When they asked, she explained perfunctorily about her work, but she found that she was most comfortable talking about Jasmine and her achievements. She was careful not to sound boastful, but she sensed a real curiosity in the women's questions about Jasmine's fascination with the theater. One woman adroitly observed that she had had a good background in drama, having participated for so many years as a dancer at competitions.

Molly had not honestly considered that idea, but she appreciated the wisdom of it. Undoubtedly her daughter was a synthesis of tribal ritual and modern performing artist, and she reflected that this could be a truly inspiring combination.

At last, when everyone seemed satisfied and well fed, unable, they all protested, to eat another bite, Nate, who had been mingling with all the well-wishers but spending the most time with the circle of young people that included his sister, walked to the front of the table. Picking up a fork he found lying there, he hit the side of the glass he had in his hand, just as they did in the movies. The ringing sound caught everyone's attention, and soon the talking ceased.

First Nate thanked them all for coming, for their cards and gifts and especially for their blessings. Molly swelled with pride at how graciously he spoke. But then, drawing himself up and looking directly at his parents, Nate spoke proudly but spitefully the words of his coveted secret.

"I wanted to tell you all," he said gravely, "that I signed up this morning for the Marines. After boot camp I'll be going straight to Iraq."

Molly, who was standing a few feet away from Red Hawk, looked over at him and saw his face blanch. In the moment of stunned silence that followed Nate's announcement, she made her way quietly over to

Red Hawk and took his hand. Their eyes met, and they saw mirror reflections of their own feelings: shock, sadness, and disbelief.

For her part, Jasmine burst forth theatrically with a loud expression of disapproval, but her remark was soon covered over by exclamations of congratulations and best wishes as the crowd moved towards Nate.

Though they knew it seemed rude, Molly and Red Hawk left soon afterwards, by mutual agreement. They drove in silence to the house, each locked into his or her bewildered disbelief. Once there, they sat together on the couch, holding each other in a gesture of mutual consolation, drawn together by the dark energy of what they already felt they had lost.

Thomas was the first to collect himself and move away. His face was grim. "I guess there won't be any need for you to talk to him now," he said bitterly, and Molly could not decide whether that bitterness was directed towards her or towards Nate.

For her part, her self-recrimination was already so overwhelming that Red Hawk's adding to it would make very little difference. Why hadn't she seen this coming? Why hadn't she forced Nate to be more communicative? Why had she stayed so aloof? Wasn't she the adult, shouldn't she have forced the peace?

Her voice breaking, the tears already forming in her eyes, she said, "Why would he do this, Red Hawk? Why on earth would he want to go over there, to such a dangerous and violent place?"

His voice neutral, resigned, Red Hawk answered, "You know full well the military tradition of our people; we have a long history of serving our country, of being honorable soldiers." And then, by way of explanation, he added, "I think it was Nate's way of getting our attention, of letting us know how angry he is at us. He's never gotten over you leaving, Molly," he added without apparent rancor.

Molly voiced the fear that she knew Red Hawk felt too but would not express. "He could be killed, Red Hawk. He could die, and all because he's angry?" Her voice rose into a wail as the tears ran unheeded down her face.

Circling

Once again Red Hawk embraced her, stroking her hair as she put her face into his shoulder, wishing with all the power of his being that there was something that he could say to comfort her. Finally he murmured, "We shouldn't think the worst, Molly. Nate's smart and capable, and he is of age. He has the right to make his own decisions. Maybe he'll be put in communications or something; maybe he won't be in combat." But even as he spoke these words, he knew they were a lie. Nate had joined the Marines, and there was no way a Marine would be on the sideline: They were always at the heart of the fray.

They kept talking on into the night, part grieving, part reminiscence, part speculation, alternatively embracing and pulling away, the emotions of both momentarily frank and open, their hearts on their sleeves. When Jasmine came back at midnight, they were still talking.

Jasmine was uncharacteristically terse. "I will never speak to my brother again," she said. "What he has done is unforgivable, monstrous. How could he do this to me?"

Red Hawk and Molly simply opened their arms to her, the three of them bereft of words adequate to their sorrow, their mutual embrace the only strength that could gather them together, their love, however broken and fragile, suddenly all that mattered.

Jasmine

It was hard for Jasmine to believe that Nate had been in Iraq for almost ten months now. At first they had heard little from him, mostly just quick phone calls to let them know that he was all right. His voice would sound fuzzy and remote, like an astronaut calling from the moon. Finally Jasmine had convinced him to start e-mailing, and since then their communications had greatly increased in frequency.

Initially his written words were like his spoken ones on the telephone, terse and impersonal. She resented the cold maleness of his communications, all logic and objectivity, never mentioning how he felt, what he saw that disturbed him. This had infuriated Jasmine, who wrote back long, emotional messages about her life, the play that had just been performed that was her drama project, her opinions about the war, her experiences as a peace activist. She recognized that in part she was taunting him, but it was prompted by love: She wanted him to admit what she was convinced had to be the trauma that he was experiencing. She wanted to pry open the shell of denial in which she presumed he had enclosed himself.

This viewpoint was reinforced by her growing involvement with the anti-war movement in Portland. Her natural youthful enthusiasm and idealism fused with her love of the dramatic gesture, and she took part in the rallies dressed in outrageous costumes, caricatures of politicians with enormous papier-mâché heads or as part of a group of women dressed in the black of mourning. She helped make signs and symbolic flag-draped coffins, attended workshops on protecting

Circling

oneself against tear gas and rubber bullets, and learned methods for dealing non-violently with the police. Her mother, although she was in theory opposed to the war, nevertheless fussed about her participation, doubting whether or not these demonstrations really did any good. But Jasmine persisted, reminding her mother that she had protested the Vietnam War as a student herself, and this irrefutable argument usually silenced Molly's objections.

As the end of school drew near and summer loomed, Jasmine began to look forward to being back in the open spaces of Montana, to participating in the summer rituals she loved at the powwows and fairs. She talked to her father frequently, and she thought he sounded depressed. She noticed that her mother took the phone from her more and more and engaged in long conversations with Red Hawk. If she sensed that the conversation was becoming private, Jasmine would go to her room or turn on the television in the living room.

In her heart of hearts, she still believed in her parents' love for one another. She knew this was typical of kids whose parents had divorced, this fantasy that they would someday get back together, but she couldn't rid herself of it, no matter how irrational it was. Nate's leaving had shaken them all, making them more aware of their need for one another. Maybe, she hoped, this new awareness would serve as a catalyst to reconciliation.

As the months went by, Nate's e-mails metamorphosed into a more honest revelation of his feelings. He still would not tell her about the horrors he had seen or his own fears in the midst of battle, but he did sound less and less like a soldier and more and more like a home-sick and confused young man. He told her too about his private misgivings about the rationale for going to war. He revealed that he was not sleeping well, that his nights were haunted by a dream of apocalypse, a dream in which a huge black wolf appeared to be stalking him, not threateningly, but almost pleadingly, as if, Nate said, the animal wanted to communicate with him.

He also mentioned that he couldn't stand the food anymore. He longed for a good meal of fry bread and coffee and venison or the giant

Pamella Hays

Napi burger that they served at his favorite café in Browning. He even admitted that he missed his father, that he would give anything to go fishing with him, to just sit beside him on the bank of the river and do nothing but absorb the quiet.

Nate's new openness obliterated all of Jasmine's remaining anger at what she had seen as his betrayal of the family. She wrote back thoughtful, insightful e-mails full of love and compassion. She told him how much they all missed him and how they longed for him to come home.

Nate

The war was nothing like Nate had imagined it. For one thing, it was boring, his days routine and regimented and predictable, the weight of his regulation gear, body armor, rifle, and boots like a continual penance. The heat took him aback; he had never had rivers of sweat run down his body before, even in the summer back home when he would hike for hours up steep mountain ridges. On the days he was not on patrol, riding around the dusty, rubble-strewn city in a Humvee, on the look-out for snipers and suicide bombers, he had the rare privilege of eating inside the air-conditioned dining hall, and this was almost worse than the heat, because he knew in a short time it would be snatched away from him, and his body would suffer even more in the furnace of the almost treeless landscape.

And his first winter here, which he was just now experiencing, was hardly any better, with sandstorms that made Browning's winds seem like puny relations. But at least the heat was considerably muted, and the nights were actually chilly.

He had relished his training, its merciless physical challenges, its hard-boiled, war-like attitude, its almost hypnotic propaganda of brotherhood: "The few, the proud, the Marines". Something he hadn't known he possessed was stirred in him; the ancient calling of the Indian warrior mixed with that of the Marine, the symbol of self-possessed, unflappable manhood, the courageous soldier protecting his own. He stood tall and straight in his new uniform, proud that he had made it into this exclusive club, ready, he thought, to take on the world.

Pamella Hays

The one thing he had not anticipated but probably enjoyed the most was the camaraderie of his fellows. There were people here of all different races, black, brown, red, white, and yellow, and though once in a while he got teased about his tribal heritage, he couldn't detect any real animosity. The uniform was a stronger indicator of belonging than his Indian appearance. It wasn't, he decided, just that they were all Marines: they were more importantly part of a secret brotherhood and the closest group he had belonged to since he had played basketball. As Marines they all faced the same fears and depression every day, and this bond, though largely unvoiced, held them together.

They were in a hostile, confusing environment where the enemy looked just like the civilians they were supposedly protecting. The more the insurgency grew, the more chaotic the situation became, and sometimes he was ordered to fire at young Iraqi men who looked just like the ones he saw everywhere, in the marketplace, on their way to school, walking with their families. He wondered how his captain could be so sure that these guys were insurgents; they had no uniforms, no visible weapons, no identifying marks except for their penetrating black eyes, filled with anger and resentment.

But as the months went by and the insurgency grew, the attacks on the patrols more frequent and deadly, Nate lost some of his aplomb. It was not a war game anymore, but a real war, implacable and irrational and terrifying, and though his fellow Marines would never say it in so many words, he knew that they too longed for home, for a reasonable and normal existence. He could see in the eyes of his fellow combatants the hollow shock of grief at witnessing someone they knew die next to them. He could feel in their hearts the unrelenting fear, the inhuman struggle to be soldiers, to distance themselves from any compassion.

Sometimes on his cot at night he would relive the birthday party in his mind, see his father's face fall and grow older in that very instant that he had announced his intentions, hear the initial silence in the room and then his sister's inappropriate and embarrassing response. "Are you out of your mind?" she had yelped.

158

Circling

Gradually, of course, all of the guests had congratulated him, risen to the occasion, especially the old men who had served honorably in other wars, in the proud tradition of native peoples in the military. Molly had said nothing at all. She looked too stunned to speak, and he noticed that she had gone over to his father and taken his hand. Now, watching not only his fellows but sometimes whole Iraqi families die, trapped in cars at checkpoints, killed by mistake, or chance victims of a random IED explosion or car-bombing, Nate began to feel for the first time some regret at the way he had told his own family about signing up. He understood now, as he had not before, their anguished disbelief, the way his announcement had taken the air out of them, had deflated them.

He began sending long e-mails to Jasmine at least twice a week. He told her about everything he saw that was not related to combat: the children playing soccer in dirt lots; a woman in a black robe with a young girl in hand, dressed in her school uniform, picking their way carefully through the rubble; Iraqi men loudly discussing politics and drinking coffee at an outdoor café. He told her about the dust and the heat and the beauty of the desert sunsets. But he tried very hard to disguise his growing sense of uneasiness at his chosen profession, and he was careful never to mention the violent, grisly incidents that he had seen.

For her part, Jasmine at first wrote back angry, critical letters, making sure he knew how upset Molly and his father were and how utterly stupid she thought his decision had been. But over time her tone softened, and she began to tell him about school, about the newest endeavors of the drama class, about her own passionate belief that the war was wrong. And more and more, at the end of each letter, she begged him to be careful, to come back to them sound and whole.

After a while Nate began to live in two separate states, the dreamlike, surreal state of combat, when he felt as if he were actually operating somehow outside of his body, and within the state that he had begun to see as real: the memory of his former life, of who he had been and how he had acted, when, despite his disappointments and anger,

159

Pamella Hays

he had felt present, alive, in control. He began to draw again, often late at night when he couldn't sleep. He drew the faces of his fellow Marines and of Iraqi civilians, especially the children with their enormous dark eyes and beautifully sculpted features, and more and more he found himself drawing scenes from his dreams, strange, incoherent images that were part real, part fantastical, and often, hidden somewhere in the background, he drew the hypnotic, penetrating eyes of a wolf.

Already reserved by nature, he retreated even further into himself. He spent a lot of his off-duty time e-mailing friends and joining the chat rooms he found on the Web. He was surprised to learn about the large numbers of anti-war activists, by the proliferation of peace activities, marches and protests, and the passion of the peace movement. It had never occurred to him to doubt the war itself: It was just there, an almost organic reality, like rain or thunder or lightning. It existed, he had thought, because it had to exist. He and his fellow Marines had to shore up its existence, which was indiscernible from the patriotic rhetoric that nurtured and surrounded it: freedom, democracy, honor, country.

At first he was enraged by the opposition of the peaceniks, thinking them the most base kind of cowards. But gradually he found himself beginning to listen to what they were saying, especially about the hopelessness of this kind of 'solution' for a human problem. He could see for himself every day that things were getting worse, more violent and uncontrolled and destructive. He could feel his former convictions shrinking, his mind beginning to nag at him, pummeling his conscience, his non-soldier self.

One morning as they were checking IDs at a checkpoint, Nate saw out of the corner of his eye a small pickup approaching at high speed. He yelled at his companions, who immediately hit the ground, as he did, firing their rifles. The truck continued towards them, ignoring their warning shots, obviously with no intention of stopping. When it was close enough that they could see the forms

Circling

of the men in the truck, the occupants opened fire, spraying the Marines with their AK47s.

Nate felt the bullet penetrate his chest and travel through to his left lung. He felt no pain or even fear, marveling instead at the way his body had been able to detect the movement of the bullet, like watching an animated science film. Then he lost consciousness.

He found himself up on the meadow beneath the mountain where he and his father had often hunted elk. He was sitting cross-legged on the ground, facing east, and he noticed that his body, nude except for a loin cloth, was painted in stripes of many colors: black, red, brown, white, yellow. He gradually became aware that he was sitting within a circle, surrounded by the stones of the Medicine Wheel. A wolf came out of the trees behind him, the large gray wolf from his dreams, and walked up very close. Somehow he was not at all afraid. The animal was deeply familiar to him, a brother and paradox like him: outcast and communal being, the hunter and the hunted.

But he didn't have time to think about anything; there was too much happening to which he had to pay attention. The wolf circled him at a distance, walking over the same ground time after time until he had created a deep rut, a crack in the earth that opened as if split by an earthquake. Then there were four wolves, and each lay down outside the circle at one of the four cardinal directions.

But Nate's attention was focused on the furrow the animal had made, for out of it were arising a multitude of people: He saw his father, Molly, Jasmine, and his Auntie, and they were all holding hands, linked together. His grandmother was there, too. She was dressed in the white buckskin garment he had seen in her wedding picture, and she was young and very beautiful.

Others came also, all the people he knew on the reservation, his friends and companions in the Marines, Iraqi women and children and men, old people, young people, Asians, blacks, Latinos, whites. They all rose up and began a slow dance around him, and he heard them singing, a soft chant that grew stronger and stronger, that became like the roar of a great wind, melodious and powerful, so exquisite that, even though he could not understand the words, he found himself singing, too, caught up in the mesmerizing rhythm, the pure joy of harmony.

Then he too began to dance in the center of the circle, spinning around and around until the colors on his body melded into one, and when he looked down at himself he saw that he was the wolf, his coat a silvery gray. His singing became a howl, the lone cry of the outsider looking for his tribe, the haunting ululation of life's ultimate longing. At the sound of his cry, the other dancers joined too, their voices full of the same urgent need, caught up in the yearning supplication of the lament, rocked in its mystery.

Nate sat down again, panting for breath, and he saw in his right hand an unstrung bow and in his left hand a sheaf of broken arrows, and all around him the cry of the people, of earth's people, rose, pleading for mercy. Then he heard above him an echoing, distant cry, the call of a hawk that was circling and circling, riding the drafts of air, drifting higher and higher into the clouds until, in a heart beat, it was gone.

There is no more need for me here now. The warrior has at last found his own medicine. It is time for me to return, to comfort his father, because he will not be able to accept what has happened.

The sea below me is tumultuous and black. I am buffeted by strong winds, so that even I, with my powerful wings, begin to tire. I face into the wind and summon my last ounce of strength in order to go on.

I can see him sleeping. His mind is at peace. Soon I will enter his dream and bring him this sorrow, this unspeakable news. Then I will watch over him as he awakens and enters a real world of nightmare. He will need me more than at any time in his life before. He will have to make use of my eyes, my vision that sees beyond the ordinary and obvious. He will have to sit very still and observe, as I do, the transitory nature of existence.

Grandmother

They buried him today, his old, sad soul, his wounded spirit. All around him soared the laments of those he left behind, their grief spiraling up to the heavens and demanding explanation. I alone understand and accept; I alone can welcome him and enfold him in my arms; I alone can heal him.

He knew, even as a child, how askew things were. I tried to explain back then, but he was stubborn and prideful and strong: He was determined to do it on his own. I watched as he turned frantically from one path onto another, each leading him farther from the truth. My old wisdom did not fit into his new world. It could not encompass the suffocating reality that surrounded him on all sides. The hardest thing is to know and not have one's wisdom trusted, to speak and not to be heard. But now there is time, the time of the universe, the time of truth-telling. And now too I must focus my concerns on the living, on that waif wandering out in the wilderness, her soul so obscured by grief that she has become a living ghost, a woman without a center. She must survive for many years more. She is a Medicine Woman with much work to do. This I must find a way to tell her.

Molly

Molly got out of bed with infinite care so as not to wake the sleeping figure beside her. She was glad to hear Red Hawk's deep, resonant breathing, to know that he was sleeping peacefully. Since Nate's death six months ago he had hardly slept a whole night through, she knew.

She gathered her clothing, laid out the night before on the armchair, and made her way into the kitchen. There she dressed, shivering in the early morning cold, and poured water into the coffee maker, and only then did she go into the living room to look out at the sun that was just beginning to break out from behind the autumn haze. The view of the prairie and distant mountains sustained her, as it always did, making it seem possible that she could live another day and face whatever came.

She had risen very early, so she had the unaccustomed luxury of curling up into the armchair opposite the window with her cup of coffee in hand to take in the vast, untouched beauty of the muted landscape, its colors still half-asleep in the morning mist.

She had decided to stay here after Nate's funeral, not just out of pity for her husband, but because she needed solace and comfort for her own grief as well. She had felt selfish, knowing that this was probably her primary motivation, but the reason for her decision was changed utterly when she and Jasmine had stepped off the plane and she had seen Red Hawk's ashen face, his eyes like black wells into which no light could penetrate.

165

Pamella Hays

The days that followed, those leading up to the funeral and the weeks afterwards, had become all mixed together in her mind. She felt as if she were in a state of permanent emotional vertigo, dizzied by the maelstrom of feelings that buffeted her. Everyone was kind and thoughtful towards their family, and she began to appreciate for the first time the value of this close-knit community, but even then she could find no one to whom she could confess her guilt, her own conviction that her abandonment of her step-son had been partly to blame for his death. But Red Hawk and Jasmine were in such a deep state of grieving themselves that she felt she had to press down her own suffering and attend to theirs. She tried to be mother and wife, friend and adviser. She felt responsible to Red Hawk and Jasmine as she had never before, and somehow in her ministrations she herself began to feel less anguished, less bereaved.

For the first time in all of their years together, she saw Red Hawk not as her knight, her patient rescuer, but as the weaker partner, as a man who had lost his center, his equilibrium. After the funeral, as the days of what was intended merely as a visit turned into weeks, and she could no longer excuse her absence from her work at the Portland hospital, she decided to quit her job there and stay with him. Before she told Red Hawk, she spoke with Jasmine about her decision.

Though it would soon be time for her to return to school in Portland, a plan to which all agreed, Jasmine felt little enthusiasm for returning to school. She was in a kind of disorienting mental fog, as if her very being had been mummified and wrapped in layers of thick gauze through which reality could not penetrate.

When Molly told her about her decision to let the condo in Portland go and to stay in Browning, however, Jasmine's eyes lit up, and she seemed genuinely happy that her parents were going to be together again. Molly explained that she intended to take care of Red Hawk and to work at the local clinic.

Jasmine was surprised, but not astonished. She remembered with a trace of bitterness her dreams of their reconciliation: silly, girlish dreams that belonged to her old life, to someone who was now a

166

Circling

stranger to her. She had never imagined, however, that their coming together would leave her alone, throwing her out of their orbit and into the cold world by herself. Yes, she had agreed initially to go back to Portland, had even in a strange way looked forward to it. Here everyone knew her family's sorrow; people responded differently to her than they had before. She would catch their eyes gazing at her covertly in the supermarket or hear a group murmur to one another about her loss as she passed them in the aisles. Perhaps in school she would once again feel that comforting old anonymity once again.

She often went out for long walks, revisiting the places she had walked with her grandmother. She knew this landscape like her own face in a mirror: she never felt alone or afraid here. As the first signs of autumn began to emerge, and the grasses turned from green to a buttery tan, she thought about the plants, especially the roots, which should be dug this time of year, to be dried and then stored away for winter. Who would do these things, she thought, now that Grandmother was gone? Who would be the storyteller, the wise one who wove the old stories through their modern, damaged culture, so that someday they would still be told for comfort and instruction?

She sank down on her knees onto the hillside and lowered her head into the prairie, smelling the primitive, ageless must of the earth. Finally, she lowered her whole body, lying prone and minuscule on the huge expanse, her arms stretched out like Christ on the cross, but her body turned downward, towards Mother Earth, the great mother who was now the only one who could comfort her. She vividly remembered Grandmother talking to her, telling her that she must never abandon this place, must always turn to the sacredness of it when she became lost and confused. She sobbed until there were no more tears that could come, feeling as utterly abandoned as a lost child. The fear of leaving, of somehow betraying her Grandmother, grew huge inside of her, creating a hollowness that she had never felt before. Now they were both gone, those two people she had loved the most. What would she gain by going back to Oregon, to a place where she was only half herself? Who would harvest the medicinal

Pamella Hays

plants and keep the stories alive? Grandmother had always told her that she was a wisdom-keeper too, but what wisdom was there here now, with no one to instruct or guide her? The fear carved out an abyss that lay dark and menacing inside of her and threatened to unbalance her mind.

But to her parents she never spoke of this or voiced her fear, and for the rest of the summer she played the faked happy family game, going to pow-wows, for hikes, having friends over for barbeques on the deck, the three of them watching movies on television and stuffing themselves with popcorn. It was only at night, alone in her room, that Jasmine gave vent to her grief, covering her face with her pillow to stifle her sobs. She tried to be brave; her parents had enough grief of their own to bear, and she didn't need to add to it. A thousand times she wished her grandmother were still here. There was no one else to talk to, and besides, her grandmother had the same gift of seeing inside that she did. Grandmother would have understood the dark weight on her heart.

Molly

In late August, after Jasmine left, Molly knew that she had done the right thing. Jasmine had seemed reconciled, if not content, with the idea of returning to school in Portland, and a counselor they had consulted had reassured Molly and Red Hawk that the activity and new environment would be the best thing for her.

Alone together, she and her husband rediscovered the wonder of their sensual selves. The one aspect of their relationship that seemed to have come through the tragedy unscathed was their passionate lovemaking. In fact it was somehow actually enhanced, or perhaps she thought transformed, by the sorrow that enveloped them. Their passion for one another allowed them to transcend time, to enter a healing void where the past and present had no dominion. They felt like the survivors of a nuclear holocaust, joined together in a last, frantic embrace that defied the ugly intrusion of the world's violence and tragedy, and each embrace restored them enough to struggle on.

And Molly herself had been changed by the gradual warming of her relationship with the whole community. Everyone at the clinic respected her as a healer; it was so small that all of the staff there consulted with one another on difficult cases. Molly's expertise as a diagnostician, based on her findings in the lab, had deepened her own sense of worth and helped her to reach out to patients who came there. Belatedly she understood that much of her former feeling of rejection had come from her side, that she had not made a sincere effort to make a contribution, to be a person whose role could be valued.

Pamella Hays

She remembered fondly one afternoon when a very old elder had come to visit the clinic with a stomach pain. After the doctor had examined him, she came into the room to take a blood sample. He looked at her respectfully but curiously, too, his long white hair reaching almost to his waist and framing a deeply lined face that must have been very handsome once upon a time. The dark irises of his eyes glittered beneath his eyebrows, almost hidden by the craters of wrinkles that lined them underneath. In the native way, with exquisite courtesy, he had asked, "You are the famous healer and the lovely wife of Red Hawk?" And then, without waiting for an answer, since he obviously knew who she was, he added, "I knew his mother, you know. She was quite the lady then." His mouth broke into a sly smile, revealing worn gums punctuated here and there by small, misshapen teeth like tiny white rocks randomly strewn about in a pink moonscape. "I used to have a crush on her," he confided.

His confession caused Molly to smile indulgently, and she teased him in kind. "So did you know my husband too, when he was a boy?"

"Oh, of course. I also wished he had been my own son," he mused. "Red Hawk was very strong-willed and a handful back then, but he has grown into quite a fine man, a wisdom keeper like his mother."

Molly winked at him, "Yes, he is a very fine man," she agreed. "Still stubborn and hard-headed, though."

The old warrior cackled, adding a ribald observation. "But men who are a handful make the best lovers, don't they?"

At this Molly burst out laughing and taped the piece of cotton on his arm, patting it affectionately. "I'll bet you were a pretty good handful yourself," she teased, and was delighted to hear him laugh once again. She reflected then that one of the things she loved most of all about these people was their keen awareness of the human condition, especially their unembarrassed and forthright observations about sex.

As her commitment to the tiny medical center increased, so did her involvement with tribal affairs. She became interested in all of

Circling

Red Hawk's efforts as a member of the Tribal Council, and she steeped herself as well in his stories of his people, which he would relate to her late at night when they lay in bed together. These stories formed a sacred bond with the memory of his mother, Stands Alone, who had spent many an evening telling them to him as a child. She snuggled closer into the curve of his arm as he told the story, watching how his face lit up from inside, like a candle in a jack-o-lantern. She knew that she understood only superficially the meaning of the stories, but she was growing fond of them nonetheless. In fact they reminded her a bit of the fairy tales one of her older sisters used to tell years ago, but there was another element in these Native tales that was distinctively different. Stories like Sleeping Beauty, one which she had particularly loved, had a magical quality, too, but the moral of the story was superficial : only very beautiful, spunky maidens, though sometimes punished for being disobedient, would find their prince charming and live happily ever after. Some of Molly's old feminist tendencies erupted when she thought about the hidden message that a woman could find fulfillment only through a man.

Red Hawk's tales, however, were more significant somehow, reflecting the lives of a whole people, and their heroes or heroines came back with a lesson or some critical knowledge for the tribe. Though they might be rewarded personally, the importance of their experience was not merely selfish. The vision they brought back to their people nourished their entire community. And, Molly noted, living 'happily ever after' was never mentioned.

"How did Stands Alone become a medicine woman?", she asked one evening as the snow drifted lazily down outside.

"She always seemed to know that that is what she would be," he answered. "She hung around old men and women who would tell the old stories and answer her questions about their meaning, and as a young girl she already was an apprentice to an old man who was a healer, who knew every plant and how to prepare it for medicinal purposes. That's why she was so powerful", he added. "Even as a kid I knew she was different, special."

"Have women always been allowed to be wisdom keepers?" she queried, stroking his shoulder as she spoke.

"Of course," he answered. "Why wouldn't they be?" Then, tired out by her endless questions, though proud that she had begun to ask him about his people, he gave her a kiss, rolled over on his side, and went to sleep.

Eventually Molly even began to attend tribal ceremonies that were open to all the public, and though she felt herself always to be somewhat of an outsider, she allowed herself to enjoy the sense of being welcomed and included. Meeting many of the people she knew in the clinic, where she had a clear identity and was respected for her knowledge, seemed to have reassured them, making her a known quantity, perhaps still a mystery, but more readily accepted. She basked in that new feeling of belonging and, though she did not actually participate in the ceremonies themselves, she relaxed and allowed herself to simply soak it all in.

Still, after a year, she could not manage to think of Nate without feeling a collapse in her spirit, as if she were a balloon pierced at random by a malignant god. Nothing she knew or believed could sustain her through this; no artificial knowledge or philosophical structure could stand against the onslaught of unholy aberration that his death represented. Finally she accepted, however, that, as Red Hawk had said, there was nothing to do but to go on. In her darkest moments she clung to this paradoxical and infuriating truth, that there was no revealing past or visionary future that could comfort them, but only the life-affirming now.

Lost in her musings, Molly had not heard Red Hawk come up behind her. Now she felt his hair brush against her cheek as his arms slipped around her shoulders, and she leaned back into the familiar, warm smell of him, needing nothing more.

Red Hawk

Every day he woke and pinched himself, thinking of his good fortune that Molly had come back. With her patient care and tender solicitude, slowly he had begun to emerge from the black hole he had dug into his subconscious, from the dark energy that was consuming him from within like a cancer.

After hearing of Nate's death he had become as helpless as a child. It was all he could do to make himself get up in the morning, shower and dress, and go through the mechanics of eating. Somehow he had gone to work at the store, but he didn't remember how he got there or how long he had stayed, or what merchandise he had sold. He was dimly aware that people treated him gently, as if he were a fragile piece of glass, and he was grateful but not able to reach across to them. They lived in that other world, the world of color and light and sound, from which he now felt forever exiled.

But Molly's presence had gradually penetrated his spiral of grief and self-recrimination. After the funeral she had stayed in Jasmine's old bedroom, but one night he had felt her creep in beside him, and from that time on they had been together, rekindling their old passion.

He could remember the day that she told him, during lunch, that she had decided to stay. She had asked him if he thought he could use his influence to help her get work at the clinic. For the first time in what seemed centuries, his heart awoke, as if coming out of hibernation, and nudged his mind out of the wasteland in which it had been wandering.

Pamella Hays

After that, they were inseparable. He took her everywhere, hiking, fishing, to the store, to eat Napi burgers, big as plates, which they shared together. They took long walks, holding hands like young lovers, waving at the people in cars that went by, neighbors who were celebrating with them their return to life.

He watched Molly blossom in her work and understood for the first time how important it was to her and how good she was at it. He often came to pick her up after work, and he smiled broadly to see how she took leave of the rest of the staff, waving and laughing as she came out to the pickup. He reflected back on the days, years ago, when she had lived here with him and the children; now she seemed like another person. No, not another person but the person he had fallen in love with: capable, intense, honest, independent.

When she had gotten into the pickup, he would reach for her and pull her close and kiss her passionately on her lovely, generous mouth, heedless of who might be in the parking lot. More than once they got a friendly honk or teasing gesture, and Molly would laugh with him, feeling like a girl again, or better, like the whole woman that she was.

It took a little longer before they could bring themselves to speak of Nate. To their amazement, they realized that they each had blamed themselves for the tragedy, Red Hawk because he had been too harsh and demanding, had not told Nate about his own personal experience with alcohol but had instead taken the scolding, parental role; Molly because she knew now that Nate's heart had become deeply scarred by her leaving, and because she had thought that he would get over it and so had not shared with him her own hurt and loneliness after she left.

It was easier to speak of the living, of their now only child. Jasmine was living with a family in Portland, finishing her senior year in high school. They missed her but had agreed that she should finish school there. Not only was it the school where she had gone all of her high school career, but she was deeply involved in the theater department there and was recognized as one of its bright stars. There was nothing similar that Browning could offer, and, besides, they

174

Circling

both fantasized that she would heal better in that environment, where there was more for her to do and where she had the company of her good friend, Patty.

Without speaking their fears aloud, they both knew too that Jasmine was not the same person after her brother's death that she had been before, but they consoled themselves that her youth and energy and her involvement in drama would bring her old self back, would restore the uncanny wisdom and enthusiasm for life that she possessed which was beyond her years. They settled for her emails, infrequent but treasured, and called her once a week. Conversations were a bit stilted, perhaps, but then their whole identity had a family had to be rearranged, redesigned. Now they were three rather than four; now their daughter was the only child, and the burden on her was greater than ever. Molly and Red Hawk didn't want to scare her away. A grief counselor they had gone to had advised them not to put too many of their hopes and expectations for her onto her shoulders right now. She needed time to heal in her own way. And, for all that they might wish it, she was not any longer merely her old self. For the rest of her life she was going to carry her brother on her shoulders as well.

PART TWO: **THE JOURNEY HOME**

A Disappearing Act

She had lied repeatedly to her parents. In fact, during the past two months she had lied almost all of the time. She was doing everything in her power to distance herself from them, and gradually her old life receded like the tide, leaving her heart brushed clean, a stretch of barren sand with no distinguishing marks. During her waking hours she kept emotions at bay, but at night she dreamed constantly.

In her dreams Nate would come back to her. He never spoke but simply observed her, his eyes full of disapproval, just the way they had looked when they were children and he was scolding her for something she had done wrong. Often he came dressed as a dancer in a wolf headdress. He would circle her slowly and warily, his feet moving gracefully in the intricate steps of the dance, the wolf costume mimicking the animal's movements as he bowed forward, then back.

She became angrier and angrier towards him. It was bad enough that he had chosen his own death. Now, why couldn't he choose to leave her alone, or if not that, at least to tell her what he was thinking? It especially infuriated her that he, who had never chosen to participate in dancing at the pow-wows, would now be so arrogant as to assume some ancient tribal identity, would put on the costume of a medicine animal. As far as she knew, he had never had one, never participated in a sweat or gone on his vision quest. Why then did he do so now? Why, instead of being so mysteriously tribal, didn't he help her to understand the feeling of betrayal that she felt from his

Circling

death, the depression that left her drained of energy, the loss of innocence that wound around her like a shroud?

All night her subconscious struggled against her growing disorientation, trying to untangle the lies and deceptions that the greater
culture had told her every day of her life: If you believe the right
things and do the right things, life will be a bowl of cherries: you
will have everything you desire, you will be successful and rich and,
of course, you will find true love. And now she knew that none of
this was true. Nor was the simple, mystical way of her tribal people
with its dogged beliefs in the old ways. And her brother, the big
brother who had always rescued her before, who had always been able
to explain away her fears, was dead, and she was left alone. Her parents had deserted her too. It was obscene how they were wrapped
up in their retrieved marital bliss, almost forgetting to grieve, she
thought unkindly. All that she knew was that they were selfishly
involved in one another and were utterly indifferent to her loneliness.

Sometimes she woke up in the morning and realized that she was
quietly singing the medicine song her grandmother had taught her
when she was a child. She remembered that her grandmother had
once told her their meaning, but all she should could call up were
the Blackfeet words, which reverberated sonorously in her mind like
the rhythmic beat of a drum. Her grandmother was excluded from
the resentful feelings she had towards other adults. She had always
treated Jasmine with respect, as if she were another adult, even when
she was little. A longing for her grandmother's kind, steady wisdom
pierced her like an arrow, leaving a pain in her chest that did not go
away. She woke in the morning on the thin mattress on the floor of
her rented room more tired than when she had gone to bed.

She had found this room only a week ago, after running away from
the Anderson's home where she had been staying since the school year
began. Ever since coming back to Portland from the Rez, she had
been unable to sleep. Her only antidote to insomnia for the past several weeks had been to sneak out through the second story window,
shinnying down the sturdy branches of the ancient oak that grew

outside her window. No one was the wiser: Patty slept soundly in the next room, and her parents snored away in the bedroom across the hall.

She slipped out to walk the streets, to hang out by the river, breathing in deeply to counteract the sensation of suffocation that was with her most of the time. Though she knew the ocean was far away, she fantasized that she could smell its salty air and envision its curve of dark blue extending off into space like the prairie at home, magnificent in its solitude.

Patty was such an innocent, Jasmine thought. She would never choose to imagine any other life than the safe, prescribed little life of school, with its stifling regimentation offset only briefly each day by the dynamic atmosphere of the theater department. After Nate's death, however, this small island of lucidity in the midst of the bureaucratic insanity was simply not enough for Jasmine. Even her former theater friends, the crowd that seemed to her the most sophisticated and tuned in to what was really happening in politics, seemed more and more bit players, mouthing lines they had been taught to say and never glimpsing the real tragedy, the truth about life's false script.

At first her sleepless nights didn't register on her behavior. Every morning she woke up after only three or four hours' sleep, showered and dressed, and ate breakfast with the family, chattering with Patty about school and the new play, Shakespeare's *Hamlet*, that they were working on for the spring show. She was in fact such a good actress that she fooled everyone; she thought smugly that it was not so difficult after all to be two people at once.

After several months of her nightly sojourns, however, she no longer bothered to come home at night at all, merely slipping in the window as dawn broke and her alarm clock began to ring. She fell asleep in classes more and more, and her grades suffered. The lovely young woman who was so 'bright' began to fall out of favor with her teachers. They removed the gold star from her forehead and instead harangued or pleaded with her to "get it together." When the report

Circling

cards came in the mail, she intercepted them and threw them into the public trash receptacle on the corner. She knew that, eventually, her parents would call and ask for an explanation, and she invented two rather clever ones in a row, but by the time the third quarter of school rolled around, she realized that her duplicity was not going to be successful for much longer. That was when she decided to make the break all together.

What bothered her most was not being able to tell Patty, a sweet girl, a sincere friend, generous and smart, but not, Jasmine decided, of the temperament that would understand. Besides, she had to disappear cleanly and quickly, to simply vanish into the city without a trace, and to tell anyone, even Patty, would be tantamount to raising an alarm.

That morning in April she got up early, packing only the most critical personal items in her schoolbag: toiletries, of course, clothing for Portland's quixotic weather conditions, a pair of good hiking boots, and her journal. She left her textbooks hidden under the bed, satisfied that no one would suspect her subterfuge until at least tomorrow morning.

At breakfast she ate prodigiously, prompting Patty's mother to remark that she was so glad to see her appetite had returned. On the bus on the way to school she tried her cover story on Patty. She told her she had to work after school and into the evening on the set for their upcoming theater production. As head of the set design committee, she said, she had to be a good example and keep up the team's energy with her own extra efforts. Of course Patty accepted this and agreed to explain to her mother why Jasmine wouldn't be home at dinner.

After that, it was easy. Jasmine hung around the theater department for about a half an hour after school got out, just in case Patty came by to talk for a minute, and when she was sure that was not going to happen, she left the building, catching the first city bus that went by.

Money, she knew, was going to be a problem. Her parents sent her spending money but paid the Andersons the money for her room

Pamella Hays

and board directly to them. She had been carefully saving her small monthly stipend and had accumulated $300, but she knew this wouldn't last long in the city.

Her first decision when she got off downtown, then, was to walk to the tenderloin district to look for a cheap room that she could rent for a week or so. Hoisting her backpack onto one shoulder and with her free hand pushing her long hair back behind her ears, she stepped off the bus and entered into the human stream on the sidewalk, feeling curiously unburdened for the first time in months.

Despair

When the phone rang at seven in the morning, Molly was sound asleep, and she was both annoyed and startled by the unexpected call. All of her senses awoke instantly, however, when she heard the frightened voice on the other end of the line.

"Molly, this is Mary Anderson. I'm so sorry to wake you, but I have difficult news." Her voice faltered for a moment, causing Molly's heart to jump erratically. Then she continued, "Jasmine has disappeared. Actually, she told Patty that she had theater practice last night and she would be home late, so we shouldn't wait up for her. She has a key, so I didn't think much of it, but when Patty went into wake her this morning, she was gone. Her bed hadn't been slept in."

The dark import of the news reached Molly's consciousness as slowly as water dripping from a faucet. She blinked, shook her head in denial, and told herself that she must be still asleep. But as the message worked its way into her emotional center, its meaning suddenly lit up, a meteor burning through the cloud of shock.

At the same time that she began to speak, Molly reached over and shook Red Hawk awake. He sat up abruptly, his eyes large and questioning, his whole body tuned immediately to Molly's fear.

"What do you mean, gone? How could that happen? Did someone take her? Was she kidnapped? Did she come home last night at all?" Molly knew she wasn't making any sense, that she was asking too many questions at once, but all of the horrific tales on television police shows and missing person accounts flooded immediately into her awareness. She felt as if she were one of those pathetic, hysterical mothers filmed when they were being told something horrible about their child, the whole world watching in a kind of surreal, quasi-compassionate voyeurism. A subterranean emotional abyss opened in front of her, swallowing her rational mind. All she could think was, "This is not happening. I must be dreaming."

Sensing her disequilibrium, Red Hawk took the phone gently from her hands and spoke calmly into the mouthpiece. "Mrs. Anderson, this is Jasmine's father. Could you please repeat what you just told my wife?"

He listened intently, without expression, as he heard Mrs. Anderson's story. He asked if she had notified the police, and she said she hadn't yet done so; she had wanted to contact them first. Then he asked if he could talk to Patty.

His voice was calm and reassuring to the girl, who was clearly in shock. "Patty, hello. This is Jasmine's dad. Could you please tell me when was the last time you saw her?"

A small, shaky voice stuttered through the wire. "Yesterday at school. She told me she had to stay afterwards and work on the sets, so she wouldn't be home for dinner. She does that sometimes, so I didn't think anything about it. I told Mom I would stay up and wait for her, but I fell asleep. I was so tired. I had had a bad day at school. And then," her voice broke into a sob, "and then I woke up and she wasn't here!"

Red Hawk spoke quietly, "It's not your fault, Patty. You haven't done anything wrong. Of course you were tired. Right now we need to concentrate on some other things, though. For instance, has Jasmine been behaving strangely lately? Do you think there is any chance that she ran away? We have to think about all the possibilities, you know."

Molly, who had been sitting still as stone, jerked her whole body into attention when she heard Red Hawk's last question. She interrupted loudly, "She wouldn't do that! That's not like her at all!"

Finger to his lips, Red Hawk shushed her wordlessly. The one-way conversation, which was all that Molly could hear, continued.

Circling

"Then you think she's been a little withdrawn lately? Do you think she might be depressed? What do you two girls talk about when you're together?" To each of Patty's responses, Red Hawk's eyes focused attentively, like a hunting dog on the trail of a scent. He sat up straighter, every muscle in his body rigid, on alert, nodding his head in assent from time to time. Finally he said, "Patty, tell your mother that we will call her right back. Molly and I need a minute to talk about this and decide what to do, alright?"

Molly sat clutching the bright homemade quilt in her hands as if to anchor herself to the earth. She ground her teeth, swallowed hard, and forced her voice to be steady. "Jasmine is gone?" she asked her husband. "How? Why?"

Red Hawk told her what he surmised by reading between the lines of Patty's monologue. The impression he had was that Jasmine had not been her self since coming to Portland. Patty had reported that they were not as close as before, that Jasmine was friendly and sweet but didn't seem to trust her friend anymore, almost, Patty had said, as if she were keeping some sort of secret. She mentioned Jasmine's diminished interest in school, something that was a surprise to Red Hawk, until his mind had leapt back to the two recent excuses she had given about missing report cards, something about a newly instituted semester system, and that a report card should be arriving soon. Patty said that Jasmine had become more and more of a loner, hanging out with a couple of the more rebellious and wildly nonconforming theater students. She said Jasmine never laughed anymore or wanted to do anything fun, but she just had chalked it up to a period of grieving that a school counselor had explained to her was a predictable and normal thing that Jasmine was going through.

"Why do we always miss the signals, Red Hawk?" Molly asked. "Why do we have to get hit over the head before we understand what is happening to our children? And where has our little girl gone? She could be in so much danger." She laid her head on her husband's chest, curling her arms around his neck, stunned into silence, too overwhelmed even to cry.

185

They were too stricken to eat, but they drank coffee in front of the fireplace, its cheery flames macabre, the antics of a pathetic jester who has not been informed that the world is coming to an end. They discussed what was, to both of them, the only obvious choice they had: Red Hawk would fly out to Portland and deal with all of the missing persons reports, the police investigation, and consoling the Andersons, who were sincerely distraught by what had happened. He also planned to interview the friends she hung out with and wanted to try to reconstruct some idea of how she had spent her last day at school and to ask other students who might have seen her outside at the end of the day. He knew that she might in fact be the victim of a random kidnapping, of a sexual predator or some other troubled individual, but he refused to acknowledge that possibility; it made him feel so insane that he was afraid he wouldn't be able to function. And besides, everything Patty had told him so far fit into the pattern of a desperately grieving, depressed young woman. He reminded himself too to talk to the school counselor about his theory that Jasmine might have disappeared of her own volition.

Molly, meanwhile, would try to continue working. Her job required her presence much more than did the building supply business that Red Hawk's employees could run without him. On the chance that Jasmine should call, or even, they dared hope, to come home, someone needed to be there.

Molly called the airport and booked an afternoon flight, and then she spoke with Mrs. Anderson, explaining what they were going to do. Molly, meanwhile, held herself together with her old stoic determination, the iron self-control that she had practiced when she was alone and struggling to survive against what had seemed a hostile world. For the next while she was going to be alone again, without the gentle, encompassing centeredness of her husband, and she might as well get used to it. As if in confirmation, the sun slid behind a bank of clouds, sucking the light from the sky and turning the world into a gloomy, threatening place.

And My Heart Falls Down

He had walked at least three miles out of town before, spent and breathless, he sank down on the top of a rise with a view of the mountains beyond. "I'm getting old," he thought. "I used to walk for miles when I went hunting, and I was never this tired."

Since returning from his fruitless trip to Portland, unable to bring back any news of Jasmine to his anxious wife, terrified in his own heart that they might never see her again but afraid to let Molly see his uncertainty, he had almost been able to watch his body aging. A ridiculous notion, he knew, but something in him, some clock that had before always ticked along regularly, began to be erratic, sometimes slowing almost to a halt and at other times accelerating so much that he felt as if he could run in a frenzy to the edge of the universe and leap over.

Wherever Jasmine had gone, she clearly did not want to be found. He had followed every possible lead, talked to all of her best friends and to her teachers, trying to find some clue to her behavior. He had of course involved the police as well, but they were politely sympathetic and distant. Ultimately they had to tell him that young people vanished every day, and there was little realistic hope that they would find Jasmine. He had stayed with the Andersons, talking and talking with them for hours about where she might have gone. What none of them ever voiced was the ominous possibility that she had met with some kind of violent end, or even, almost worse, had been kidnapped into a nightmare life of prostitution from which she could not escape.

Even with Molly he had not been able to give expression to an idea so monstrous. It was as if, once they voiced it, the idea would grow in power and take over their lives, snapping their last tiny thread of hope. And so, even though he knew full well that Molly sometimes thought about this possibility, too, they never shared their fears with one another. Each one sank into his or her rationalizations, into habitual actions that kept them within the borders of sanity.

Molly threw herself into her work, spending long hours at the lab, fighting every evidence of disease on the microscope as if it were the very symbol of evil in the universe, as if when she solved this specific mystery she would somehow be able to solve the mystery of her daughter's disappearance.

Red Hawk had responded in an entirely different manner, preferring to be by himself as much as he could without giving up control of his business, missing so many council meetings, that had his friends not known about his personal anguish, he might have been asked to step down. The only comfort he could seem to find was in these solitary wanderings. When he was utterly alone, contemplating the natural splendor of this place, he could pull himself together enough to go on, or, more accurately, allow his surroundings to quiet his anguish enough so that he could live. He had often heard the expression 'a broken heart', but now he thought it was totally inadequate to the actual feeling: It was more a charred, burnt out husk, like a home that had experienced a fire that gutted its interior but left a shaky frame unaccountably still standing.

He tried to practice the meditation that he had honored in his youth, when life was all promise and beauty, when he could meld with the whole of nature, but now, he realized, the real art of meditation was how to reach that state when one was bound up in sorrow and loss, and that was so much harder to manage.

In his meditations he fought off the temptation of self-blame. He had now lost both a son and a daughter, and he couldn't escape the possibility of his own complicity in that loss. Had he been such an imperfect father? Had he been blind to signals that he should have

Circling

seen? Had he failed to let them know how much, and how unconditionally, he loved them? His rational mind's answer was always
"Yes." We all are, he thought, somehow guilty, somehow to blame,
less loving than we should be.

But despite the weight of this knowledge, despite his new insight
that he was, and always had been, so far from perfection, there was
some grace that he was granted here outside, looking at the mountains' unassailable certitude, that softened his grief.

With his eyes focused on the distant hills, he did not look up, but
if he had he would have seen a tiny speck, a hawk riding a draft of air,
at last spiraling out of sight into the vast reaches of the sky.

Grandmother

What are you thinking, child? How could you do such a thing? This is no solution to your grief. It is time for you to return back to your land, to your roots. I will take you by the hand and lead you back. The people are waiting for you there, people who need your skills as a medicine woman. True, I could not wait long enough to teach you all that you needed to know, but I planted the seed. Hear my words. Turn away from this madness, this destruction. Who ever profits from confusion and self-doubt? Who gains in stature when they run away from what is calling them to their purpose? I will give you a spirit guide so that you can find your way back, but you must travel the hard road by yourself. You must find what you seek by trusting your heart, not doubting it. Reach inside and pull up your courage. Though you do not know it, I will be walking by your side.

Hiding

After her small nest egg ran out, Jasmine found a job in a second hand store in her rundown neighborhood. The manager didn't ask questions, and her pay came as cash in an envelope at the end of the week. Jasmine liked the people who came in; they were either street people looking for a warm place to hang out or perhaps some cheap item of clothing, or, less often, well-heeled upper class women, their hair fashionably coiffed, their clothes impeccable. She could see that such women, who almost always came in groups of three or four, were excited by their daring, by slumming in this poor part of town. Sometimes they were looking for something specific, something they called 'antique', not second-hand, such as a table lamp from the 1920s or a vintage hat or fur. Jasmine understood that she was invisible to them. They glanced at her when they answered their questions but took no further interest, so Jasmine left them alone. They chattered excitedly over the items they found, like magpies clawing and tearing at a choice road kill.

Most of the men who came in were part of the neighborhood, homeless or nearly so, disheveled from a night sleeping on the street or in a shelter, wrapped in several layers of sweaters and vests for warmth. Jasmine had noticed that one of the first clues of home-lessness was a pungent, earthy odor that formed a protective shield around the person, isolating them from others. Most people avoided the transients, passing around them on the sidewalks or in the store as if they were not human. After a while Jasmine became used to their appearance and was no longer offended by their smell. She liked the whimsical touches of individuality in their clothing: the World War I leather pilot's hat with sheepskin-lined flaps, the insouciant air of a pair of highly polished dress shoes, the tattered splendor of a colorful silk scarf. Occasionally a man would appraise her surreptitiously, but she didn't really hold their attempts at flirtation against them. She was, she realized, only a paycheck away from being amongst the homeless herself, and she understood their loneliness.

What did unsettle her deeply was the vacancy, sometimes tinged with madness, in some of their eyes, eyes whose spirit had wandered so far into some dark place in the interior that no light came up to the surface. She wondered what had happened to them, what abyss they had stepped into that left them so dazed and bereft of purpose. She recoiled involuntarily from these lightless eyes, a pang of pure fear ricocheting from her stomach to her brain, recognizing that she herself stood teetering on the edge of her own unfathomable abyss.

After being there for about a month, Jasmine began to recognize some of the local types who stopped by on a regular basis. She even learned some of their names and gradually heard a little of their life stories. One man in particular, a middle-aged, kindly looking person who, despite his old clothes and rundown shoes was nonetheless always clean and tidy, caught her interest. Above all she was drawn to his eyes, a dark, rich brown that beckoned with a mesmerizing quality, like a the depths of an unplumbed lake. Unlike so many of the homeless men she had seen, he maintained his dignity and remained somewhat aloof. He would not talk about himself but showed a keen mind that was aware of current events. He spoke with the vocabulary of an educated man and spent most of his time looking through the few old books they had on a 'sale' table.

Once, noticing that he had chosen a book on Vietnam, she ventured to ask, "Are you a Vietnam vet?"

His face revealed the answer before he spoke. "Yes," he said.

Jasmine felt chagrined that she had asked him such a nosy question, so to soften its impact, she added, "My brother was in Iraq—a

Circling

Marine." Then, to her great surprise, because she had never told this to anyone before, she said, "He was killed about a year ago."

The man's reaction was not what she had expected. He put a hand on her arm, very gently, and nodded his head in sympathy. He did not speak for a moment, but then offered, "My name is Mark."

After that he came into the store more often, and when she could slip away from the manager's watchful gaze, she would visit with him about his war experiences. She knew somehow that he was not telling her the whole truth, and she was grateful that he spared her those details, but she also was bizarrely comforted by having a clearer picture of war, of what a soldier actually saw and felt and went through every day. She never mentioned her brother again, but she began to understand for the first time what he might have experienced.

One night, when Jasmine finished her day at the store, Mark was waiting outside, and he fell into step beside her as if her were a spouse picking her up after work. Jasmine accepted his presence without question; in fact she rather welcomed it. She was not in any way fearful, for though she had lost most of her ability to see inside people, she still trusted her common sense, and it told her that this man was not threatening. Besides, she was in a permanently benumbed state, wandering through her days like the lost, abandoned spirits her grandmother had told her about who could never rest. She often cried out voicelessly to her brother, but her pleas hit the stone wall of his death and bounced back like an echo that gradually diminishes until it vanishes into the air. She despaired that he could no longer hear her.

When she and her quiet companion arrived at the downstairs door of her apartment building, she glanced at him inquiringly, and since he made no gesture to leave, she asked, "Do you want to come up?"

Mark nodded his head affirmatively and surprised her by taking her hand as they walked up the stairs.

The tiny second-floor room, with its swaybacked bed, hotplate, and a patched orange armchair that she had gleaned from the second hand store, seemed to fill up with their presence.

"Would you like some tea?" Molly offered nervously.

Mark seemed taken aback. "No, no, not really." And then, less abruptly he added pointlessly, "So this is where you live?"

Jasmine sat down uncomfortably on the edge of the bed, removing her shoes. Now that he was here, she had no idea what to say to him. What in the world was she thinking to invite him here?

Mark sat down next to her, but he was careful not to touch her "How did you end up here?" he asked. "Where's your family?"

Unable to respond, Jasmine leaned her head onto his shoulder and wept. The tears wouldn't stop, and neither would her body stop shaking.

Later she wouldn't have been able to explain how they ended up in her bed. She remembered his awkward attempts to comfort her while she cried, patting her head gingerly, and then a longing so overwhelming that it swept over her like a tidal wave, a desire not sensual but visceral, to touch someone else's body, their contours, the solid evidence of a living, breathing human being. Their coupling was brief and awkward, reminding her of the few times she had slept with one of the boys in her drama club. Then too there was this hurried ineptness, the sudden awareness of a stranger's skin against one's own, the gradual sensation of a floating alienation. Mark's need was so great, and her grief so profound, that they drifted into their separate universes even before the brief instant of climax. Then her erstwhile lover rolled immediately away and in no time was snoring loudly.

Jasmine couldn't remember when she also fell into a fitful sleep, but the pounding thrum of the music woke her at around two o'clock. It came from across the street, from a bar she knew was there but that she usually tried to ignore when it woke her in the wee hours of the morning.

Coming fully awake, the first thing she realized was that her companion was no longer there. She glanced over at the upturned blue-plastic egg crate that served as a night table, and noticed a wadded ten-dollar bill lying there. The whole experience had been so surreal

Circling

that it had never occurred to her to see it from his point of view, and her first impulse was a raw anger that he could have been so unaware that she had simply needed some basic human warmth. And then, reluctantly, she realized that perhaps sex had been his only intention all along, that he interpreted her loneliness as availability, that to him she was a commodity that he could purchase, use, and then throw away, or, even worse, that the money was left out of pity for her situation. She staggered into the bathroom, pulled her long hair away from her face, and vomited violently into the toilet.

Now wide awake and shaking with shame and rage, she focused her attention on the nearby bar. She threw on a pair of jeans and a sweatshirt and tore down the stairs and across the street. Even from the street outside, she could smell the smoke and sour beer and sawdust. Through the swinging doors, like those of an old-fashioned saloon, she could see the dim outlines of figures hunched up against the bar, some standing and some who sat on the high stools, hooking their cowboy boots onto the rungs. The floor was strewn with sawdust that bounced with the loud beat of the drums. She could not tell if the sound came from a real band or a jukebox, but the place didn't look prosperous enough to be able to afford a band, she reasoned, so it was probably a jukebox.

As suddenly as it had come, her anger left her, and she felt both vulnerable and ridiculous standing there. Hadn't been being mistaken for a prostitute once before that night been bad enough, she scolded herself? What if some drunk were to come out now and proposition her? Vowing to return in the morning, she scurried back across the street, taking the stairs two at a time, and rolled herself into the cocoon of her sleeping bag. Pulling the pillow on top of her head to muffle the music, she fell into a troubled sleep.

After her solitary bowl of oatmeal the next morning, which she cooked over the one-plate electric stove she had bought at the Salvation Army, she dressed quickly and went down to the street below. It was early enough that only a few cars were out on this side street, and the brisk air teased her nose playfully. Across the street, the bar that had been so noisy the night before was silent, the entrance locked and gated. It occurred to her that waking someone, if there was anyone there, would be difficult to accomplish, but then she decided she should try so that they would get the same treatment she had received the night before. It was only fair.

She thrust her face in between the iron bars and called out, "Hello, hello. Anybody home?" Hearing no response, she rattled the lock on the gate, banging it against the rusting metal. Again she called, this time with more force, "Hey! Anybody in there?"

She was just about to turn away in frustration when she heard the wood in the door creak and the door open the slightest bit. In the crack of light she discerned a slice of a face, a segment of eye and half a nose and mouth from a Cubist painting. It was impossible to guess the age of this apparition, but something told her it was male. A voice snarled, "What the hell do you think you're doing waking me at this hour of the morning?"

Undeterred, Jasmine replied, "And what the hell are you doing every night keeping me awake at all hours with your damned music?"

The door opened slightly wider, revealing a long, wrinkled face framed by gray hair that hung to broad shoulders. Suspicious black eyes registered astonishment as he took in the appearance of his angry caller, and gradually his broad mouth broke into a huge grin that transformed his stern face, pulling up the corners of his eyes and emphasizing his high cheekbones.

"Well, well," he said with great amusement. "So, do you want to come in and talk about this dispute we apparently have?"

Jasmine hesitated for only and instant and then answered, as casually as she could manage, "Yes, I do."

The old man struggled with the key that opened the padlock, cursing softly under his breath. Gradually the stubborn, rusty mechanism gave way, and he unwound the long chain that held it in place. Gesturing gallantly, his long gray hair sweeping forward over his face, he showed her to a stool that faced the bar. Jasmine stepped awkwardly onto the bottom rung and hoisted herself onto the seat.

Circling

Without preamble, the old fellow took the seat next to hers, pivoted, and sat facing her, until she turned and did the same.

"You look Indian," he said. " Probably a half-breed, but I would guess Blackfeet?"

Pulled suddenly out of her self-pitying anger, Jasmine realized with a start what should have been obvious: this old man was native, too, probably Cheyenne or Sioux, she thought. "It takes one to know one," she answered unkindly, and then, regretting her rudeness, especially considering his age, which called upon a younger person to be impeccably polite, she continued sheepishly, "Yes, I am Blackfeet, from the Rez in Montana."

"A long way from home." The dark eyes lit up, not with merriment, but with a knowing and not unsympathetic recognition. "How long have you been in the city?"

"Only for a couple of months," Jasmine answered. "I," she hesitated, "I just needed a little space. I was tired of school."

Rather than the scolding or inquisition that she expected from her confession, the elder patted her arm consolingly. "Sometimes a person just needs to go away and get their head together," he observed kindly. And then added, "I'm the cook and bottle washer around here. Could I scramble you up some breakfast?"

It was all Jasmine could do not to break into tears. This unexpected kindness and solicitude almost unraveled her. But she managed to hold back her tears and, smiling, answered, "I'm just starved. Thank you."

The Question

Over the next two months, Jasmine saw Charging Elk almost every day. They took walks together on her days off from work, often going to the local park that, despite the number of homeless people and addicts sleeping on park benches, had the only green space in this part of the city. A small, sad pond, ringed by carelessly tossed paper cups and pop cans, was populated with a ragtag group of ducks who would dive half-heartedly into the scum that covered most of the pond, looking for some edible food.

The old man knew many of the homeless people in the area, and he gradually introduced them to her. Some of them were Indian, too, and they would sit down and talk with these new acquaintances all afternoon. The Indians were there for a lot of reasons, but the biggest one seemed to be that, like her, something bad had happened in their lives that caused them to be lost.

For the first time in her life, Jasmine began to think about her father's time in Seattle years ago and wondered why he had gone there. Had he quarreled with Grandmother? Had he felt frustrated about the lack of jobs and opportunities on the Rez? Or had he merely wanted to have an adventure, to take his new bride to a more cosmopolitan, exotic place? Above all, she wondered how long he had been there before he began missing home. Or perhaps, she told herself, he hadn't missed the Rez but only came home when he needed Grandmother's help to take care of his son.

She watched the handsome face of the Indian man that Charging Elk had just introduced her to and reflected that he was probably

Circling

about the same age as her father had been when he came to the city. Her heart filled with a kind of singing, as if for one moment she saw her father as he had been then: proud, serious, thoughtful. And perhaps, she thought, feeling as well the constant outsider, the one who could never fit in, not just because of the bronze of his skin and the aquiline set of his features, but because he carried in his bones, as all tribal people did, the communal memories of a deeply different and wholly encompassing ancient culture.

Gradually, Jasmine found herself telling her new friend all about her days growing up on the Rez, about her grandmother's lessons on herbal medicines and her calm, steady presence in Jasmine's life. She even began to share the pain of the last year: the death of her brother; her parents' reconciliation; her own flight from school and her work at the Salvation Army store.

Charging Elk listened intently, watching her face closely, and he rarely interrupted. More importantly, he never scolded her or questioned her decisions, though he did sometimes tell her about his own youth and how he had come to be in the city. He told her he was a "displaced Sioux warrior" but said little about his years living in Portland except for his present circumstances.

He slept there in the bar, a part-time night watchman, and slowly took over cooking the hamburgers, hot dogs, and fries that late-night drinkers wanted. She noticed that, despite the way he lived, he didn't seem bitter or resentful; in fact, she thought that he was one of the most serene people she had ever met.

But her favorite days, because they were so rare, were when he told some of the old stories he remembered from his youth. Jasmine didn't know if it was the stories themselves or the fact that he, too, was very old, that reminded her so much of her grandmother.

Gradually Jasmine realized that she trusted him not just because of their tribal backgrounds, but because, like her, he also lived in a separate reality, unable to connect with the 'real' world around him. The difference was, however, that he seemed calm about this displacement, and she continued to be unnerved by it. She had lied to her parents and betrayed them. She had no money, and a miserable job. And she was young, she reflected. How should she live the rest of her life? If her parents didn't want her after what she had done, where should she go?

At last she got up the courage to ask. "Charging Elk, what happens now? Should I go back home? Would my parents accept me back, or are they so angry that they wouldn't want me there? And how would I make my way there, without money?"

Charging Elk's harsh answer stunned her. "I don't know what is in store for you, Jasmine," he told her. "You need to go on your own vision quest; that's the only way to find your way back. And I think that, now that you know the question, it is up to you to search for the answer. I have been waiting for you to come to this place, to the moment where it is time for you to go, to move on."

Jasmine stared at him in disbelief, flooded with a red rage that distorted her face and left her gasping for air as she spoke. "What right do you have to tell me what to do or not do?", she screamed. "And what does that mean, 'going on my vision quest'? No one does that anymore. What the hell do you mean?"

He took her by the shoulders and held her firmly. "Go," he said. "You have yet many mountains to climb. Don't be afraid. Your grandmother will be with you." And then he walked away.

Jasmine was too shocked and hurt to go after him. She just watched as he disappeared into the crowds. Her mind turned somersaults, her sense of reality spinning. What had he meant that her grandmother would be with her? Her grandmother was dead! She felt that she too ought to just die right there, on the spot. What use was she to anyone? A stream of people going by parted around her on both sides, as if she weren't even there, and she realized suddenly that she was an island and the current of life was passing her by.

She hadn't eaten all day, and as she stood there swallowed up in her despair, her head became so light that it felt detached, as if it were floating off somewhere above her. She tried to move, but instead sank down onto the sidewalk, clutching her backpack desperately, as if it were a parachute that wouldn't open.

Wandering

The sun was relentless today, beating down on her neck and back with a ferocious heat, burning her exposed skin not covered by the handkerchief she wore over her hair. She stood up, stretched, and surveyed the progress of the other migrant workers around her. She had been with them long enough to learn a little Spanish, and she turned to Guadalupe, who worked in the next row.

"Tienes agua?" she asked, hoping for a drink of cool water. But Guadalupe just shook her head and pointed far down the row behind her.

"Allá en la casucha," she answered, indicating the shack where the boss hung out and counted their filled boxes as they brought them back.

Jasmine smiled, shrugging her shoulders to indicate her reluctance to walk so far, and stooped again to her task, picking the strawberries carefully from the vine and placing them into the cardboard box. Jasmine knew that she was still, after a month of picking, too slow, and she feared being fired, but this was a time-sensitive crop, and she had the advantage that not many people were eager to take her place. In fact, she was the only non-Latino in the entire camp.

Once they had established her as a reliable companion, someone who would help them speak to the boss if their sparse English failed them, and someone who would play with their children while the women cooked their meals in the evenings, they treated her as family. Jasmine loved the evenings, the sun setting on the flat horizon, the air beginning to cool, and the smell of refried beans toasting in a skillet on the fire. Best of all, though, were the handmade corn tortillas, their slightly smoky, toasted flavor as good as any bread she had ever eaten except, perhaps, for the fry bread her grandmother had made. She learned about making fresh salsa with all of the fresh tomatoes, onions, and peppers readily available, and in turn she made some fry bread for them to taste.

These were a people, she reflected, who had almost nothing and yet had almost everything: family, camaraderie, music, good food cooked over an open fire, a lilting, beautiful language that seemed to roll off their tongues like some kind of delicious honey, soft and yielding and sweet.

After dinner, when the guitars stilled and the songs ended, and everyone went to their tents, Jasmine would sit alone for a while longer by the fire and struggle to keep her composure. Something here, everyone here in fact, reminded her of home, of her own people, her own rituals and music and dance and laughter. How long could she keep doing this? How would she make enough money to get back? And, her greatest fear, would she be welcome when she returned?

Tired to the bone, her back and leg muscles aching from being stooped all day over the low-lying strawberry plants, she rolled out her sleeping bag and settled down to sleep. The family she had grown closest to had offered her room in their tiny shack, to protect her from being harassed during the night. Comforted by the children's soft, even breathing and the smell of the rich black earth beneath her, she soon slept.

After a few weeks, as they were finishing the strawberry harvest, Jasmine spoke to her friend Consuelo. "Where will you go next?" she asked. And then, struggling to get across the idea in Spanish, she queried, "A dónde ahora?"

"Vamos to beets," Consuelo answered, smiling proudly at her English, and then added, "You?"

To this, Jasmine only shrugged her shoulders and lifted her arms in response. "I don't know," she said. "I just don't know." She tried to look cheerful and confident, but in her heart she felt quite the

Circling

opposite. She was afraid to keep going and afraid to stop. The money she had earned was so small, despite her hard labor in the fields. At this rate she would never have enough to go home, and besides, she didn't know if she wanted to. She felt like a sleepwalker, moving through a make-believe world where everything had the appearance of reality but did not have meaning for her personally. She might has well have been one of those fat green grubs that they picked off of the leaves of the plants and crushed beneath their heels.

Grandmother

There comes a time in everyone's life when one must choose between life and death, the death of the heart and spirit. My granddaughter has lost the spore of meaning, of her powers. There will be a great void in the family if she loses her way. She does not yet understand her medicine, the healer that is inside of her. No one can make this choice for her, not even me. I must trust her innate strength and courage. If she chooses rightly, she will bring joy to many people.

Lost

It was much easier, Jasmine thought, to lie down than to try to sit up. The effect the drug had on her was one of a kind of dizzying euphoria, worth the racking nausea and pain of withdrawal she knew would come after the high.

Her companion, wandering unconscious in his drugged state, sat in the filthy brown armchair that was the only other piece of furniture in the room aside from the bed. His legs were splayed out in front of him, his eyes closed, his huge bald head, like a giant pool ball, gleaming in the half-light coming from the window. The pervading smell was of mold and dirt and the sweat of other people whose presence still haunted the room, a smell someone had tried to overcome with the sickly sweet smell of an air freshener, making matters worse.

Jasmine paid no attention to the man in the chair. In truth, she couldn't even remember his name, even if she had been straight. He was valuable to her because he had supplied the drug; that was all. She was vaguely aware that they had been in this cheap downtown motel room in Portland for about three days.

She had abandoned migrant work because things had steadily gone from bad to worse. After the strawberry harvest, she had roamed through California, following the migrants who were guided by the seasonal rotation of the crops. She didn't mind the outdoor work; in a way it reminded her of the days spent foraging for herbs in the hills with her grandmother. Gradually, however, drifting itself, the sensation of being nothing more than a piece of flotsam on the human current, began to unsettle her. Despite the kindness of the simple family that had sheltered her, or perhaps almost because of them, she had begun to feel a longing for home that cut to the bone. She would look in the mirror and see an alien creature, gaunt and hollow-eyed, her pride and joy, her long, shining dark hair, unkempt and dull. One day she simply left without saying goodbye, heading north towards Oregon.

For a short time she had tried working in a small café in Portland. Despite the gruff but kind efforts of the older woman who owned the café to show concern for her, however, Jasmine stayed for only three weeks. Her floating sense of disconnection, of being alone in an alien world, became more and more acute, and finally she abandoned all pretense of normalcy and sought out the escape offered by the drug.

Jasmine was haunted continually by strange, chaotic dreams. At first she attributed them to the effects of the drug and tried to ignore them, but one night a dream that was clearly from home, a dream that could not be dismissed, came to her. In this dream she was free falling through the air, the wind spiraling around her body in a tunnel of elemental force. Somehow her body was spinning, too, and she recognized that when she landed she would have absolutely no control. Then, in the grip of utter terror, she heard the unmistakable sound of huge wings cleaving the air, an echo of the heave and retreat of waves in the sea as they hit the shore. She felt herself lifted up, her body wafted along like a feather in a gentle breeze, buoyant and joyful, able to look all around at her leisure, aware of the green earth below her that summoned her into its soft emerald embrace. Far below her she could see her home and her family, miniature figures like porcelain dolls, standing outside on the prairie, unmoving. The expression on their faces was anguished, their arms lifted as if in supplication. Her parents looked old, their skin deeply lined, much older than she remembered, and their gray hair blew loose in the wind. She wanted to get down and comfort them, to go to them, but the great bird's wings beat up and down, leaving them quickly behind. Suddenly she was over the ocean, and the powerful waves beneath her seemed as if they could reach out and pull her down. Her heart beat so fast that

Circling

she thought it would explode out of her chest and tumble down into the ocean below.

Then she was in a strange place that she had never seen before: It was a great desert, at first seemingly endless in its austere whiteness. After a while, however, great fires appeared, smoke billowing out from them, black and full of malice, fires burning in cities that were half-destroyed, their buildings in ruins. She saw great armies moving across the landscape and heard the screams of the people below, running in terror from their houses into the streets. And then the great bird swooped low, and she saw her brother. He was leaning against a Humvee parked by the side of the road. A small truck was careening towards him from the south. His face was partly obscured by his helmet, but she could see the expression of fear on his face. Then she heard a staccato sound like firecrackers exploding, and without warning, he fell.

The bird spiraled precipitously upward then, and she saw the whole earth beneath her, the globe patterned with blues, greens, and tans like an enormous marble, as astronauts see it from space. Circling the globe in bright-colored costumes danced people from every corner of the world, with her brother in the center like the hub of a wheel. They were laughing and singing, their faces shining. And then she woke up.

Jasmine shuddered, the dream still reverberating in her mind. She knew better than to ignore such a dream, a visionary dream that was speaking directly to her. Suddenly, somewhere in the deepest recesses of her mind and heart, Jasmine understood that she had come to a crossroads. She could either choose the way of this new, harsh world in which she found herself, where she would soon become an addict, a homeless person, or perhaps a prostitute plying her wares, or she would have to take the biggest risk of her life and choose to once again become fully human, with all of its risks and fears. She would have to give up the drugs that had provided a temporary shelter from her worst imaginings, would have to face her own elemental self, the mixed race girl who was lost in a world that made no sense to her,

Pamella Hays

who had abandoned but not forgotten the stories of her people. It would be, she knew, an irrevocable choice. She remembered the words from *Hamlet,* the play they had been rehearsing when she ran away: 'To be or not to be.' For the first time she thought she understood the meaning of those words.

As the sun was just coming up, Jasmine woke and stirred in the disheveled, hammock-like bed, its springs protesting loudly with every movement. She disciplined herself to move with agonizing slowness and managed to sit up and put her feet over the side. She hastily gathered up her jeans, sweatshirt and sneakers, and grabbed the old canvas pack that held all of her worldly belongings. She tiptoed out of the room and softly closed the door. Her snoring companion never stirred.

The sensation produced by her unusual dream had stayed with her poignantly, and as she walked down the cracked sidewalk, unaware of the traffic going by, indifferent to the stares of the passersby, she was hit with a longing so deep and so strong to be alive again, to find her place again, that she groaned out loud, and her whole body wanted to collapse under the weight of it all.

A well-dressed man in a business suit saw her sway and reached for her elbow, but when he saw her agonized expression, her eyes filled with grief, he grew alarmed. Steering her to a bus bench nearby, he thrust a twenty-dollar bill in her hand and walked quickly away.

Muddled but somehow clear-sighted too, Jasmine stood up and looked around for the nearest diner. Inside, she settled gratefully into a small booth, her pack beside her, and treated herself, thanks to the stranger's generosity, to a hearty breakfast of waffles, ham, and eggs, and drank cup after cup of black coffee. Somewhere in the back of her head, a voice was speaking to her, or perhaps she was just talking to herself, but for the first time in a long time she knew what she had to do. With the clarity brought by the dark coffee and the food, she suddenly realized fully how close she had come to losing herself utterly. She began to sob, tears running down her face, and the old, tough-seeming waitress, alarmed, came by and asked her if she was all right.

Circling

"You need some help, honey?" she asked gruffly.

Jasmine looked up, and seeing the wrinkled old face above her, thought of her grandmother, and began to cry even harder. But she managed to answer, "No, thank you. I think I'm going to be fine." She slid out from the seat, leaving her payment on the table, and ran out the door, feeling the sun on her face and noticing the world around her for the first time in a very long time, as if she had been far away, visiting another planet. She walked back to the park bench and waited for the bus that would take her by the Goodwill store.

She hitched a ride north after spending a few hours in the store where she had bought elemental camping gear: a bedroll, a one-man pup tent, two battered old cooking pans, and a suitable, though used, pair of leather hiking boots. She was going on autopilot, trying not to question the forces that appeared to be moving her, feeling drawn to the mountains, to the clean, untroubled air of high meadows and the tranquility of effervescent streams. It felt unutterably wonderful to be alone, to feel once more in charge of her life, however inchoate that life might be.

Her driver, an unfriendly and taciturn woman, seemed uninterested in conversation, so Jasmine slept deeply and innocently, like a child, for the first time in so long that she had almost forgotten the healing sensation of untroubled sleep.

Sojourn

Jasmine waked up when the car stopped moving, and she felt someone shaking her shoulder vigorously. "This is as far as I go," the woman's voice said, gradually waking her into consciousness. "There's a gas station about a mile down the road, but here's where I turn off," the woman added.

She quickly gathered her few possessions and, thanking the woman for the ride, stepped out onto the two-lane highway that was winding its way up the mountain pass. The air hit her lungs, cold and bracing, and as the car pulled away she felt an exhilaration unlike anything she could remember in a long while. It was the kind of cold that she remembered when she had hiked alone in the foothills around the reservation in the late fall when she was a girl.

She looked below her and could see the road they had come on performing looping acrobatics as it doubled in on itself, carving great 's' curves as it wound its way up the mountain. The colorful patterns of autumn foliage lay all about: burnished orange bushes on the side of the road tumbled down the steep embankment and nestled amongst the evergreens, cloaked now in their gray-green dullness. Interspersed amongst them, slender aspen, their leaves shining in the late afternoon sun, spread like a golden carpet, highlighted here and there by the scarlet and copper of maple and mountain ash.

It occurred to her that if the bird with the giant wings in her dream could swoop down and pick her up right now, sailing over the vast, unbroken forest beneath her and set her down on the forest floor, she would be the happiest person on earth. She could be alone in the

Circling

great, silent woods, beholden to no one, far away from all the world's deception and heartbreak. Yet the other part of her dream, the part that had called her back to the world, to sanity and wholeness and a kind of unimaginable courage, had stayed with her too.

So taken was she with these strange, conflicting sensations, that she had not considered what she should do next, here and now, in the real world as it presented itself. Shaking herself out of her reveries, it now occurred to her to wonder why she had been left off here, in this stunning but isolated place. Then she remembered what the woman had told her and realized that the driver must have taken a dirt road visible not too far up on the right.

Jasmine thought about the gas station up the road, and shivering in the cold wind, suddenly mindful that it was growing colder by the minute as the late afternoon sun began to slip behind the mountains, she lifted her pack, slinging it over her right shoulder. With her left hand she picked up her sleeping bag, cooking pots jangling, and headed up the road.

The old timer in the quaint, old-fashioned gas station and general store could not have been kinder. Cozying up to the wood stove inside, which was beaming a welcome heat, Jasmine explained that she needed a place to stay the night. "Well," he opined, his lively blue eyes full of sympathy as he spoke, "that's gonna' be a bit difficult around here. Aren't any houses for miles. Only thing up here is that there Buddha place, you know, where they have those priests that wear gowns." His observation was not given unkindly, but simply stated in a matter-of-fact way.

Jasmine, who had finally begun to be a bit worried about her situation, perked up. "Do they let people stay there, I mean women?"

"Don't know," he answered. "Never had occasion to ask. Worth a try, though," he offered. "They seem like nice folks when they come in here. I don't think they'd turn anyone away in this weather. It'll turn real cold tonight, if I don't miss my guess."

"How do I get there, then?" Jasmine asked.

"Here, I'll draw you a map," the old fellow said, taking a brown grocery bag off of the counter and retrieving a pencil stuck behind his ear.

Shelter

By the time Jasmine got to the broad dirt lane described on the map, it was already dark. She was grateful for the small flashlight she had bought at the last minute. Its narrow beam illuminated the road ahead, keeping her from stumbling on the uneven, stony surface. At last she saw a light in the woods up ahead and realized that she had come to the large log house that the storekeeper had described. Smoke curled up out of the chimney, and there was a light on the porch, but the rest of the building was dark. She approached cautiously, hoping that there were no guard dogs, and then smiled to herself as she realized that this was a Buddhist enclave, a place where no violence of any kind would be tolerated. Still, because the residents within were apparently fast asleep, she hesitated. Should she knock on the door and disturb them?

Then, out of the corner of her eye, she noticed another, smaller building that stood alone on a rise a few yards away. It was very different than the pioneer-style log house, much smaller and built, from what she could see in the darkness, of planed wood. Its roof was curious: a kind of sloping style that curled on the ends. Too tired to consider further, she headed towards it, hoping it was something other than a residence and might not be occupied. The wind had begun to pierce her old jacket, and she was aware that hypothermia could set in quickly at such an altitude.

She pushed open the heavy, carved wooden door and murmured quietly, "Hello? Anyone here?" As her eyes adjusted to the meager light from a bank of windows that looked out over the mountains

Circling

and the glow of two oil lamps on what appeared to be an altar full of intricately sculpted icons, Jasmine's tired legs refused to sustain her any longer. She took out her sleeping bag, placing it in a corner of the room where she hoped it would not be offensive in this sacred place, removed her boots, and crawled inside. Jasmine didn't know then that the temple was left open for precisely this reason, in case someone needed shelter, but something within her resonated with the sense of peace that she felt all around her, and she fell almost instantly asleep.

Months of sleeping in strange places had made Jasmine a light sleeper, and when she felt someone's presence standing over her, she sat up with a start, frightening a young man dressed in long robes who stood beside her bed even more than he had frightened her. He immediately stepped back, lowering the blanket he had in his arms to the floor and putting his hands together in the Buddhist gesture of greeting. Though her rational mind was fully awake, the dream must have still been hovering, too, because the first thought that went through her mind was that this comely man with such dark eyes was from a dream she had been having. For one thing, his features looked like her Dad's and Nate's, and his skin had the same burnished copper glow.

Gradually she recovered her wits enough to speak. "I'll leave right away. I shouldn't be here."

A soft voice tinged with an unidentifiable accent reassured her, "No, no, please. You are welcome. This temple stands as a shelter to anyone who needs it. You may stay as long as you want. I only wanted to give you this blanket," he said, gesturing towards a colorfully patterned wool blanket on the floor. After a brief pause, he added, "Indeed, if you would like to go back to sleep, I will leave you until morning. You would be welcome then to share our meal with us."

The wind had come up, rattling the windows and howling through the pines, and, more tired than she had ever been before, Jasmine simply nodded in assent and lay down and shut her eyes.

Pamella Hays

Before going back to sleep, she had a fleeting sense of the strangeness of her reaction; she had learned in the last several months not to trust anyone, but with him somehow she had felt instantly safe. The next thing she knew, it was morning.

Snowstorm

Jasmine awakened as the early morning sun bathed the tall windows in a golden light and stretched her arms and legs, luxuriating in the warmth of the room where she had slept. Then she heard the door open and someone coughed conspicuously. Pulling the bag up to her chin, Jasmine sat up in her improvised bed and watched the young man from the night before carefully remove his boots at the door before he approached. He wore the dark red robes of a Buddhist monk, and his head was shaved in the traditional fashion, but he still had, even in daylight, a remarkable resemblance to her father and brother, she thought. From a respectful distance he bowed as he had the night before, and then said, "I hope you slept well?"

"Very well, thank you," Jasmine replied.

"Then perhaps you would enjoy some breakfast?" her companion asked.

"Oh, that would be great!" Jasmine enthused, and then, a bit embarrassed by her obvious hunger, she added, "If it's not too much trouble."

Smiling, he replied, "We would be pleased to have you join us. When you are ready, please knock at the door of the main house, and someone will attend to you." Then he added, "There is a bathroom there also for the use of guests."

Jasmine dressed in fresh, though badly wrinkled, jeans and a turtleneck and wool vest, and then walked over to the residence. She used the large metal knocker on the door and was shown inside by a very old monk with a kind, beaming face. First he indicated the location of the bathroom. When she emerged, he seated her in a kind of front porch outfitted with windows instead of screens. Then he brought her a breakfast of rice, fresh sautéed vegetables, and yogurt and some kind of wonderful whole-grain bread. Bowing as he left her, he backed out of the room. In an instant the young man arrived and asked if she would allow him to eat with her, and she quickly nodded assent. Jasmine was confused, as she had assumed that she would be eating alone, since the monks lived in a monastic order. But as if he could read her mind, in his lovely, formal English, the young man explained.

"You are wondering why I am here," he said, not questioning but simply stating the obvious. "You see, the monks are not allowed to eat with our women guests, but I am not a monk. I am only a *pabbajja*, an acolyte. I chose to study Buddhism for two years as a layperson, and in my second year I am allowed to wear this robe, but I am only a novice, and I do not intend to take my vows as a monk. Because of this, my brothers have given me the responsibility to explain our way of life to our lady guests and to make them comfortable."

"And for now, please eat before the food gets cold," he added. They ate the meal in companionable silence. Jasmine was so hungry that she had to remind herself of her manners; it was very hard not to stuff the aromatic, warm food in as fast a she could go. Usually nervous with strangers, Jasmine was struck by the calm that emanated from the young man, and she happily ate every last bit of food on her plate, sighing gratefully as she finished.

"I suppose I should be on my way," she finally said, breaking the silence. "Thank you so much for your hospitality. Please tell the others as well."

A look of concern settled on the young man's features. "Are you sure you would not like to stay a bit longer?" he queried. "Though it is only autumn, the weather being predicted tomorrow is for a few inches of snow," he offered. "And you are walking alone, are you not?" he added, obviously puzzled.

Circling

Jasmine was used to being looked at askance as she had carried her motley camping gear through the city streets, and she knew that people either stared unabashedly or turned their faces away, quickly hurrying by her, but this gentle young man was not behaving in that way. His face was genuinely concerned, and his demeanor was respectful but confused.

As a result, she decided that she needed to be, if not totally honest, then at least somewhat forthcoming. "Yes," she answered. "I am alone. But I grew up in Montana, and I am used to cold weather," she added reassuringly.

"May I ask where you are going?" he added.

This is going to be harder than I thought, Jasmine observed. Taking time to arrange her thoughts, she spoke. "I know it is unusual for young woman to be out alone in the mountains," she said. "But you see, I am a Blackfeet Indian, and I have been on my own for several months. My family lives far away, and I am," she hesitated ever so slightly, "I am on a little hiking trip to see this country before I go back."

Though his eyes spoke otherwise, the young Tibetan nodded in assent, and he said politely, "Then you are an experienced hiker, and I will trouble you no further." "Although," he added with a gentle smile, "as an experienced hiker you know that the coming storm could be dangerous. Even though it is early autumn, there will be several inches of snow, perhaps. Not the best footing for walking, even though it should melt rapidly."

Then, rising from his chair and placing his hands together before him, he added, "My name is Jumpa, and I would be pleased to know yours as well."

Smiling at his formality, Jasmine answered, adding to her name her sincere pleasure at meeting him and her thanks for his help. She too stood as if to go, but thinking better of it, she reluctantly admitted, "You know, I am afraid that you are probably right. Perhaps I should delay for a day or two. Would it be all right for me to take

Pamella Hays

shelter here for a bit longer? I hate to be a bother, " she concluded apologetically.

"You are welcome to stay here as long as you need," the young man replied, smiling the first genuinely delighted smile she had seen.

That evening Jasmine had trouble sleeping, in part because she was surprised at her ready capitulation to the young man's suggestion that she stay with them that night. Her streak of obstinate independence had crumbled quickly, and she was upset with herself that a stranger could so easily influence her decision. Outside, however, the snow, revealed in its hypnotizing splendor by the floor to ceiling windows, seemed a benign presence, and gradually she forgot her irritation and succumbed to its magic. Flakes, crocheted like tiny lace doilies, floated lazily down, so delicate that she knew they would probably not last until morning. The storm had come so early that the ground was still warm enough to melt them, and the air itself was barely cold enough to conjure snow instead of rain.

She remembered how her mother had told her that each snowflake is utterly unique, that no matter how many billions of flakes fell, there were never two that were identical. As a child she had tested this theory, which she thought could not possibly be true, by studying the frost on the windows in her room, looking at each snow crystal that had frozen there. To her surprise, she found that, in fact, no two ever were the same, the geometric pattern of each flake a miniature white kaleidoscope of unique design.

She snuggled deeper into the sleeping bag, and thinking of Jumpa's kind face, so foreign and yet so familiar, she pondered the universal qualities of the features of the human face. Like the snowflake, each face had the history of one's life painted there, each feature uniquely carved by experience, revealing one's ethnicity, character, and beliefs, and yet all faces showed the same basic emotions, especially through the eyes. Jumpa's eyes, in fact, had reminded her of her grandmother's, whose gentle, tranquil gaze never judged and never seemed to doubt one's essential goodness. Comforted somehow by this thought, she closed her eyes and soon slept.

Circling

At breakfast in the morning, which she once again shared with Jumpa, he was quite eager, now that his tenure at the monastery was coming to an end, to find out what the city was like and everything she could tell him about the reservation.

Gradually Jasmine warmed to the subject, surprised by how fervently she cared about her home, and especially about her people and their culture. At one point, Jumpa, who was fastidiously polite, actually interrupted her.

"The ceremony you are describing, the elaborate costumes and the drums and the dancing, those remind me so much of home!" he enthused, adding, "It makes me even more eager to return to my land. I have been here perhaps too long, although living here at the monastery I have been using my own language and practicing my religious beliefs," he added quickly.

Then, switching quickly to another topic, he said, "There are many good things here, of course. I do love your technology, especially the Internet. And I will miss the American enthusiasm for doing things. In Tibet the people are always busy too, as their lives are often very hard, and they must work on their farms from dawn to dusk, but still they take more time for prayer and contemplation than most of your people do." Then, looking somewhat embarrassed, he asked, "Or do you consider yourself to be American? I mean, do you see yourself as a separate people?"

Jasmine hesitated, not sure herself of the appropriate answer, but then she spoke. "I myself have an American mother, as you would say, and an Indian father. I live in both cultures, which are indeed quite different in some ways, and yet not in others. It has been a long time since native peoples had their own ancient way of life. Some of our ceremonies and traditions have survived, and others have not. Some Indians live in cities and don't practice them at all. I feel in-between: I have some of my mother's pragmatism and some of my father's dreaming." She smiled then, thinking that those two characteristics were not easily reconcilable, and yet for the first time she realized how much each meant to her, how much they had formed her.

Jasmine stood up suddenly, aware that much of the morning had already flown. "I had better get going if I want to catch a ride and get back to Portland," she said, adding warmly, "It has been so much fun talking to you."

Then, impulsively, she added, "Would it be possible for us to email one another? Would you mind giving me your address? I have no computer, but I can access one in the public library."

Beaming, Jumpa nodded, hurrying into the house and returning with a pencil and paper. "Be so kind as to give me yours, too?" he added.

A few minutes later, backpack once again stuffed, with the addition of some crackers and fruit at Jumpa's insistence, Jasmine walked down the steep road to the highway, stopping midway to turn and wave at her new friend.

Reunion

Jumpa's emails, in their quaint but beautifully crafted English, intrigued Jasmine. She had asked about his religious beliefs, and the first thing he had said was that his was not a religion—it was a way of life. The Buddha was not an all-powerful God, nor was he interested in punishing people for their sins. Rather, Buddhism's beliefs were simple and straightforward: Each of us is capable of achieving enlightenment by choosing to be mindful, honoring our responsibility towards ourselves, towards all other people, and the earth itself.

As she read his messages, Jasmine began to consider more and more the beliefs with which she had grown up. She thought of the vision quest, and how it challenged the seeker to pull up his or her greatest courage and find one's truth and then bring it home for all the people to share. It was a system of mindfulness much like what Jumpa had described, a way to enhance the spiritual awareness of the whole tribe. Yet the vision could not be gained until a person had made a huge sacrifice, a giving up of selfishness.

A month later, Jasmine met Jumpa at the local train station. He looked different in his American clothes, his slender form emphasized by his jeans and sweatshirt, and his hair was just beginning to grow out into a soft, ebony down. He smiled at her shyly, unsure of how to greet her, but she embraced him warmly.

Jumpa was hungry, so she took him to the nearest vegetarian restaurant where, over rice and sautéed vegetables and tea, they talked for hours. Gradually it dawned on them that the sole waitress was

221

looking at them crossly, having cleaned all around them. Obviously the place was closing, and they needed to go.

Unsure of what to do, Jasmine offered him a space on the couch in the small room she had rented over a movie theater. "It's pretty noisy," she warned him. "There's a movie theater just below us, but it's warm and safe."

Jumpa's face flooded with relief. "Oh thank you, Jasmine. I was not yet prepared to find a place to stay." And then, a little embarrassed, he added, "I have lived here in this country only in the monastery. I'm not very good at knowing how to find a room."

In the morning, over breakfast, he told her about his dream to return to Tibet. Jasmine immediately felt his homesickness and his longing to be amongst his own people, a sentiment with which she could easily identify. Jumpa thought he would need about $2000 for the trip. Jasmine suggested that he look for work on a construction site. The money was usually fairly good, and they always needed a 'gofer', a term that puzzled Jumpa until she explained its meaning, someone who learned quickly and would be able to organize tools and building supplies and bring anything a carpenter might need, from a cup of coffee to a measuring tape.

Jumpa's face lit up. "I could do that!" he said enthusiastically. "I helped to build the temple at the monastery."

He assured her that he would find a place of his own after he had found a job, but one week went by, and then two, and even though he was working now, neither of them mentioned his moving out. For her part, Jasmine enjoyed his company and loved learning about his country. Jumpa, though quite shy and still reserved, began to show as well a new side of himself, as a young man who enjoyed teasing her, and laughing at the terrible movies they sometimes went to see in the theater below. He was also a very good cook, and they alternated nights for preparing their evening meal, although Jasmine had difficulty finding ways around serving the meat dishes that her own family had always eaten.

Circling

Sometimes when they shared the cleaning up in the tiny kitchen, they would inadvertently bump into each other. For her part, Jasmine was utterly disconcerted by this physical contact; she knew he had never taken the vows of a monk, but she didn't know what, if anything, he thought about romance. Perhaps he intended to stay celibate? She couldn't deny that she was attracted to him, but she avoided that thought scrupulously and struggled to suppress her feelings for him.

Then one evening at suppertime, when they were sitting on the couch with their plates on their improvised 'table' of boards and boxes in front of them, Jumpa simply reached over and took her hand and, without speaking, pulled her up and walked with her into the bedroom. Jasmine kept silent as well, afraid to break the spell. Wordlessly, he undressed her, his touch lingering on each curve and hollow of her body, slowly, alertly, like a man walking through a wilderness. His lips brushed her hair, her eyes, her mouth as gently as a whisper of wind.

Jasmine had never before felt such tenderness, and she shed all of her previous hurtful encounters with men as easily as a branch sheds snow. She was new, she was whole, and she would never again be ashamed.

Radiance

"So this is what it feels like to be seen," Jasmine mused, as she lay curled against her lover's lean brown back, remembering with a rueful smile her own notion of seeing inside of people when she was a girl. Now, for the first time ever, someone had actually seen and recognized her and loved her for her strength, her vision, and the commitment to her people that she held to so tightly in her heart. Until Jumpa had seen them, she herself had begun to doubt that those best parts of herself still existed, but with his unfailingly kind and calming reassurances, her own innate self, or perhaps, she thought, some gift from the ancestors, had begun to manifest itself again.

Jumpa slept soundly as he always did after their lovemaking, his narrow hips and broad, thin shoulders familiar now to her as her own body. She outlined the slope of his back with her fingertips, memorizing his shoulder blades and the small of his back so that she would be able to recollect them perfectly when they parted. Their relationship, startlingly frank from the beginning, had already contained within itself the outlines of fate. Jumpa was an ardent nationalist and believed deeply in his obligation to go back to Tibet as soon as he was able. He had never hidden from her his unswerving and irrevocable conviction to work towards his country's independence. They never spoke of plans for the future together.

Each night in their dingy, cramped bedroom they dumped their day's earning on the bed, her tips from waitressing, and his from his construction job, putting aside every possible cent left after food and

Circling

lodging to add to their horde. But even as their savings painstakingly grew, the time they had left together inevitably diminished.

On this particular evening in March, Jumpa counted his pile, frowned, and then counted it carefully again. Satisfied with the results, he looked up at Jasmine and smiled engagingly, like a child who has just realized he has enough money for an ice cream cone. "Jasmine! Do you realize that this is enough to get me to Lhasa?" he crowed. "I could work only one more month and have all I need for the trip!"

Jasmine felt a shock of despair overtake her breathing, but she composed her face and said hesitantly, "Well, that's wonderful. But, but....are you sure that this will be enough to get you all the way to Tibet?" The anxiety in her voice betrayed her attempt to look matter-of-fact.

Jumpa pulled her to him, holding her gently against his chest. He stroked her hair but did not speak, as he knew there was nothing he could say that would be of any comfort. It was, he realized, harder for her than for him. He was returning to his home country with zeal and high expectations of working towards his goal; she, on the other hand, though she had said very little, was, he thought, unsettled about going home. The more he had learned about her flight away from the reservation, the more he understood how worried she was about her parents' reaction when she arrived there. His emotions felt pulled taut, and he had a haunting feeling that, on leaving her, some intrinsic part of his being would be lost, and his self would never be completely whole again. And yet, he reminded himself, she had never questioned his decision or asked him to stay, and he had never faltered in his determination to return. He had total faith in her strength and resiliency and knew she would be able to go on without him. He kissed her eyes, her nose, her lips, the tips of her ears, and pulled her down gently onto the bed.

The next afternoon, as she swept the floor or filled ketchup dispensers during the relatively quiet hours of the afternoon in the café, the looming reality of their parting made Jasmine wonder how she

Pamella Hays

would react when the time actually came for Jumpa to leave. In her rational brain she believed that she was prepared, even stoic. He had never deceived her. She had known this was coming, and she would never break her word to peacefully let him go. But another, frightened part of her knew that when the time came, her heart would be torn loose in her chest, like a prairie tumbleweed tossed by the wind, abandoned and disconnected from the earth.

She had been there before, buffeted by emotions too painful to endure, and a small fissure of pure terror would open in her mind, remembering how it had been when she was alone. Still, she had grown, she had learned to trust herself, she had accepted that with a great love sometimes comes great sorrow. And the little being, small as a walnut in her belly, needed her and would need someday to hear his father's story, and she was the only one who could tell it. This was her one and only secret withheld from Jumpa. Otherwise there existed an emotional honesty and remarkable synchronicity between them that left her in a state of almost euphoric peacefulness.

So she would see him off on the plane in four weeks, and she would keep her counsel, knowing that such a revelation would trouble him so deeply that he would hesitate, would feel he needed to stay with her, and she knew it was inevitable that he return to his life as a native of his land, just as she must return to hers.

Now, watching him as he slept, she felt him stirring beside her, and as he rolled onto his back, his generous mouth lifted in a tender and embracing smile. She responded by kissing his lips passionately, her long dark hair covering his face, a silken waterfall. This moment, this immersion of two people into one was all that she would need for the rest of her days, she thought. There would never be any separation.

Leave-taking

As the plane rose up and up into the sky, becoming the size of a child's toy, and finally disappearing into the vast expanse of blue, Jasmine's heart fell down and down, coming to rest on the ground. She cradled her stomach in her hands, instinctively comforting the small being within her. Her emotions, so carefully guarded for so long, threatened now to undo all of her resolve to be brave and accept her choice. But she straightened, dried her eyes, and forced herself to breathe evenly, thinking how much this child would depend on her to be a warrior.

Fortunately, in anticipation of this day, she had made a plan. When they had left the apartment that morning, she had packed as well, putting her small belongings into her old pack and leaving behind the camping equipment on the kitchen counter in case some other wanderer might need it. She would catch the airport shuttle into the city and take a bus to the restaurant where she had worked so many months ago, in hopes of finding work there.

She had told Jumpa a circumscribed version of the truth, convincing herself that technically she had not lied to him. She was in fact going to Portland, to a small diner where she had worked briefly before she had gone with the migrants. She needed a while longer to get some additional cash and then planned to head for home. But she did not tell him that that event would be months away, six months in fact, and that she didn't quite know how she would manage this on her own.

Pamella Hays

Slipping her pack onto her back and adjusting the shoulder straps, she walked over to the shuttle service area. Tears threatened again to pool up in her eyes, but inside she was singing to her grandmother, asking for her guidance and help. The sensation of comfort that provided her gradually quieted her, and by the time she got on the bus, she had regained her composure, at least outwardly. She was mindful suddenly of Charging Elk's last words when they had parted so abruptly on the street so many months ago: "You will have many mountains to climb, but your grandmother will be with you." Putting her pack at her feet, Jasmine settled into the seat, and had a silent, earnest conversation with her grandmother, telling her about everything that she had been through.

At the stop nearest to the small neighborhood café, Jasmine alighted and walked the last two blocks. It was early in the afternoon, and only three customers were in the café, sitting together in a booth. Margaret, the crusty old owner, cranky as a bad-tempered mule on the outside, and tender as a new lamb on the inside, surveyed her from head to foot without saying a word. Then, her appraisal complete, she spoke.

"I see you're back. No big surprise. I thought you would change your mind about roamin' around by yourself." Her husky smoker's voice, deep as a man's, growled her pessimistic outlook. Without preamble, she added, "I suppose you want your job back?"

"Yes, if I could," Jasmine stumbled, her impulse to hug Margaret held back by only a thread of self-discipline. "Can you give me some hours?"

"Come in tomorrow at 7:00," the older woman barked. "And don't be late." And then, as an afterthought, she added, "I suppose you don't have a place to stay?" Without waiting for the response, she continued, "The apartment upstairs is vacant. Haven't had a chance to clean it up yet, but you're welcome to it if you want it. I'll take the rent out of your wages."

Circling

Unable to any longer control her impulse, Jasmine gave the woman a long, heartfelt hug. When she stepped away, Margaret merely harrumphed with a snort and sailed back into the kitchen, swaying like an old, rusty battleship.

Transition

By the fifth month Jasmine's pregnancy was obvious. Margaret, for once the ultimate diplomat, did not speak of it, but she could not hide her concern. Jasmine seemed dispirited and withdrawn; she seldom spoke and almost never smiled.

Finally, unable to stand the tension, Margaret spoke one afternoon when the incessant, gray rain outside had left the café almost bare of customers. "So what do you intend to do when this baby comes?" she asked in her straightforward way, without preamble.

Startled, Jasmine looked up from the magazine she was leafing through as she sat at the counter. "Do?" she asked sharply. "Have it, I suppose. Any other suggestions?"

Margaret had never known Jasmine to be rude, and this response took her aback. Taking a deep breath to overcome her pique, she spoke softly, "Jasmine, it won't do you or that baby any good to be angry. Of course you'll give birth, but where? Who will be with you?"

Jasmine looked abashed and ashamed. "I'm sorry, Margaret. You didn't deserve that. In fact, I've been thinking about nothing else lately. And I've decided that, once the time is close, I'm going to look up a friend in town who could be with me." Then, seeing the suspicion in Margaret's eyes, she added, "No. He's not the father," managing a weak smile as she spoke.

Margaret looked at her for a moment and then, before going back to the kitchen, she observed, "You'll be a good mother, Jasmine. I have no doubt of that. But a baby needs a father, too."

Circling

Jasmine lowered her cup of coffee and set it in its chipped saucer. "I'm afraid his father is gone," she explained. "But I am going to go home, and the baby will have grandparents who love him. Or at least I hope so."

Three months later, unable to work any longer, Jasmine said goodbye to Margaret and left to find Charging Elk. On the bus across town, she sat alone, fingering in her pocket the five twenty-dollar bills that Margaret had insisted on giving her as a bonus before she left. When Jasmine had protested, Margaret merely said, "Consider it a down payment on all of the letters and pictures you're going to send me. I'm kind of its Godmother, you know." So saying, she hugged Jasmine fiercely to her for just an instant, and then turned quickly away, wiping her eyes with the edge of her cook's white apron.

Jasmine felt the little person kicking inside of her and smiled to herself. She thought of Jumpa, so unreachable and so far away, and wondered if he would ever meet his son someday. Then she watched for her stop opposite the bar where she hoped fervently that Charging Elk still worked and wrapped her arms around the bottom of her belly, reassuring her unborn child.

The Journey

They prepared carefully for the journey, using almost all of Jasmine's painstakingly guarded savings for necessities. At only three months old, the baby didn't need anything but breast milk, but she and Charging Elk would need money for food and one or two nights' lodging and some new footgear. They would be hitchhiking as often as they could, but they also would undoubtedly be walking a great deal. In addition they needed warm jackets, since spring in the Rockies could be almost as cold as winter, though hopefully the threat of a serious snowstorm would be unlikely now. They also took a small amount of cash for unexpected circumstances, which Jasmine sewed into the lining of the baby's snug pack, a new-fangled sort of papoose-carrier that could be used on the back or on the front.

For his part, Charging Elk seemed like a delighted child going to Disneyland. He braided his long hair into one plait down his back, attaching an eagle's feather to it with a piece of leather. He had given notice to his boss two weeks ago, and had seen to his delight the look of sheer astonishment in the man's eyes when the old Sioux told him he was traveling east with a girl and a baby, heading for tribal country. Though he knew that baby Tenzin already had a grandfather, he could not resist adding, "I have a godson, you see. I need to take him and his mother home."

Realizing the possible hazards of the journey and concerned about the safety of her child, Jasmine was less cheerful than her companion, but deep inside, despite her worries, she was extremely excited about seeing her parents again. Tenzin was so fetching, so mellow

Circling

and engaging, with such incredible dark brown, penetrating eyes. Surely her parents would fall in love with him?

They set out on a crisp morning early in March, stepping briskly along the city pavement, eager to get out of town before the morning rush hour. Charging Elk was carrying the large backpack with all of their gear, and of course Jasmine took the baby, snuggled down in his carrier close to her chest as he slept. By mid-morning they had already stopped for breakfast at a small diner on the edge of the city and were beginning their trek through orchard and farm country. They had decided to take only secondary roads to avoid the hassle and noise of the interstate highway, and to provide them with more places for stopping and resting as they went.

As they hitchhiked, Charging Elk, with his tall, lean frame, leather leggings, and long white braid, provided quite a sight, and several cars slowed, staring curiously at the little trio, but they did not stop. Within an hour of their having eaten breakfast, however, a van stopped for them. The driver, a middle-aged man with a scraggly gray beard and thinning, disheveled hair, opened the back door with its seat full of odds and ends: a guitar, old clothes, sacks of empty pop cans, and random camping gear, and threw all of it helter-skelter into the back, apologizing for the mess. They thanked him profusely and piled in. Jasmine liked him right away, a sort of throwback, she thought, to the era of the sixties.

Taking off the carrier and settling gratefully onto the bumpy springs of the seat, Jasmine tickled Tenzin under the chin, getting his classic burbling response. This was only the beginning of a long journey ahead, she knew, but she felt comforted and reassured by this first gesture of kindness, and she could feel Grandmother's presence beside them. Before long she and the baby, worn out by the stress of their first morning on the road, fell fast asleep.

The miles slipped away magically, the time going much faster than Jasmine had anticipated. They spent their first overnight in an old-fashioned 'mom and pop' motel, the ancient neon sign blinking intermittently, its vacancy message prominently displayed. The

Pamella Hays

elderly couple who owned the place were taciturn but kind enough, given that their guests were quite an unusual threesome. The air in the room smelled stale, but it was very clean and tidy, even offering an ancient black and white television. Jasmine settled herself and the baby in one of the beds, and her companion, after trying out the other bumpy bed, opted for the floor instead.

The nearer they got to Montana, the more the countryside changed. There were trees and mountains and streams in Oregon, of course, as well as in Idaho, but something about Montana was different, Jasmine thought. The stretches of forest seemed vaster, the rivers more raucous, the mountains higher. And, Jasmine smiled to herself, the people fewer. Yet their ability to catch a ride didn't diminish; with the exception of only one day, when they had walked for almost all of the early afternoon without being picked up, they had amazingly good fortune. Some of the drivers were quiet, offering little conversation and apparently uninterested in their passengers, but most wanted to chat, and women especially were entranced by their story, in its edited form of course, and wanted to hear all about the baby.

On the last day of travel they caught a ride with a voluble traveling preacher on his way to an isolated congregation out on the prairie, who dropped them off in the center of Browning, waving goodbye in the rear view mirror as he drove away. As she stood arranging the baby in the pack, Jasmine surveyed the familiar surroundings from her childhood: the cracked sidewalks, the meager hodgepodge of businesses with their rundown exteriors, the derelict cars parked sparsely on the street. She felt a chill run up her spine like a bolt of lightning: fear or excitement, she couldn't tell which. She was home!

Unbidden, the whole trajectory of her life came into clear focus, as if some essential link in an invisible chain had suddenly locked into place. She saw herself coming round full circle from where she had been for the past two years of self-imposed exile, as an outcast and stranger, back to this place, where she utterly belonged. And yet she knew she was more complete from having wandered, from

Circling

finding and loving Jumpa, from choosing to become the mother of this remarkable child.

As they left the downtown and began climbing up the steep hill towards her house that stood above them on a promontory overlooking the town, solitary and it seemed to her brooding, like a small, beleaguered castle, her fears for what she might find there coalesced into an almost paralyzing terror. She stumbled, nearly falling, and Charging Elk reached out a hand to steady her, looking at her questioningly. She gave him a hesitant little smile and shook her head as if to say, "I'm all right."

Her companion nodded his head in response, but his sharp old eyes, nestled under the unruly white hairs of his eyebrows, looked skeptical. After that he walked closer to her, taking her elbow when they walked over a particularly rocky, uneven part of the dirt road.

Gradually, as the wind playfully tugged at her hair and the morning sun warmed her back, Jasmine began to breathe more easily. Surely, she thought, studying her son's sweet face, now awake and alert to everything around him, surely her parents, however hurt and angry, could not reject *him*.

When she finally stepped onto the wooden porch at the side door they had always used as an entrance, she hesitated, took a deep breath, and then knocked softly, calling her mother's name. The door opened, and Molly stared at her as if she were a chimera, stumbling back from the door with a little cry and barely managing to right herself. Then she began to weep convulsively, great tears pooling in her large blue eyes and running down her cheeks. For her part, Jasmine said nothing, but knelt in the doorway and removed her son from his pack, placing him on the floor in front of his grandmother like an offering.

Molly recovered her composure enough to kneel and touch the face of the smiling infant. Only then did she look into her daughter's eyes and pull Jasmine towards her, their embrace forming an arch over the child, who was so delighted to be out of the restraining pack that he waved his arms and pumped his legs and squealed with pleasure.

The two women stayed in one another's arms, swaying gently, not saying a word, until Molly finally recovered herself sufficiently and found her voice, "Red Hawk! Red Hawk!" she cried. "Come here! She's come home!"

Jasmine's friend, meanwhile, had stood quietly on the porch in the rambunctious wind, his long white hair blown across his face, observing the scene before him. His eyes too seemed moist, but whether from the cold wind or the emotional scene before him one could not tell. Around his shoulders he carried a Hudson's Bay blanket pulled tight around his neck, and beneath that a plaid wool shirt, blue jeans, and moccasins. His large pack, belted at his waist, towered over his head. After a time, he got the clasp loose, and, working one arm free from the shoulder strap, he bent almost double and swung the pack down in a practiced gesture, leaving it at his side.

It was at this moment that Red Hawk came into the room. He looked much older than Jasmine remembered, and the now familiar pang of guilt constricted her windpipe. Unlike his wife, however, Red Hawk seemed less stunned. He took in the three people before him as if they were somehow expected, and then he took the child up in his arms. He pulled Jasmine to him with his left arm and rocked both mother and child together in a long embrace.

Reconciliation

Molly woke the next morning as if she had been asleep for a thousand years. For the first time since Jasmine had disappeared, Molly had slept the restorative, innocent sleep of a child. No nightmares, no long, painful attacks of sleeplessness, no endless dialogues with herself full of blame and recrimination for her failures as a mother. Only once in the night had she awakened, but so profound was her sleep that she imagined that she was dreaming when she heard a baby crying.

Then, awake, she smiled to herself as she realized that it *had* been a baby crying, and her heart lit up with the anticipation of once again holding her grandson. She got out of bed hurriedly but quietly, as Red Hawk was in the same state of utterly restful sleep that she had been, and grabbing her old blue robe from the foot of the bed, she tiptoed out of the room and into the open living room. Jasmine was nursing Tenzin, the two of them curled together on the couch, the fire already built and warming them. The baby's tiny head, crowned with a thatch of dark black hair, seemed perfectly fitted to the crook of his mother's arm, their lovely brown skins aglow with the fire's light.

Molly slipped in beside Jasmine, careful not to disturb the child, and put her arm around Jasmine's shoulders. Jasmine responded by resting her head on her mother's arm, nestling in as if she had been there forever.

Later, while the baby slept, mother and daughter prepared breakfast together in companionable silence. Molly realized that she felt

Pamella Hays

no need to question or interrogate; rather, she felt assured that some-day Jasmine would tell her story. If Molly had learned one thing from her husband's culture, it was the importance, the critical significance, of a story. Molly knew that stories were sacred not only because they held the connection of the tribe to its ongoing history, but because stories were the linchpin for all understanding between people. A person without a story was as lost and isolated as a lone shipwrecked man on an island. And certainly she could wait for her daughter's contribution to their family's story.

A phrase she had once read came into her mind: "the song of the family." Years ago she would not have understood it, but now it was clear to her that her own family had a song, and that that song had just yesterday taken on a new rhythm, a redeeming significance.

For the rest of the day, the four of them were hardly ever parted, eating, smiling, and admiring and cuddling the baby in turns, an infant who was, of course, the most beautiful child they had ever seen. There was no need yet for talk; that would come with time. But now they had this peace, at last, after so much sorrow.

What more could they ask? Red Hawk thought to himself. He had awakened a new man, full of vigor, of plans for the future, life itself stretching out before him like a green, open field, where only yesterday there had been a barren, rocky desert.

Healing

Red Hawk loved nothing more than going out to his old workshop to visit with Charging Elk. Well, perhaps 'visit' was stretching the term a bit; often they simply sat in silence for long periods of time, smoking a pipe that they passed between them and listening to the wind as it invaded the stove pipe with a rattling, hissing sound, like a disgruntled spirit.

After ten years of living with them, the old man had become almost completely blind, but as he lived most of the time now in his memories, his blindness did not trouble him in the least. When in the right mood, and especially when prodded by his godchild, when Tenzin accompanied his grandfather out to his lodgings, Charging Elk would launch into a tale from his own childhood, thrilling Tenzin with a glimpse of a world that had long since disappeared.

When he and Red Hawk were alone, however, the old man sometimes talked about the time he had spent with Jasmine. Then he would sit back in his rocking chair, covered with the ancient Hudson's Bay blanket that had come home with them years ago, and, tapping his moccasin-clad feet gently on the weathered boards of the floor, would reminisce. He seldom said anything that was in chronological order, but Red Hawk quickly adjusted to this, and when he was alone afterwards, he could usually figure out the actual sequence of events. What impressed Red Hawk most from the old man's elliptical stories, however, was an awed awareness of his daughter's remarkable courage.

Thomas had never been one to stir up the water until it became muddied with self-doubt and fear. Even when he had sat on the hillside one afternoon long ago and agonizingly accepted that he might not ever see his daughter again, he had never questioned her integrity and goodness. And though he never spoke of it to Molly, who would have dismissed his idea as nonsense, he gradually began to nurture a small hope that she might in fact return. He thought about her flight from them, about her disturbing silence, and yet he remembered too the astonishing gift of her insight, a kind of wisdom that she has learned, or perhaps inherited, from her grandmother. Sometimes he even allowed himself to hope that she was on her own form of a vision quest to find her own medicine and her own purpose, cost what it may.

When she had appeared at their door, he had seen, not to his surprise, a changed, transformed woman. And since then he had watched her as she worked her way back into the community, studying for several years until she got her master's degree, becoming an honored and respected counselor at the school, a wise woman who could see into the children's souls, into their essence, and who never disrespected or doubted their basic worth. It was this last thing, he thought, that had been her greatest tool for healing. Having been in some deep confusion herself as a young woman, she did not judge them, nor did she doubt that they could be made whole.

But his greatest joy, the focus of all of his life now, was his grandson. He had looked at the small bundle on the floor before him that day that Jasmine had come back, and knew that he had been given another chance. This time he would be a better caretaker, a worthy grandfather for this child, who, he could not help but think, was somehow redeeming him from the agony he had always felt over his inability to connect with his own son, with Nate.

As the old man slept, nodding off as he so often did now, Red Hawk heard the door cautiously open and turned to see Tenzin tiptoeing across the squeaky boards, his black mane of hair shining in the light that filtered in through the small framed window on the

Circling

side of the workshop, the miniature bow his grandfather had made him clutched in his hand. The young boy smiled with that spontaneous joy that only children seem to call up so easily, and slipped onto his grandfather's lap, throwing his arms enthusiastically about his neck. Then, in a whisper so as not to waken the old man, Tenzin asked, "Grandfather, could we go look for elk today? You said it was almost hunting season, and we need to know where the herd is. Can we? Can we?"

Red Hawk felt a quick, almost painful tug on his heart, as the memory of a hunting trip long ago appeared suddenly in his memory like a still-life painting. He sighed quietly, but then said, "Absolutely, my grandson. How about this afternoon?"

Forgiveness

Molly had always loved mornings most of all, perhaps because, the earliest riser, she had the house, which was suffused with its spectacular morning sunlight, all to herself. Her steaming coffee, so thick and black that it could, Red Hawk always claimed, retain its form without the mug, nestled comfortingly in her hands, warming them. Her thoughts circled back through the years to the day when her life had begun again, when Jasmine had come home. She remembered vividly her sensation of almost fainting, swooning, as the old romantic novels would have said. The world had gone into a vertiginous downward spiral, like a carnival ride out of control, and she had had, for one fleeting moment, the terrifying feeling that she was losing her mind. But then the baby wrapped so tightly in his blanket had made a sound, a melodic, purring gurgle that instantly pulled her out of the slide and focused her whole being on the bundle in front of her. She had heard people of a religious persuasion talk about being covered with a mantle of light, but until then, she had never experience such a thing.

In the years ahead, as she had lifted her toddler grandson into the air and had swung him around in a circle, loving how his voice cackled and screeched with utter delight, Molly would always hear the words of Jasmine's story echo over and over in her mind. She smiled ironically when she realized that she at last was part Indian, because she had a traditional story that she would carry down through the generations, part of the lore of her family's trials and tribulations, and, yes, she reflected, part of their joys as well.

Circling

Each day with this remarkable child, this mysterious being, seemed miraculous, as if he were the answer to her agonized, angry prayers after Jasmine disappeared. Despite her innate skepticism of the cosmos, she mumbled a contrite and deeply felt thanks to whatever Being had brought her daughter and grandson back.

Her old yen for absolute answers had not entirely deserted her through the years, and yet, though life itself had been at times captivating, at times terrifying, she had been with Thomas's people long enough to know that their spiritual beliefs, bare of dogma and theology, were as real to them, as everyday and necessary, as the air they breathed. Molly supposed that, even in the dark time in which Jasmine had vanished, she had subconsciously clung to the tribal assurance of life's essential rightness as a person floating at sea would cling to a piece of driftwood.

Tenzin's presence gave Molly, for once in her life, the grace not to ask questions, not to badger her daughter about what she had done and where she had been. There were times, it was true, when Molly had literally to bite her tongue not to let the fear she had experienced for her daughter metamorphose into the old, sad accusations of betrayal that she, despite herself, had felt. But something in her, having broken when Jasmine had disappeared, mended again in her grandson's dancing eyes and irresistible smile. Anger over the elusiveness of what it all meant, the old angst that had badgered her for years and years, causing her to judge harshly both herself and others, melted away in Tenzin's bear hugs.

In the summers Molly took him for walks in the meadows and the surrounding hills, often accompanied by Red Hawk, and in the winters they bundled him up and went flying down the hill beside the house, the wind biting their cheeks and turning them a deep pomegranate red. Tenzin was a fearless child, so much so that Molly found herself being very watchful of him, to the degree that Red Hawk finally told her she was smothering the child's survival instincts, the warrior side of his male self that was to her husband something matter-of-fact and necessary as the sun coming up every day. Rather than

Pamella Hays

arguing with her husband, Molly, to his astonishment, acquiesced, trying to allow the child more of his own intrepid explorations.

But her favorite time with Tenzin was, surprisingly, in her own lab at the hospital, where she took him when she had extra work to do on the weekends. To her astonishment, he was fascinated by the whole process of scientific research into the causes of illness. As the years went by, his interest only increased. By the time he was a high school student, he spent many hours with her in the lab, seeking her knowledge about the field of medicine, asking for the advanced professional help that his grandmother could offer above and beyond his high school science teachers' abilities. When he announced to the family, on graduation day, that he intended to pursue a career in medicine, Molly's heart glowed with pride, warmed by her own deep sense of connection with her grandson.

Though her relationship with Jasmine was now more intimate than it had ever been before, Molly sometimes berated herself that she had allowed that small estrangement, a tiny fissure of doubt, to develop between them long ago when Jasmine was little. Despite her sincere attempts to accept and understand, Molly would be haunted the rest of her life by her daughter's bizarre flight away from the family, away from her tribal identity, away from, as Molly thought, the values she had been taught. But then, Molly would remind herself, Jasmine had inherited the trait of flight, of running away, honestly. Her headlong search for meaning mirrored her mother's years ago: a chip off the old block, as Molly's own mother would have said.

Eventually, of course, Jasmine had shared her story, telling her mother about the events of her self-imposed exile, though Molly suspected that Jasmine had spared her the details she thought her mother might not be able to handle. Jasmine's story of Jumpa, the great love of her life, whom she had let go with sadness and an aching heart, was like the great, epic love stories of all time, Molly reflected. It was astonishing to her that, even afterwards, Jasmine insisted that she had not regretted her decision, though Molly knew that when Tenzin grew older and asked questions about his father, Jasmine felt

Circling

the full impact of what she had done. She still, however, defended her actions and believed that Jumpa would have forgiven her. For her part, Molly would never completely understand Jasmine's decision to let Jumpa go, but she kept silent. She approved that Jasmine had raised her son in the native way while telling him as well the traditions and beliefs of his father.

Lost in her morning musings, Molly did not hear her husband's approach until she felt his arms enfold her and find that special spot on her neck at the hairline where she so loved to be kissed. She suddenly and unquestioningly felt as if she had come home, forgiven and forgiving, attached by an invisible umbilical cord to something too beautiful to name.

Connection

Jasmine turned into the hospital parking lot at four o'clock and walked up the stairs to the small, empty lobby, its oppressive green décor about as appealing as a fetid swamp, she thought. Fleetingly she wondered why institutions seemed fixated on providing visual environments that were both depressing and impersonal, just when their clients needed some warmth and affirmation.

She took a right turn into the hallway where the lab, its door ajar, radiated the steady hum of overhead fluorescent lighting. Her mother and Tenzin stood close together, their heads bent over a microscope, animatedly discussing the specimen on the slide before them. Molly's curls, now highlighted abundantly with grey, contrasted with Tenzin's carefully barbered short black hair. None of the tribal long-haired stuff for him, he had insisted, opting for both practicality and, amongst his more radical school mates, a much remarked conformity.

A high school senior, Tenzin had long ago turned his back on the social mores of the small, ingrown high school he attended and was already accepted for a pre-med program in a prestigious school back East. Jasmine recognized that the help of the doctors at the hospital, who knew him from his work with his grandmother and wrote him glowing recommendations, had probably tilted the balance in his favor. Even as the sterling student that he was, a graduate from a tiny Montana school, and especially a school on the Rez, had the odds against him from the start. Much as she would miss him, Jasmine knew he would be doing what he loved.

Circling

The pair hadn't even heard her come in, so engrossed were they in their conversation. Jasmine cleared her throat and commented, "Don't you two ever quit? I need to take you home and then get back to school for a meeting."

Tenzin turned first, his shining almond eyes almost taking her breath away, as they always did. He was very much his father's son, and seeing him both thrilled and unsettled her, sometimes causing a little spiral of grief to rise briefly in her heart. She missed his father every day, every hour.

But to him and her mother, she merely smiled and shook her head, adding, "You two are sure a pair to draw to."

Molly, her lined face lifted by a rare, happy smile, shrugged her shoulders. "What can I say? I have a grandson who is a genius," she said with deep pride in her voice.

On the way back to the house, Molly asked Jasmine about the meeting she had to go to and wanted to know when she'd be home for supper.

Jasmine frowned. "One of my kids has gotten into some serious trouble with drugs," she replied. "I'm especially upset because I thought we had really been making progress in our counseling sessions. But his family is so screwed up——pardon the unprofessional expression——that maybe there isn't any hope. I'm not sure, but at least I can tell the school and police authorities that I think he's worth saving."

Tenzin chimed in with a grin. "You always think everyone's worth saving, Mom," he said with a skeptical pride.

Jasmine smiled back. "You're right, I do," she said. "What's it all about if we don't take care of each other? Like Grandmother always said, every life is sacred. I just try to let my students know that."

She pulled into the gravel path outside of the attached garage but didn't turn off the motor. As her passengers got out, she told her mother not to wait supper for her. She would grab something on her way home, as there was no telling how long the meeting would take.

Driving back to school through the busy after-school crowds of kids, dogs, and mothers on their way to the store, she allowed herself a brief moment of self-scolding. What, indeed, was she accomplishing as a school counselor in this often despairing and always schizophrenic culture, suspended between old spiritual traditions and the siren song of modern greed and willful ignorance? But this internal monologue was merely a brief indulgence of her usually quiescent skepticism. Surely her own improbable life, from the Rez as a young woman to the shadow she had been for two years, and then back to this place, was proof enough of life's astounding ability to heal itself, to circle back to the unnamable mystery that kept it in such breathtaking balance, like an angel dancing on the head of a pin.

Wisdom Keeper

Her gnarled fingers, silken as driftwood turned incessantly by the river's waves, grasped the medicine bundle that her father had left her not long before he died. The worn leather pouch was softer than a baby's skin, its weight insubstantial as a feather. She could remember as clearly as yesterday the moment he had given it to her, twenty years ago.

Though her old eyes were less acute than they used to be, her inner eye could see in vivid detail the day Red Hawk had given her his medicine pouch.

"You are the Wisdom Keeper now, Jasmine. You are so much like your grandmother that I can see her every time you smile. And soon you will be a grandmother, even as I will be a great-grandfather. How happy your mother would have been if she could have seen her first great-grandchild!" Then he had handed her the bundle with both of his hands, and she had accepted it with both of hers.

She smiled to herself as she remembered that moment, the wrinkles around her eyes folding like the pleats of miniature fans. Now she had come full circle, her life almost completed, and every nuance of her experience could be perused by her mind objectively, as if it were the story of someone else. She knew without hesitation her virtues and faults; she knew what hurts she had caused to others and what blessings she had brought to them. There was no perfect life, she reflected, only a path that sometimes led one into terrifying quicksand and at other times forced one to climb over mountains or allowed one to meander through meadows filled with wildflowers.

249

Her own path had been one that she chose, yes, but also one that had taken her to unexpected places. Along the way she had left her joys as well as her grief and guilt, and now the traveled path stretched far in the distance behind her, and only a little farther ahead she could see the end of the path as it disappeared into the white light of the horizon. Still, she was not afraid, because she at last had learned the final lesson: how to forgive herself and others. She would welcome passing to the other side when her time came.

On the day her father had given her his medicine, her mother had been dead for three years. Jasmine always wondered if her own selfishness, when she had disappeared for almost two years, had hastened her mother's death. That thought caused her the greatest sorrow that she had to bear and the one it had taken the longest to forgive herself.

Jasmine sighed, wiping the tears from her eyes. To forgive was not the same as to forget, she mused. The amazing healing that took place when what she had dreaded most, the anger or even rejection of her parents, became instead pure joy and gratitude that she had returned. That memory was as fresh as if it had happened only yesterday.

The old Sioux warrior, as Charging Elk had called himself, was buried in the cemetery near her mother's grave. He had requested and received the ceremony that his own tribe practiced for those who had crossed over to the West. Later, her father would be buried there too, next to Molly.

It was her father's medicine bundle, which she was unconsciously stroking with her fingertips, which brought her back to the present.

Outside the autumn clouds gathered ominously. Lightning zigzagged across the yellowed grasses of the prairie, and the fire in the fireplace leapt and crackled in imitation. Jasmine looked around her at the familiar room, one that she had been absent from for only a small portion of her life. It was on the Navajo rug, bright against the polished oak floor, that her son Tenzin had taken his first tentative steps towards his grandfather. Red Hawk's shout of delight had

Circling

brought her and her mother running from the kitchen where they had been preparing supper. Outside of the bay window, on the steep hill that sloped west towards the mountains, Molly had taken Tenzin on his first sled ride, the two of them screeching with delight as they plowed through the unbroken snow in their little ship. And it was here, too, that Tenzin and Sarah had married that Christmas that he came home from his studies at medical school.

How many times, she wondered, had she held Tenzin in her lap, or, as he got older, watched him as he sat across from her on this very rug, and told him stories about his father? As a small child he had accepted the absence of his father as a given; it did not occur to him to question that fact. But as he reached his teens, their conversations turned more serious. Jasmine had to face the difficult task of trying to explain why his father had left them when Tenzin's anger flared over what he considered his father's abandonment.

Ultimately there was nothing to do but to tell him the truth, that she was to blame, that it was she who had made the decision to keep her pregnancy a secret. Tenzin couldn't believe his ears. "You mean my father didn't even know?" he had yelled at his mother, incredulous and furious. "How could you do that?" And then, cutting deepest of all, he had added, "I thought you were so wise, such a great counselor. You know better than anybody what happens to kids who don't have a dad. I will never forgive you for this!"

Jasmine had had enough. Yes, she deserved his questions and even his anger, but she did not, she thought, deserve his derision and self-pity. She waited for a moment, collecting her thoughts and calming her feelings, and then she explained. "Tenzin, unfortunately we are not born with wisdom: we have to earn it. I was very young then, only 18, alone and frightened. To tell you the truth, I don't even know what I would do differently if I could go back in time, even though now I know much more about life. I may be considered to be 'wise', as you say, but that does not mean that I am anything other than human. All I can do is to ask your forgiveness for having made this decision that has so affected you life."

She had paused for a long moment, and added, "But I will defend myself in this way: You have had the unconditional love and support of three adults in your life, more than many children do. Your grandfather has been as much a father to you as anyone could be." Her eyes filled with tears. "You are old enough to see me as someone other than just your mother, Tenzin. You need to see my own suffering, too. Do you think that I don't miss your father every day, that I don't wonder what our lives might have been like had I told him I was carrying you? Whether I made the right or wrong decision so long ago, I do know this: Your life is as it is. It is up to you to make something of it or to live in anger and bitterness. You are the only one who can decide."

He had not spoken to her for weeks, and she had kept silent also, waiting for his response. Tentatively, gradually, their relationship had thawed, and even though he had never spoken about their conversation, Jasmine was happy to see that his longing for the father he had never known prompted him to explore the philosophy of Buddhism. He read everything he could get from the library loan system at his high school, and later, at college, he had taken a series of classes on the subject. One of Jasmine's greatest joys was when he had told her that he had discovered a Buddhist myth with symbols much like those in a tribal myth she had told him.

Over the years Tenzin had come, she thought, to love this place as much as she did, but he had never felt as if he belonged there, and though she had told him all of the old stories and the lore of the Indian side of his inheritance, she knew that he had not bonded with that part of himself, despite his deep affection and respect for his grandfather, and she was not surprised when he chose to go to school back East and to live his life there.

Here in this room as well, she had first seen her grandson, Ben, when his parents brought him home at three months of age almost twenty years ago. Her love for him, so complete and instantaneous, was bigger than any she had ever known, for she knew immediately in her heart that he would be a credit to his people. Her own gift

Circling

of insight she no longer questioned. Of course as a grandmother she loved this child unconditionally, but as Wisdom Keeper she also envisioned his role as the next shaman, who would carry on the tribal traditions and stories.

For Jasmine the past was a complex pattern that, now from the perspective of age, she could finally discern as a master design; or at least that was how she saw it. Each person, each event, whether perceived as good or bad at the time, now was clear to her as a necessary ingredient of the design, part of what had made it whole.

Her musings wound their way back to the small apartment in Portland she and Jumpa had shared so long ago, evenings spent talking or making love, learning each other's deepest desires and fears.

She reflected on the trip home that she had taken with Charging Elk, and how Tenzin had proved to be a resilient traveler, content to be wrapped warmly in the backpack, and sleeping most of the time. He had waked only to eat and smile up at her engagingly as he nursed. When they had crossed the summit and were heading down into East Glacier, only a few miles from the reservation, Tenzin had awakened suddenly and gurgled with delight. How did her son know this place, she had wondered? Perhaps, she thought, there are sacred places that exist not only on this earth but in the heart and mind as well. She sensed this because she herself had been for a time a homeless waif, bereft of the sense of belonging that such places create in us, estranged from her own internal landscape.

The sound of her grandson's voice calling for her as he came into the house awakened her from her reverie. She placed the medicine pouch on the table beside her and rose slowly to greet him. She smoothed the hairs that had escaped from the tight braid that hung down her back and, smiling, waited for her grandson to come into the room.

Though she had never told him so, every time that she looked at him she felt as if she were looking at her brother, Nate. True, her grandson was taller than Nate had been, and his features showed his Indian and Tibetan heritage as well as the Scandinavian heritage

Pamella Hays

of his mother. The similarity between Ben and Nate was hard to describe, more a presence of character than an actual physical one. Gratefully, however, she acknowledged that Ben had utterly escaped the anger that had driven Nate towards hopelessness. Though she knew that Ben Walks Softly was his own distinct person, for her he was always, secretly, in some part her brother, a living reminder of all that was good in him, of all of his unrealized potential.

Like Nate, he was a gifted artist, and he had taken an early interest in his uncle's drawings that the military had sent back along with his other personal effects after Nate's death. As a child Ben had pestered his grandmother about the pieces, asking who the people were and what the strange, half-rendered image of the wolf meant. Jasmine could only guess at their meaning, but she told her grandson everything she could, even telling him about her own astonishing dream when her brother had appeared as a wolf-dancer.

Ben had gone to school in New England, where his father practiced medicine, and, luckily for him his father recognized his son's aptitude, agreeing to send him to a high school for gifted students and then on to a school of art. When Ben visited his grandmother in the summers, he spent almost all of his time hiking in the nearby mountains and making pencil sketches, which he would then turn into paintings over time. He had already gotten a reputation as a talented artist, perhaps because his work combined the natural beauty of this part of Montana with the haunting images of faces and half imaginary animals that seemed to populate the landscape, now appearing in a cloud, now amongst the grasses of the prairie, again outlined in a rocky crag.

As he entered the room, Ben noted his grandmother's serious face, and always quick to read her moods, he frowned and asked what was bothering her.

"Just a foolish old lady living too much in the past," she said, smiling up at him. And then, sensing that he had something on his mind, she added, "Why did you call me?"

Circling

"Grandmother," he said, addressing her formally, "I need to ask you to begin telling me the old stories so that I can start my training. When I was a child you always told me that I was to be a shaman, a Wisdom Keeper. What do I need to do? I am almost twenty now, and it is time."

Jasmine's heart skipped a beat as she contemplated the earnest, handsome young face before her. She lowered herself into her chair and patted the footstool in front of her. "Then let us begin," she said, smiling.

Grandmother

Now my task is done, and I can rest at last. Jasmine will be joining me soon, and then the circle will be completed. It is the new generation that must carry the stories forward. They will go through suffering, too, as we all have, and if they are wise, they will learn from it. The old days are gone. It is clear that the Earth itself will not last unless all people share their stories, joining one another in the last great battle to preserve humankind. Only in that way will the thread continue on unbroken and the people's dance move in harmony with the sacred rhythm of the drum.

Made in the USA
San Bernardino, CA
16 March 2013